Southern Spirits

God, she wanted him. Wanted to feel those lips on hers and those hands on her ass and hear that voice grunt obscenities. But she was certain that he wouldn't take it that far. A moment later, when his hand moved behind her as if for a refill of his glass, reached down and squeezed one of her cheeks, she thought differently.

She glanced around, ensuring no one was watching, before she rose up onto her toes, tottering on the points of her new high heels, and whispered, 'Let's find someplace quiet.'

He grinned, and then made a show of nonchalance as he started towards the corridor, Cat waiting a respectable minute before following him.

The corridors were dark except for around the elevators, but Nathan waited near the door for her, leaning against the wall for support. 'Hey, thought you'd sent me out for a joke.'

She swayed into his arms. 'I don't joke about some things.'

He seemed to tower over her, even more so as he lunged towards her and kissed her passionately, full on the lips, his hands moving up to touch her hair, which she had pinned up before. A few deft moves and it tumbled free, his fingers through it. He pulled back to whisper, 'It looks much better down.'

By the same author:

The Pride

Southern Spirits
Edie Bingham

BL

This edition published in 2008 by
Black Lace
Thames Wharf Studios
Rainville Rd
London W6 9HA

Copyright © Edie Bingham 2008

The right of Edie Bingham to be identified as the Author of the Work has been
asserted in accordance with the Copyright, Designs and Patents Act 1988.

A catalogue record for this book is available from the British Library.

www.black-lace-books.com

Typeset by Palimpsest Book Production Ltd, Grangemouth, Stirlingshire FK3 8XG,
Printed and bound in Great Britain by CPI Bookmarque, Croydon, CR0 4TD

Distributed in the USA by Macmillan, 175 Fifth Avenue,
New York, NY 10010, USA

ISBN 978 0 352 34180 8

1 3 5 7 9 10 8 6 4 2

Prologue

To the hard pounding rhythm of the train that carried them, the lovers moved their bodies together like pistons: the man driving deep into her, again and again; the woman clutching and squeezing him as another climax rushed through her.

The heat in the berth was stifling, unrelieved by the ceiling fan directly above them, and sweat matted the tips of her russet hair to her neck, before rolling down beneath the salmon-pink silk of her teddy. She wanted to take it off and be as naked as her lover, but he refused to unwrap his huge arms from around her, refused to stop using those full, strong lips and tongue.

She had no problem with that.

She sat in his lap, her thighs straddling his hips as he pushed up into her repeatedly, the tip of his shaft stroking the walls of her sex in all the right places. She felt like such a small thing in his embrace, but protected. One of his hands had descended along her spine to cup her cheeks, squeezing hungrily and sending tiny jolts through her like sparks on the rails.

Her teddy had become distracting enough for her to pull back and motion silently, until her lover got the idea and relaxed his hold on her. When she cast it aside, however, he bent her backwards until she thought she would fall from him, then he bent forwards and engulfed one of her nipples in his mouth, sucking sharply and making her yelp. Her hands gripped his arms for support, and she stared upwards, the whirling wooden blades seeming to mesmerise her.

And still he drove into her, even as she drove back, meeting him thrust for thrust, while his free hand manoeuvred between their bodies, touching her bush, then her clit, his thumb providing a gentle but insistent teasing that made her weak with the sensations running though her.

'Oh sweet God!' Riding the crest of it, she leant forwards once more, wanting to kiss him again, to push him harder, faster. She wanted him to lose control, wanted him to surrender to her for once, and fill her with his seed. She knew it would all be over, before either of them knew it.

Neither of them heard the berth door open ...

1

'His name is Jonathan "Jack" Wheeler, thirty-nine, born in Willoughby, Georgia, grew up in various foster homes, school record distinguished by a number of petty criminal cautions. From high school, he enlisted in the army, where he trained as an electronics engineer, earning an administrative discharge a year before his expected release date, the reasons for which remain unclear. Since then he has operated a number of confidence operations throughout the South-east, including telemarketing, property development and pyramid schemes. No arrests...'

Catalina Montoya, Special Agent for Criminal Investigations in the Internal Revenue Service, paused as she saw the high pink brow of her supervisor crease, a familiar sign that her words, at least for now, had reached the point of diminishing returns. She stood before his desk, blinking at the strong morning Miami sun pushing through the beige vertical blinds, caressing the potted plant in the corner.

Her attention returned to her supervisor, who was now turning a page in the report. Michael Hausmann was a short, unassuming man in his late forties, forever hiding behind small wire-rimmed glasses, and sporting a bald pate that creased with every smile or frown, as if seeking to amplify his particular state of mind. 'And he currently operates this... Southern Spirits Tour?'

'Yes, an alleged haunted luxury train that tours the back-waters of the Deep South, though given the places he advertises, it primarily serves as a mobile swingers' party.' Catalina paused and added, 'When couples meet to exchange partners for –'

'I know about swingers, Catalina,' Hausmann noted dryly, never looking up. 'I even kissed a girl once.'

'Yes, sir.' *Idiota*, insult your boss's intelligence, why don't you? She felt the sweat bead down her back beneath her blouse, resisted the urge to reach under her dark dress jacket and attack it. 'It's operated for the last year out of New Orleans, taking couples and parties on weekend tours. The last return received indicated he was barely making a profit.'

'Any evidence of money for sex transactions?'

'No, sir. There are legal provisos in the online application form which stress that the fee is simply for the train tickets, accommodation etc.' She watched as he turned to a set of downloaded photos. 'Those are from his website.'

Hausman's eyes narrowed at some of the photos of revellers. 'I wonder if my wife is free this weekend.' He looked up, his face remaining deadpan. 'That's a joke. At ease before you sprain something.' He turned the page, settling on a medium-sized photo of a blond man, with rugged facial features and a nose that looked as if it had been broken and reset. 'And is this Mr Wheeler?'

'Yes, sir.'

'How did he come to your attention?'

She'd already thoroughly explained this in her report, but understood his preferred method of operating. 'During the Lateece audit, I found an amount of eight thousand paid as an out-of-court settlement from Wheeler to prevent a lawsuit regarding food poisoning. Then the Fitzsimons audit indicated "gambling winnings" of nine thousand while onboard the train. And the Valdez case declared an eight thousand dollar refund from Wheeler for a cancelled trip.' She breathed in. 'I know it's just a hunch, sir, but . . .'

'But nothing. Hunches like that keep us on the top of the chart.'

She nodded. The chart listed the various Federal agencies' conviction rates, and CI had the highest conviction rate, even higher than the FBI or Homeland Security. Moreover, in the year she had worked there, she had surprised herself with her hunger for noteworthiness, her diligence and attention to detail. She undertook all additional training offered. She made sure every report she filed was complete, concise and clear, all the metaphorical *t*s crossed and *i*s dotted. Hausmann couldn't find fault with her work.

However, that didn't stop him from asking questions. 'And your reasons for requesting an undercover operation?'

'The named cases are noted for untraced assets. The amounts are all conveniently below the usual Federal minimal reporting levels. Given Wheeler's criminal background, and the interstate operative sphere of his business, it is probable that Southern Spirits Tours is being used for money laundering –'

'No, I mean why have you requested to conduct the operation yourself? The Special Investigative Office has trained agents on hand.'

'None of whom are currently female, sir. Wheeler's literature indicates that he accepts only single females or couples on his train.'

'The SIO can request an appropriate female agent from another field office.'

'Unnecessary, sir. I have the proper undercover qualifications already. It would be a Class III operation, intelligence gathering only, low risk and limited to the weekend. And the suspect has no criminal history involving firearms or violence.'

Hausmann leant back in his chair, regarding her directly; for a man short in stature and slight of build, he had an intimidating, penetrating gaze when required. 'Is that your only reason for recommending yourself, Catalina?'

She swallowed, now regretting not taking up his initial offer to sit down. 'Sir?'

The director let his favourite gold pen slip down his hand to the tips of his fingers, then twirled it around like a miniature baton. 'Are you looking for excitement? Danger?'

'No, sir.' She had learnt long ago that despite her badge, despite the physical fitness and weapons proficiency training, the bulk of CI work involved following audit trails, recovering assets and decrypting records. No TV producer could ever make a show about her work that was both truthful and entertaining. 'I'll leave those sorts of puerile desires for the boys.'

'Well then, is it curiosity about swinging? Intrigue about what goes on?'

'I know about swingers, sir. I even kissed a boy once.'

The corners of Hausmann's thin lips rose slightly. 'You've recommended on-site investigations before, but now you're requesting personal involvement. I can't help but play on my own hunch that this has something to do with Adcock's promotion.'

Despite herself, Cat bristled, mostly because he was spot on. Harry Adcock and she had joined the Miami field office at the same time, had possessed identical qualifications, applied for the same promotions – but somehow they selected him for promotion to Special Investigations. The feedback she had received following the interviews had been perfunctory, told her simply that Adcock's overall presentation had been marginally better. However, it made her re-evaluate how she could stand out more next time.

She hadn't discussed it with Hausmann before, and she chose to be honest. 'Yes, sir. An undercover operation, even a low-risk one, would demonstrate more effectively my dedication to the job –'

He raised a hand. 'I have no problems with ambition among my agents. Your dedication has never been in dispute. If anything, you sometimes come across as ... overzealous. You don't show enough of that sense of humour I know you possess.' Now he leant forwards, his expression softening into an avuncular suppleness. 'You're more than just your work here, Catalina. You should show it more often.'

'I'll ... try, sir.'

'Good.' He closed the folder. 'I'll pass this on to Simon for a threat assessment, and let you know when I know.'

Cat bypassed her office, and ventured to the ladies' room by the elevators. She checked to ensure it was unoccupied, and then swore as loudly as she thought she could get away with. Her heart still thumping, she turned and looked at herself in the mirror, glared at the reflection of a woman quietly creeping into her thirties, with a lean face inexorably softening with time, a Latin complexion that brought out her bright, challenging olive eyes, her shoulder-length ink-black hair drawn back behind her ears.

Puta! It was fine for Hausmann to tell her to lighten up. He, and the other agents beneath him, all male, didn't have to fight against the thinly veiled chauvinism of their profession, constantly judged on their gender, their looks, their attitudes. He was symptomatic of the invisible hurdles around her, the cliquey network that would keep the little woman in her place.

She returned to her office, a stark enclosure of cream-coloured walls, bottle-green vertical blinds and matching carpet, and framed diplomas and certificates. Her only personal photo was from her graduation, when her parents put aside their acrimony to present an image of marital harmony. All for the sake of their daughter and, more importantly, their image.

Cat would have preferred the truth, however, even if it meant one or both of them hadn't shown up. She found such hypocrisies an insult to her intelligence, a lie, and she dealt with more than enough of those in her life, let alone her work. To her, it was a fact of life that most people were dishonest: dishonest to their employers, employees, colleagues, family, friends, lovers, themselves. Some called her cynical for such an attitude, but she preferred to see herself as armoured, tempered to face such realities.

'Overzealous'? *Besame el culo*, Hausmann.

A flash on her PC alerted her to an incoming email. A part of her hoped it was Hausmann, already approving her request, though she knew paperwork never flew that fast. Then she saw the sender's name, and recognised it as a response to an earlier request, made a couple of days ago, to the interstate police. She opened it, examined and absorbed its contents. She felt she took the news better than she thought she would.

Wanting a change of thoughts now, she returned to her work. She knew she was no stick in the mud, no unfeeling bitch. She just didn't suffer fools, thieves or liars gladly, whether it was obvious predators like Jack Wheeler ... or ones closer to home.

It was still light when Cat left the building, a modest structure compared with the taller neighbouring glass towers like International Place. She was eager to get home, but avoided her usual route on I-95 to make a detour along a boulevard closer to the ocean. Miami was like Venice, built on several hundred natural and artificially created islands interconnected by bridges. She drove north on Marriot Boulevard towards her favourite Chinese takeaway, glancing across the water to one of the wealthier islands.

The sky had deepened to a blush by the time she reached her home, an apartment overlooking the verdant enclave of Billings Island Country Club, a haven for people who would feel less welcoming to someone like Cat, though it would be close as to what would ostracise her more, being Latina or an IRS agent.

She juggled her briefcase and takeaway as she entered her apartment, a stark interior of tiled floors and stucco walls and ceilings. She heard the TV playing in the living room. 'Cliff?'

He didn't answer, and she switched on the lights, saw his shoes and socks discarded in the middle of her hardwood living-room floor, drinks glasses leaving rings on her glass-topped coffee table, and the air conditioning on full. One thing you could say about him, the man knew how to make himself at home – even when repeatedly told not to. 'Cliff, where the fuck –'

'Hey.' As she started, he shuffled in from the hallway. 'Why are you shouting? I was in the john.' Then he smiled and drew closer. 'How's my little accountant?'

She pulled back, wrinkling her nose. 'Couldn't you have gone home and showered first?'

He ran a hand through his thick blond hair and smiled that cheetah's smile. 'Yeah, I *do* stink a bit, don't I?' He approached her again. 'Let's shower together . . .'

She backed away again, setting her briefcase down by her PC. 'Let's not.' Then she took her takeaway into the open kitchen area and placed the cardboard boxes in the microwave for later.

He was leaning against the back of her couch, grinning. 'Got some Chinese for me, too?'

Cat took off her jacket, hung it up and switched on the

overhead light. When she was closer, she folded her arms across her chest. 'Tell you what, you do something for me, and maybe you can have your fill of something Cuban instead?'

His smile blossomed into a grin on his unshaven face. 'Anything, babe.'

She smiled. 'Take off your clothes.'

His eyebrow rose. 'Man, I love this side of you –'

'That's because you don't have to work for it. Now shut up and strip.'

Cliff eagerly obliged, casting his shirt and trousers to one side, his erection rising already inside his briefs, his lean runner's body hairless except for a diamond cluster of curls in the centre of his chest. He grunted, and then he was easing off the briefs, too, letting his long thin shaft spring upwards, unencumbered. He was proud of it, and what he could do with it. Naked now, he leant back against the couch again, his cock pulsing further to life. 'Is this what you want?'

She offered him a smile as she slowly stepped towards him. 'For starters.' When she was just inches away, he moved as if to kiss her, but she pressed her forefinger against his warm chest. 'Now I want you to go and shower.' Her finger trailed down along his lean belly, until she almost touched the base of his cock. 'And be thorough.' She watched him quickly depart, and then she cleaned up around the living room, readied for later.

She padded quickly into her bedroom, all pastels and yellow, dominated by the huge four-poster bed. A purchase of sheer indulgence on her part. She drew the curtains shut, glancing once out into darkness and squares of light from other windows, other lives. She undressed quickly, her cream blouse and navy-blue slacks dropped carelessly onto an adjacent chair, then padded about in her frilly blue satin bra and panties.

She had a full-length mirror mounted on the wall facing

the foot of her bed; when she was feeling self-voyeuristic, as she did now, she could watch herself, with Cliff or alone. She stood before it, running her hands slowly, admiringly over her body. She would never say she was perfect – her breasts were just a little too big, that slight roll around her middle would probably be airbrushed out for any magazine covers and her legs weren't quite long enough. Some days, when she looked, there seemed to be nothing but dissatisfaction, but today, the image of her was pleasing. She smiled. She didn't have many moments like this, and she enjoyed them while she could.

Her hand moved over the front of her panties, lingered, brushed teasingly across her pussy through the gossamer satin, making her shiver. Her hand still there, she stepped back, until she was at the foot of the bed, and sat down, her legs spread. Now she looked down to see her fingers gently peel the lace trim aside, slip beneath the satin, touching her bush, feeling the heat radiating from her sex, and the hairs closer to her folds. Her middle finger eased up and down, tentatively at first, and then more boldly. She was wet; what would happen tonight had excited her more than she had expected.

Her finger moved upwards, pressed at the base of her clit, and the familiar tingle blushed outwards for a moment.

'Yum.'

The sound broke the spell, and she looked up to see Cliff, fresh from his shower, his hair combed back with his fingers. He had a thick red towel wrapped about his waist, and a bulge had begun to rise at the front.

Cat ignored him, watching her reflection as she touched herself some more, her other hand now stroking the tops of her breasts with her fingertips, until goosebumps rose and her nipples puckered beneath the satin. She leant her head back, letting her hair tumble off her shoulders.

Now Cliff stepped forwards, blocking her view. 'So, what do you want? A little –'

'A little quiet.' She reached out and undid his towel, casting it aside to watch his cock pulse back to insistent hardness. Then she grasped it, gently stroking it, loving the feel of it, its firmness and heat. 'Just do as you're told.' She looked up at him, her gaze equally firm and hot. 'This is for me. I don't care if you get off or not. Understood?'

He grinned, reaching out to stroke her hair. 'Sure, babe. Whatever you say.'

Cat released his cock, then reluctantly removed her other hand from her panties before slinking backwards along the bed. When her head was on her pillow, she raised one knee up, the foot flat on the mattress. 'Whatever I say? Well, I say start at my feet, and work your way upwards.'

Without further ado, he followed her, descending to kiss her toes, her feet, her ankles, his fingertips blazing a trail ahead. As his lips reached her inner thighs, his finger touched her sex through her panties, then slipped beneath a leg band to touch her pussy, lightly stroking her, making slow, tight circles around her clit, while his thumb brushed hypnotically up and down her groove. He was kneeling up now, straddling her raised leg, his shaft twitching against her inner thigh as if seeking attention.

Tingles and sparks ran through her, and their eyes met. She slipped her hands behind her head wantonly as Cliff masturbated her, his hand shifting so that his thumb now massaged her clit, and his middle finger gathered the juices she was producing, moistening her puffy, sensitive outer lips, delving further into her as he continued.

Cat squirmed, kept her hands above her – *Dios*, this was lovely! – willing the satin panties to fade away, longing to feel more naked. Not that Cliff would have the sense to . . .

Suddenly he was removing his hand to do just that. Smart boy, for once. She took the opportunity to remove her bra as well, enjoying the air on her skin. She watched him watching her as he returned to his work, watched his fingers and thumb, glistening, listened to the soft wet sounds which increased as she ground her hips upwards off the mattress, adopting a rhythm that complemented Cliff's. She let herself wallow in the sweet sensations, building on them as they radiated outwards from her.

She came, suddenly, almost without warning, making her pull back from his now-overwhelming touch, the blood rushing to her head. Her hands snaked down to her parted inner thighs, her fingers framing her sex as if to try to contain the heat. Then her forefingers parted from the rest enough to reach down and gently draw back her folds, the cool air barely soothing the inner flesh. Her voice was husky as she urged, 'I need your mouth, here.'

Cliff looked impatient, impatient for some relief of his own. Still he obediently dropped his head between her legs, gently nuzzled, then lapped and moistened her some more, tasting her juices and delving deeper into her with that gorgeous thin tongue of his, before rising to her clit, the tip of his nose nestling in her bush, drinking in her scent. His eager attitude was welcome, sending little jolts of pleasure which fed on the lingering embers of her recent climax, fanning them back to life. She grew warmer and wetter as he alternated between his tongue thrusting and circling her clit and his lips sucking on her folds.

As he returned to her clit, and she felt the pressures building once more, Cat squeezed her thighs against his head until she made him groan into her sex. He was pushing down hard now, and she met his resistance as she pushed her hips upwards, and received another, stronger orgasm, waves washing over her.

She felt Cliff rising from her pussy, drawing up closer to her head, his intentions clear, but she didn't protest, wanting this as well. She raised her legs again, helping him into her. Slick and hot as she felt, she enjoyed being filled and, as he almost lay upon her, their eyes met again as he thrust into her, hard and fast, as if seeking to punish her for keeping him waiting for this for so long. His words confirmed this. 'Yeah, about time –'

'Shut up.'

He listened, and she relaxed, strings of climaxes erupting within her, not overwhelming like before, but still very satisfying. She almost told him to slow down, make it last, but thought better of it. As his control eroded, she wrapped her thighs tightly around him, using her remaining strength within to squeeze him, until his face contorted and his limbs galvanised, his pace quickening, and then he erupted in her with a strangled gasp. He collapsed onto her, his chest sweaty, heaving, breath huffing from his mouth next to her ear.

She gave him a moment like this, also strengthening herself, her resolve strong with the warm satisfaction of her climaxes. Then she slapped him on the shoulder. He withdrew, rolling onto his back beside her, even as she was rising, reaching for her panties and blouse.

Cliff stared up at the ceiling, smiling beatifically. 'God, I needed that. You were good. Now, how about that Chinese?'

She was up on her feet, slipping back into her blouse. 'No time. You have to get dressed and leave.'

He grinned and jumped up, cocking a salute. 'Your wish is my command. Where am I going?'

She slowed down a little as she climbed back into her slacks. 'That's your business.'

'Huh? What's the problem?'

'No problem. You're going, and you're not coming back.'

Without looking at him, she left the bedroom, then stopped at her desk and turned when she heard him follow, his cock quickly wilting. 'Cat, what's going on? Did I . . . did I do something wrong?'

Leaning against her desk, her hand reached out blindly and touched her briefcase, resting there. 'Why didn't you tell me I'd moved into your apartment?'

Cliff's mouth opened. Then he swallowed hard and she could almost see the wheels turning behind his eyes, spinning lies. 'What? I don't . . . I don't know what you mean . . .'

'Oh, sure you do, honey. Apparently, I moved in six weeks ago. At least, that's what you put on that credit card application. The one "we" applied for.'

His face paled even further. 'How did . . . How did you find out?'

'An overly friendly customer service rep tracked down my work number this week to offer me an upgrade to Gold. It was the first time one of those annoying calls became useful.' She lifted the paperwork from her briefcase now, though she'd perused them thoroughly that afternoon. 'You stole payslips from my files here for the verification. You forged my signature on the application. With my added income you were able to get quite a substantial credit limit.' She glanced up again. 'Put your clothes back on, you look ridiculous.'

Cliff's breathing quickened, and he hurriedly dressed, still trying to make eye contact and project some air of sincerity, or regret, or something else he didn't really feel. 'Cat, I'm so sorry about this. I've been behind in my bills, I couldn't ask you for money –'

'So you committed credit card fraud instead. Yes, that was a much better choice, congratulations, *idiota*. I explained the situation to them, and they've closed the account and started recovery proceedings.'

His face was ashen now, looking thoroughly stunned – at least, at having been caught out. 'Cat, I swear to you, this was just the one time, and I'd have paid it all back. You have to believe me.'

'I don't have to do a damn thing, Cliff. And it was no more a one-off than all the other times you've done this, with other women, in Virginia, North Carolina, Pennsylvania, using other aliases.' At his disbelieving expression, she dropped the paperwork on her desk and continued, 'You may see me as just your "little accountant", Cliff, but I'm more than that. I'm a *criminal investigator*. I deal with dishonest people like you all the time and I know all the tricks of the trade. I think it's that insult to my intelligence that hurts most.' She reached behind her again, produced his key ring and tossed it to him. 'I've taken my key back. So, off you go, don't call and don't return.'

He swallowed again, his arms falling to his side. 'Look, Cat, I know you have every right to be angry with me –'

'That's just it, Cliff. I'm not.' In recent weeks, she had become more and more conscious of his many negative traits: his complacency, his laziness, his condescension. However, the sex had been great and she had been prepared to forget the rest because of it. Now, however . . . 'I'd have to possess some remaining emotion to be angry. You're not worth that.'

He managed a self-pitying look, and then asked warily, 'Then why did you . . . Why did we fuck? Why didn't you just throw me out?'

'Because whatever else you are, you're a good fuck. Nevertheless, even the best fuck isn't going to help someone if he disrespects me as much as you have. So I thought I'd get some last moments of fun out this sorry relationship.'

She watched the disbelief, the disbelief that the user was used as well, boil – boil into resentment, and then anger. He drew closer. 'Goddammit, you can't just –'

She held her position, her face taut, and her voice dropped low. 'You take one more step, I'll knock you on your sorry ass. You know I can do it.' He stopped, but she continued, 'Then I'll have you charged with attempted assault on a Federal officer. I'll use all my influence to make sure you end up in a cell playing the *puta* for some three-hundred-pound tattooed bank robber.' She nodded towards the front door. 'Try to leave with some dignity, Cliff.'

Then she saw it: the acceptance that he couldn't salvage anything more, and it was best he moved onto his next victim. He departed; to his feeble credit, at least he didn't slam the door.

She stood there, staring at nothing in particular, almost sorry that she didn't mention she'd already alerted some local bounty hunter friends of hers to collect Cliff for his outstanding warrants.

Almost. *Adios*, Cliff.

She wouldn't miss him, just miss having her libido fed so much. She had a strong drive, but her luck with men was bad, and her work and attitude made it more difficult. But she'd rather stock up on some batteries for her vibrators than put up with the likes of him.

She heated up her takeaway and settled down on her couch, just in time for the midnight movie.

2

Cliff had gone, and in the following days, she had been able to put him out of her mind and focus on her work. In fact, such was her focus that she almost didn't respond to Hausmann's summons.

She entered to find Hausmann, and Special Agent Nathan Ames, sitting there grinning. Ames was older than Cat, not tall but broadly built, like some ex-football player who still kept in shape, with dark, flattering features and just a hint of grey at the temples.

Wary, Cat said nothing as Hausmann motioned for her to take the seat beside Nathan. When she did, their supervisor took his own. 'You'll be pleased to hear that the department's approved the Wheeler investigation, and with you serving undercover.'

She nodded, still wary. 'Thank you, sir.' She left it at that, waiting for the 'however'.

'However, we feel that this will require an additional agent and, with that in mind, I've asked Nathan to work with you, now that he's returned from leave.'

She tried not to show her displeasure. She failed. 'Sir, with respect, I don't need any help with this case.'

'And with equal respect, Cat, I disagree. Nathan has considerable field experience, and the threat assessment suggested on-site back-up would be prudent.' He paused and added, 'This will still be your case. You've raised it, and you'll remain the primary.'

She felt like she was tumbling into a ravine, but grabbed hold of this assurance like a lifeline. 'So, I will remain in operational command?'

'Yes, ma'am,' Nathan interrupted with some amusement. 'You will be in total command of the entire two-agent team.'

She ignored him. 'Sir, this won't –'

'Prepare the appropriate forms, Agent Montoya,' Hausmann concluded, in a tone that would brook no further discussion. 'You'll need to make amendments for your new partner.'

Her face went taut. 'Yes, sir.' She rose and departed, closing the door just a little too forcefully before returning to her own office and pacing around like a caged animal, her insides feeling like coiled springs. *Cabrón!* That bastard as much as said she couldn't handle the case alone! Even worse, he'd assigned Nathan Ames, of all people ...

An unwelcome face almost immediately followed the knock on the door. 'Can I come in?'

'*Veta al infierno.*'

'Been to hell, thanks: crap weather but interesting company.' Nathan stepped inside, quietly closing the door behind him. 'You'll be glad to know Hausmann's door is still on its hinges.'

'*Hausmann es una grande puta.*'

'Well, I'm sure his mother still loves him.' His expression sobered. 'Cat, I want you to know I didn't ask for this assignment.'

'Oh, really?'

'Yes, really. What, you think I don't have cases of my own?'

'No, I think you heard that this was taking place on a swingers' train, and you were jumping at the chance to get me alone in an environment like that.'

He crossed his arms over his chest. 'Sorry to burst your bubble, Kitten, but I didn't exactly retire my piece after the Christmas Incident.'

Cat was ready with an acid reply, but then thought better of it. Whatever had happened between them before, he was no liar. And in the cooler light of reason, it made sense to have back-up, especially if they were crossing state lines. She felt the tension in her muscles ease, a little. 'Sorry.' She walked around to her chair, feeling the beginnings of a headache.

'Listen, Wildcat.'

'Don't call me that.'

Nathan smiled. 'Well, we *are* supposed to be playing the part of a couple. Couples have pet names for each other, to demonstrate familiarity. I can call you Wildcat, you can call me –'

'*Pajiero*?'

'My Spanish is rusty. That means "handsome", right?'

'No, but a hand is usually involved.' She offered him a cocktail-shaking gesture with her fist, in case he still didn't get it.

He grinned. 'See? *That's* familiarity. How else would you know that was one of my favourite hobbies?'

'Because you're a man?' She set the folder down again. 'I'll bring the copies over this afternoon –'

'Tonight.'

'Excuse me?'

'Tonight. We'll discuss things over dinner.' He smiled. 'I make a wicked seafood platter.'

She leant forwards, resting her chin on her hand as if regarding him for the first time. 'Oh? Dinner at your place? Maybe with some soft lighting, music? And then we can pick up where we left off on that desktop –'

'You know, for someone who wanted that matter buried, you keep reaching for the shovel.' He reached into his shirt pocket and produced a business card, then set it on the edge of her desk. 'My address and number. I'll have dinner ready for eight. And just so you don't feel the need to strap on a chastity belt, I'll make a gentleman's promise not to put any moves on you while on assignment.'

She raised an eyebrow as she accepted his card. 'A "gentleman's promise"? How gallant. The trouble is, men make piecrust promises: they seem sound, but crumble easily.'

'You're very young to be cynical.'

'Must be the company I've been keeping.'

'Maybe you need new company.'

'Maybe.' Despite herself, there was something about his old-fashioned, persistent charm that was appealing. 'Eight, then.'

Her headache worsened after his departure, and she rummaged through her desk drawer for her bottle of aspirin. She downed two without water and grimaced at the taste.

She was returning the bottle when she found the tightly rolled band of shocking-pink paper, torn, bound with elastic . . .

Last Christmas.

It was a tightly bound band of tissue in shocking pink, bound with elastic. However, Cat didn't have to unfurl it to identify it, so she set it down on the linen-clad table beside the plastic magnifying glass and tiny jumping frog, the other prizes she found in the gaudily wrapped cardboard tube. Christmas crackers were some British custom, and Hausmann's wife had brought back a load from a trip to London a week ago. Around Cat, her colleagues pulled theirs, wore the paper hats and read the terrible jokes, all of them enjoying the novelty.

She wished they'd taken to her with the same enthusiasm. She'd been in the department for four months now, and while people were friendly enough, it seemed like a polite friendliness, an acknowledgement that she was there and no more. No one had even asked her out, leaving that paranoid corner of her mind to tell her that they had dismissed her as not even worth talking to, except on business.

It didn't help, she felt, that she was the only woman currently assigned there. The others had all brought women along tonight, wives and girlfriends who regarded her with varying levels of coolness. She felt alone as she stood apart, her third champagne – no, fourth – in hand, summoning up the courage to leave quietly. Maybe she'd been there long enough . . .

'Hey, there, Catalina!'

She turned, encountered a smile that had more welcome than she'd expected. 'Cat, *por favor*, Agent Ames.'

Nathan Ames sauntered up to her, clad in a handsome black and tan striped shirt, the sleeves rolled up almost to the elbows and the buttons undone to the top of his chest. He wore a baby-blue paper crown and his skin had the pinkened hue of a few friendly beers downed. 'Hound, *por favor*. No need to stand on ceremony, it never stood on me.' He grinned. 'Where's your crown?'

She had been attracted to him from her first day, though she saw very little of him as he had been off on more than one field assignment. He both interested and intimidated her, usually, but it wasn't so bad now, seeing him in his cups like this. Blindly she reached out and lifted her still-bound crown. 'It's pink. Pink is for little girls.' She indicated her outfit for the night: an expensive black Melissa Massie sleeveless dress with a sharp V neckline, an indulgence from her first pay cheque with the department. 'Do I look like a little girl?'

'Nope.' He leant in closer, swayed slightly as his voice lowered. 'You are very much a woman.'

It was both flattering and patronising, and as she swayed too, leaning in to catch and approve of his aftershave, she accepted it more for the former than the latter. 'And you are very drunk.'

22

He pursed those full lips of his with mock indignation. 'Darlin', you'd be surprised what faculties I still have.'

She raised an eyebrow. 'Is that a challenge?'

He smiled. 'Find out.'

And it went from there for the next couple of hours, the music and drinks consumed blurring the specifics of the conversation, like watercolours in a heatwave. Their hands touched, more than once, sometimes with the excuse of reaching out for another drink, or more snacks. Sometimes not, and then the touch would linger, his fingertips brushing along hers.

God, she wanted him. Wanted to feel those lips on hers and those hands on her ass and hear that voice grunt obscenities. But she was certain that he wouldn't take it that far. A moment later, when his hand moved behind her as if for a refill of his glass, reached down and squeezed one of her cheeks, she thought differently.

She glanced around, ensuring no one was watching, before she rose up onto her toes, tottering on the points of her new high heels, and whispered, 'Let's find someplace quiet.'

He grinned, and then made a show of nonchalance as he started towards the corridor, Cat waiting a respectable minute before following him.

The corridors were dark except for around the elevators, but Nathan waited near the door for her, leaning against the wall for support. 'Hey, thought you'd sent me out for a joke.'

She swayed into his arms. 'I don't joke about some things.'

He seemed to tower over her, even more so as he lunged towards her and kissed her passionately, full on the lips, his hands moving up to touch her hair, which she had pinned up. A few deft moves and it tumbled free, his fingers through it. He pulled back to whisper, 'It looks much better down.'

'*Si.*' Then she ripped off his crown, tossed it aside. 'And that looks much better off.' Then, with a rush that ran through her like a wave, making her head spin, she was kissing him back as hard as he was kissing her, tongues caressing each other. The sensations shot down to her sex; this was spontaneous, rude, forbidden – and quintessentially delicious.

But they were still too close to the main party, and she drew back, 'Let's ... let's find a quieter place, *bruto*.'

They staggered into the darkness, found and entered one office but left the lights off. Cat kicked a waste bin as she ventured further inside, then yelped as Nathan slapped her on the ass, the sound sweet and deep in the room.

She spun around in mock indignation. 'Agent Ames, you're no gentleman.'

'I'm so sorry,' he slurred, moving closer, 'I've wanted to find out if your ass felt as slappable as we thought.'

Cat stepped back until she pressed against the desk. '"We"?'

'Did I say "we"? Oops, my bad. Adcock and I had been talking about it.' Now he seemed to focus on her again. 'Forget what the guys say about you.'

She smiled, relishing the notion of his lack of inhibition almost as much as the thought of getting him alone. 'Oh? And what have they been saying about me?'

He chuckled. 'Oh, I'm batting a thousand here. Cat, I ... I couldn't possibly say.'

'Yes, you can.' She smiled at him, her hands dancing lightly, casually, up along her front, over her breasts, lingering along her bare skin deep in her cleavage. 'Anyone say anything about my breasts?'

Nathan's breath was husky as he replied, as if mesmerised. 'Yeah. Chaney thinks they're your best feature. But Leewood loves your lips. Can't stop talking about them.'

'Oh.' Outwardly she maintained an insouciance, but inwardly

she thrilled to learn things that none of them would dare raise openly. 'But . . . But no one's ever even approached me.'

He chuckled. 'They wouldn't dare. They all think you're way out of their league.'

She parted her legs, slightly, letting the hem of her dress rise just above her knees. 'And what about you, Hound? Am I way out of your league, too? Maybe you shouldn't even bother trying.'

Now he stepped forwards, placed his hands on her hips. 'Honey, the one thing you can know about me is that if I go to hell, it won't be for not trying.' And they were kissing again, this time with his hand sliding up between them, gently but insistently cupping one of her breasts through the material of her dress, his moans into her mouth confirming his delight.

He helped set her ass on the edge of the desk, her head dipping back as she stared upwards. His lips moved down along her smooth olive skin, as he reached up and skilfully slipped one shoulder strap down. His mouth worked on the soft flesh above her lacy bra, then licked and sucking on it, biting it so softly and growling. Cat's body shook as he slipped her breast from her bra, then licked around the sensitive nipple, and she rode the sheer sensation of pleasure she was feeling through her body. Still kissing her, Nathan moved his hands to her hips and slid them down along the soft fabric of her dress, then dipped them beneath the hem to touch her stockinged thighs.

Cat moaned aloud, gasping, but still asked him, 'And what part of me do you think is my best feature?'

Almost before she realised it, he was easing her back, onto her elbows, raising and parting her legs while still supporting them, and drawing up the hem of her dress. His voice was a whiskey purr. 'When I've sampled them all, I'll tell you.'

Cat leant back further as he disappeared under her dress,

and she felt his hands, his head, moving up between her thighs. Her breath quickened as she felt his breath through her silk thong on her pussy, and her pulse skipped a beat when she felt his fingers draw aside the strip of fabric barely covering her sex.

He murmured with mild surprise, enough to distract her into asking, 'What's ... What's wrong?'

His head rose from under her dress, but his hands remained where they were, his fingers slipping under her thong. 'Hampton thought you might have a Brazilian.'

She giggled, then yelped again as his thumb found her clit, seemingly making her heart accelerate more. 'R– Really?'

He teased her clit, his other fingers holding aside her thong, or brushing along her pussy lips, never entering her fully, while the sounds of their breathing filled the room. Her arms spread out once or twice, knocking things over, but she didn't care, so caught up was she in the frantic rush of body and ego.

Then suddenly – 'Puta!' She bit her lip, wondering how loud she'd been, though inebriated enough not to care too much. The climax washed through her, and her hand reached up behind her to grasp the edge of the desk near her head. 'Get ... Get it in me.'

She set her head back fully, staring upwards as she listened to him undo his trousers, unzip and lower them. She felt his hairy thighs, his hands gripping her by the hips again and sliding her closer. She felt the hot silky head of his cock, a thick staff, brush against her inner thigh, and she licked her lips, gasping again as he ripped her thong. 'Hey!'

'I'll buy you more.'

'Fucking right you will.'

Then he guided himself into her, supporting her legs easily, and she gasped at how wet she felt as he slid in, with so little resistance.

Nathan quickly entered a rhythm, pumping his cock into her, with an urgent hunger. Cat yelped and cursed again, in Spanish and English, her voice resounding, the sheer animal nature of what they were doing taking hold of her. Something nearby crashed as she came again.

She couldn't remember when he'd come, but knew he had, felt his hot seed deep inside her. She remembered her head spinning as they had detached themselves from each other and did their best to clean up. They leant together, drunk and satisfied, kissing again, before she felt Nathan fumble with something in his hand. 'If ... If that's a condom, I think you're a little late.'

It wasn't. He unfurled her pink paper hat, having picked it up when she hadn't noticed, and fumbled a little as he fitted it on her head. 'There, your crown. You're definitely royalty.'

She wore it proudly – for a second, before tearing it off. '*Besame el culo.*'

His apartment was in one of the higher, newer buildings in the Pebble District, overlooking the Atlantic. She arrived on time, and was pleased at his reaction to her outfit – the same black Melissa Massie she'd worn the night of the Christmas Incident, with her hair pinned up again. 'Ah ... oh. My. Yes. Lovely.'

'*Gracias.* Am I allowed in then?'

'Of course.' He smiled and stepped aside. To her mild surprise, the living room turned out to be tastefully decorated: a minimalist approach with muted colours and furnishings, low leather chairs and reproductions of French expressionist paintings. A small square table with white linen, polished silver and crystal ware sat near the open doors to a balcony overlooking the ocean, as classical music played in the background.

He wore a plain black shirt, with the sleeves rolled up, and charcoal trousers. 'Not what you expected?'

She glanced back suddenly, catching him staring at her rear. 'I expected buffalo heads and Confederate flags.'

'I'm from Texas; they weren't part of the Confederacy. And my ex-wife got the buffalo heads in the divorce.' He reached out and tentatively touched her arm. 'Want to take a seat? Don't know about you, but I'm starving.'

Cat had brought the Wheeler file with her, but she set it down on a desk and sat down at the table, smirking at what was on offer. 'Oysters?'

He sat down and reached for a bottle of Merlot. 'Scalloped oysters in cream sauce.' At her expression, he asked, 'Don't tell me you had it for lunch?'

'No, but ... *oysters*? Not very subtle. I'm surprised you don't have avocado slices and truffles, if you wanted to stuff me with aphrodisiacs.'

He smiled. 'Sometimes a cigar is just a cigar. I remember you hogging this dish when we all went out to the tapas bar for Adcock's farewell.' He leant in conspiratorially. 'You know, they're made for sharing.'

'Not when I'm around.'

Nathan poured the wine. 'Tell me about yourself, Catalina.' At her expression, he explained, 'We'll need to know about each other for our cover.'

That made sense; much of their individual cover stories were better based on truth, to avoid slip-ups. Still ... 'For a start, people only call me Catalina when they're trying to scold me or bed me. Don't try either.'

'Heaven forfend.'

'Besides, I told you everything about me on the night of the Christmas Incident. How soon they forget, once they've had their fuck.'

'Refresh my memory.'

'OK. I was born in Orlando. My mother's a soap actress and

my father works in the local DA's office, but mostly my grand-father, who missed being a fisherman in Cuba, raised me. He taught me to swear, the best thing he ever did. I graduated from Florida U, spent six years in the accounting department of Petrox Chemicals, then two more with Miami PD. From there I enrolled in the CI division of the IRS. And the rest, as they say...'

'There must be more to you than your parents and career. Any siblings? Pets? Hobbies? Boyfriends? *Girlfriends*?'

She rolled her eyes. 'No siblings. No pets. No hobbies. As for boyfriends or girlfriends...there's just you now.'

'Well, yes, that's our cover, but what about in real life?'

She looked away, stared out at the ocean, darkening with the encroaching night, lit with salmon streaks. 'There *was* a boyfriend. We split up a week ago.'

'Sorry to hear that.'

She looked back. 'Don't be. He was a serial fraudster who used my details. I found out about it, had a last decent fuck with him and then dumped him.' At his expression she elaborated, 'Hey, Cliff was good at it. Just bad at everything else.'

He pursed his lips and nodded, ate some more food and, after another moment's silence between them, announced dryly, 'Thanks for asking about me. I grew up in –'

'Madisonville, Texas,' she finished. 'You have four sisters, all older than yourself, all of whom used to pick on you mercilessly, but you feel it was worth it as you ended up learning a lot about women, although you still ended up divorced two years ago. After college, you worked with the FBI for four years before moving into Internal Revenue. People think you got the nick-name "Hound" from your prowess in the bedroom, but in fact it came from your allegedly uncanny dog impressions...'

'Whoa,' he breathed out, looking stunned. 'Is there anything you *don't* know?'

'Well . . . any girlfriends? *Boyfriends*?'

'Oh, hundreds. How the hell do you know all that about me?'

'You told me the night of the Christmas Incident.'

'But we were both drunk to the point of staggering!'

'I never have any loss of memory. No matter how much I drink.'

'See? Looks like we were destined to work together.'

She snorted. 'Destiny's bullshit. Destiny, fate, kismet, Hand of God. All of it.'

'That's cold. Don't you believe in a higher power that guides us?'

'No. It's all crap designed to abrogate us of responsibility for our actions, or for changing what can be changed.'

He leant in, smiling teasingly. 'But what about when two people who are made for each other seem to beat insurmountable odds and get together to live happily ever after? Surely there's a case to be made for destiny there?'

'Odds are never insurmountable where people are concerned; the Six Degrees of Separation phenomenon is a proven fact. And besides, where's the triumph of two people meeting and not growing or developing for each other? That's why so many relationships break up, no one wants to work at it.'

He sat there, still looking pensive. 'So . . . you remember everything that happened that night?'

'All the gory details.'

For a few heartbeats, there was just the music and the gentle clink of their cutlery on the plates. Then he asked, 'Did I . . . Did I embarrass myself?'

Cat had expected such a question. She set down her cutlery and gazed at him. 'You were charming. You were honest. You were considerate. You were driven with lust for me. And we had a fun, drunken fuck. And except for how loud I was – and for our choosing Hausmann's office – I don't regret one bit of it.'

Nathan set down his own knife and fork, rested his chin on his hand. 'You seemed regretful enough the next morning, when you came to me and practically threatened me into silence about it. I understood why, you didn't want a bad reputation.'

'Well, there was that,' she conceded. 'But my primary concern was because you told me things about the others, things that I didn't want them to know that I knew. It gave me an advantage. And built up my confidence.'

'Well, glad I could help.'

She smiled.

The evening progressed through the main course and a light dessert of tiramisu. They discussed very little of the background to the case, but Cat ignored that, expecting they could talk again later, or she could leave him what she'd brought.

After the meal, they sat on his couch, a space apart, facing each other, Cat cradling her wine glass.

Finally, Nathan set his untouched glass aside. 'Cat, about that boyfriend...'

'Ex-boyfriend, Agent Ames. What about him?'

'It's Nathan, please. And I...' His gaze dropped for a moment. 'After the Christmas Incident, I kept my distance, didn't want to remind you of what happened, or make you believe I was after you again. Now I think maybe I took it too far. And that maybe I could have been there, if you needed a friend to talk to, about anything.'

The look in his eyes and the sincerity in his voice moved her to overcome her embarrassment about the matter. She shrugged, though her flippant attitude seemed forced, even to her. '*Gracias*. But I'm fine. If I believed in a higher power, it'd just be telling me to avoid any more complications in my life.' She swirled the contents of her glass with her hand, watching the dark liquid whirl and eddy, surprising herself with her own candour, before looking up again. 'And what about you? How's your love life? Little black book onto its tenth volume?'

He finished his drink, set the glass aside. 'Let's just say I'm between women. And not in the way I'd prefer. Maybe I should be avoiding any more complications in my life as well?'

'It's easier,' she found herself concurring as she set her own glass aside and reached for the Wheeler file. 'So, we're agreed: don't trust each other's genders, just each other.'

As she moved the file to her lap, Nathan reached out as if to take it, but instead took both her hands in his. His unblinking gaze, and low voice, took her full attention as well. 'Exactly. Cat, where we'll be going, we can't trust anyone but each other. Trust to watch each other's backs, to do our job – and to remain professional.' He squeezed her hands gently. 'I know I can trust you. I just want you to know you can trust me, too.'

She nodded, agreeing with soft sounds, believing him. And wanting him – even as she drew closer to him, closer, slipping out of his hands and drawing him into a kiss. She felt him gasp as her tongue snaked into his mouth, exploring, before he pressed back against her, their arms encircling each other, Cat's breasts aching against his chest as her hands moved up behind his head, then down to his shoulders. The file spilt out onto the floor.

They half-knelt like that for what felt like ages, his hands moving down to cup her cheeks through her dress. Cat knew this was wrong, but felt dizzy with the wanton passion as she let him ease her back, still kissing her, his leg slipping between hers as his hands cradled the back of her head, her hands grasping his broad shoulders, her lips and pussy buzzing and tingling. She felt his erection through his trousers, against her inner thigh, and she moaned into his mouth, so wanting to take this all the way.

But knowing better, and knowing to stop immediately or it'd be too late. The spell seemed to break with him, too, simultaneously. He withdrew as she pushed him away, gently but decidedly, both regretting and not regretting taking it in that direction. Nathan quickly untangled himself from her and withdrew, wincing as he manoeuvred himself into a sitting position, hiding his erection, his face dark with acute embarrassment. 'I, ah ... sorry ... that's, um ...'

She felt flustered, and aroused, and didn't want to lose the feeble advantage by showing either state to him. 'That ... was just our getting accustomed to each other, in preparation for our undercover work.'

Nathan swallowed, and then nodded. 'Yeah. Yeah, that's right. I think we've shown we can do that convincingly. If we need to.'

She nodded back '*Bueno.*' Cat got to her feet, straightening herself up quickly. She had to leave, to go before it was too late. He started to rise, but she raised a hand, offering a weak smile. 'Gonna go. No need to get up.'

As she exited, she hoped she'd make it home before having to pull over to the side of the road and quickly relieve herself.

She was wrong.

3

'So . . . a double bed, huh?'

Cat was meeting Nathan for lunch, but stopped outside his office when she heard the question. The voice belonged to Leewood, one of their colleagues. She kept silent and listened further, not caring about breaking office privacy protocols. In the days since Hausmann approved her assignment, details had leaked out to the rest of the Department, inviting the expected puerile jokes and gag gifts – all directed to Nathan, who relayed them to her.

And his irritation was showing. 'Yes, Denis, a double bed. We're posing as a couple. Couples use double beds. Someday when you get a girl that doesn't need inflating you'll understand.'

'Come on, Hound,' snickered another voice – Chaney, Cat recognised. 'You're trying to tell us you won't be sampling any of the goods again when that sweet little ass is up against you.'

'I'm trying to tell you two dicks, once again, that I never "sampled the goods" in the first place, that all that talk about what happened last Christmas between Cat and me was bullshit. As for the assignment, we're both professionals. In fact, she's more professional than some clown shoes I can name around here, and deserves more respect than she gets.'

Leewood spoke up again. 'Respect, huh? Does that mean you're gonna excuse yourself before you slip it in her?'

'Don't you children have something better to do?'

'Aww, Hound.'

'Let me rephrase that: *find something*.'

Nathan's tone had changed, grown sharper than Cat had ever heard before from the usually laid-back man, and she wondered just how much flak he'd been receiving about this assignment. To the sounds of mock indignation, the two men left his office, their chuckling dying out as they saw Cat standing there, staring back. They departed almost as quickly as their faces had reddened.

She ignored them and entered Nathan's office. He was behind his desk, rubbing the bridge of his nose, but on seeing her he stopped and smiled, pushing aside the irritated look on his face. 'Morning, Wildcat, you're just in time.'

She closed the office door and took the seat in front of his desk. 'Just in time to catch the last moments of your boys' club meeting. So, the official line is that you never "sampled the goods"?'

'A little disinformation never hurt anyone.' He looked up. 'I hope you don't think I'm encouraging anyone to talk about us, or the assignment?'

'No. I don't.' In the days since that visit to his flat, Nathan had been true to his word, behaving professionally and treating her with regard and decorum. And as they worked, planned, and talked about anything and nothing of consequence, she found they were forging a satisfying working relationship.

The trouble for Cat was that it made him all the more desirable to her. She'd watch him secretly whenever they poured over paperwork, or sat outside for lunch. She was almost glad that they kept their contact limited to office hours, except for the odd late-night phone call about a forgotten matter.

Her attention returned to the here and now, as he set out two chunky-looking cellphones. 'Just signed these out from Equipment, had to beat up a British secret agent to get them:

secured signalling, digital recorder/camera, forty gigabyte high-density encrypted memory and leech programs, Word and Excel –'

'I know the specifications.' She pocketed one phone. 'Who'll be our contact?'

'Gordon Green.'

Cat rolled her eyes. 'Gordy the Geek. *Puta.*'

'What can I say? He's on the rota for the weekend.'

Cat was less accepting, never having any patience with the über nerd and his effusive, schoolboy-level prurience. On the other hand, while it was standard operating procedure for field agents to have a contact for information and assistance, that didn't mean she had to use him. 'So, still think you can control yourself this weekend?'

'Sure. Why not?'

She glanced at his PC screen, saw the logo of Southern Spirits Tours on Wheeler's homepage: a figure resembling an ornate Celtic cross with a second circle inside the first, and a serpent, in the shape of an elongated S, mounted on the extended vertical bar below. It was suitably Gothic, like a piece of church railing. 'Well, with all your friends teasing you here, and the pressure you'll get from the swingers onboard the train, it might all get, if you excuse the expression, hard for you.'

'Pressure?' He regarded her with a mixed look. 'Do you know anything about what really goes on in these places, Catalina? It's just that you might want to enter the environment with fewer preconceptions.'

Cat hated to admit that he might have a point. So she said nothing, and in the following days considered doing some research on the subject, before concluding that it was irrelevant to the issue. She wasn't interested in swingers' parties, just in the man organising this particular one.

* * *

Wheeler's instructions had been suitably cryptic, but boiled down to Cat and Nathan reporting on the scheduled Friday afternoon before sunset, at a place called Verge, an abandoned train station in rural Georgia. Cat's initial nerves had settled down during the short domestic flight from Miami to Jacksonville, in the northern part of the state, where they took a rented car further north into an anonymous landscape of dark-green foliage and winding black ribbons of roads, thankful for their satnav system.

And now they stood in a large, weed-tufted clearing, with a small ramshackle wooden building sitting by a set of railroad tracks. A weather-beaten, bullet hole-marked tin sign barely hanging on the side of the building said simply VERGE, and there were a few vehicles of different makes parked outside.

'*Dios*, what a dump.'

'It has atmosphere,' Nathan quipped.

'Yes, just don't breathe any of it or you'll get swamp fever or something.' Cat stretched, glad to be out of the car after what seemed like days rather than hours. The heat made her black T-shirt and jeans cling to her body. She collected her case as did Nathan and proceeded inside, where the original purpose of the building as a station was more obvious, with the wooden benches and counters, a cracked chalkboard on the wall for departure and arrival times, and a ticket booth mounted into one wall. But the furniture was unpainted, the chalkboard empty and the ticket booth unmanned, with life and activity provided by the five people sitting about.

'Southern Spirits Tours?' asked one of them, a woman younger than Cat, short and shapely, with skin the colour of polished walnut, full lips and a mischievous grin to match her tight white T-shirt and torn black jeans. She offered her hand. 'Of course, who else would come out here? Hiya, I'm Tara Gilbrand.'

Cat shook first. 'Cat Montoya. This is my boyfriend Nathan Ames.'

Tara nodded. 'Happy to meet you both. Excuse my forward-ness, but as you'll find out, there's no reception committee waiting for us here, just some food and champagne.' She nodded to a large open wicker picnic basket on the floor. 'And a note from Mr Wheeler, inviting us to make ourselves comfort-able until sunset.'

Cat watched Nathan walk over to the note, turning back to Tara. 'And this is it? Here's hoping the train accommodations are more welcoming.'

'They are,' said an assuring, educated male voice behind Tara. The woman moved out of the way to reveal an older, silver-haired man of light frame and saturnine expression, dressed in a well-cut dark suit. He sat alone, paperback in hand, never looking up.

'Mr Richard Newholme, of Boston,' Tara introduced. 'He has ridden on the Silver Belle many times, he has said. But he would prefer to let us discover the mysteries ourselves, first hand.'

The older man turned a page in his book. 'That is her diplo-matic way of saying I'm a decrepit old grump who wants to be left alone.' But though he tried to sound terse, he couldn't help add a hint of amusement to his words.

A couple approached, hand in hand like teenagers, unable to go long without glancing at each other. They appeared a perfectly ordinary middle-aged white couple: the man was slight of build, with receding tight curly black hair and a strong Roman nose, and the woman looked a little younger, with long gamine limbs and a bob of bright honey-blonde hair. 'Hello! I'm Benjamin Oliver, this is my wife Hannah.'

The woman, too, was friendly and charming. 'This is our first time on the train. Yours?'

'She's one of the Imperial IIIs,' Ben noted, before Cat could make a reply. 'A real beauty!'

'Uh huh,' Hannah agreed, grinning. 'And it's got a genuine Cartier observation car, with an upper deck! Have you any idea how rare they are nowadays?'

'None whatsoever.'

'They're very enthusiastic,' Tara noted, smiling.

Nathan returned to Cat's side, a flute of champagne and some Beluga caviar on a tiny biscuit for each of them. 'Here you go, sweetheart.'

'No need to go all romantic on me, Hound, I'm sure you'll get some this weekend,' said Cat. Tara smirked as Cat ate the biscuit, wrinkling her nose at the incredible saltiness of even a tiny amount, and downed her champagne in one. 'Is this all of us? I expected more.'

'Mr Wheeler collects the others at different points,' Ben replied, 'for the sake of convenience and security.'

It made sense. But Cat remained puzzled by something. She handed Nathan her glass. 'Is there a ladies' room here?'

'Outside,' Tara replied. 'Round the back.'

The conditions inside weren't exactly first class, and Cat finished quickly, emerging to run into the last passenger, one she'd seen watching her in the station. 'Hey, darling.' He was young, a pretty boy with short straw-coloured hair and a smooth, tanned face, clad in a black silk short-sleeved shirt and beige trousers. He lit up a smoke. 'You're too good looking to be a hick. You must be here for the swinging.'

'The train, anyway,' she said with a nod. 'Cat Montoya.'

She could almost see the Charm turning up to eleven in him. 'Donnie Kolchak.' He had an attractive swagger that teetered on arrogance. 'So, you've been a player long?'

Cat leant back. 'Why do you want to know?'

'Well, if you want to learn a thing or two from a pro, see me. Been at it for years.'

His body language – a barely concealed nervous excitement – told a different story. 'Really?'

'Yeah. You like Rolex? I own a dealership in Tampa.' He reached to his wrist and withdrew a gleaming silver model, handed it to her. 'I can get a discount for you. I've had this one for three years now, never had a problem.'

'Interesting.' She examined the crystal, hologram and band. 'No girlfriend with you?'

'Riding solo.' He leant in. 'Now, if money's a problem –'

'No.' She handed it back to him. 'I just don't buy shit, that's all.'

'Hey, it's not –'

'Well it's not authentic, any more than you are. Serial numbers on Rolex are engraved, not printed like on that one, and the holograms in the back are designed to wear off after a time, so yours shouldn't still be there after so long. Nice try, *cabrón*.'

Donnie's brow furrowed with sudden irritation as he regarded her, then he grunted and returned his watch to his wrist. 'You a watch expert or something?'

'An accountant.'

'Wow.' The daylight had almost disappeared, as had his interest in her. 'Sounds like the train's finally here.'

He departed, as Cat picked up the distant, steady rumbling, which she had put down as retreating thunder, begin to grow in intensity. She followed Donnie to the front, as the others emerged from the station house. Nathan ambled up to her. 'You OK?'

'Of course, I'd been potty trained for years.'

Then he turned with the others towards one end of the tracks, where the approaching sounds were growing louder, stronger, like a stampede, or an avalanche. Thin trees of stark branches lining either side of the rails swayed in a dusk breeze as if trembling at the approach of the intruder into the bucolic setting. Cat was no child, and yet she couldn't help but feel anticipation, an excitement that others seemed to be experienced openly, like the Olivers standing by Tara. And what was that older man's name? Newholme? Even he had seemed to shake off his dour expression for one of almost childlike wonder – no, not childlike, like a man returning home.

Like Kolchak, he was on his own, too, seemingly flaunting Wheeler's rules.

A chill ran up her spine as she glimpsed the single light cutting through the growing twilight, heralding the thunder, glowing stronger, even as it became clear that it was slowing down, the screech of powerful brakes on steel sending goosebumps along her skin.

And then she drew up to a stop by the depot: the Silver Belle. Cat had seen the pictures in the promotional items, of course, but nothing could have prepared her for the reality of it. And though Cat had never subscribed to the romantic notion of vehicles referred to in the feminine, she had to concede now that this train was a 'she'. It was like it had slipped out of the nineteenth century, with polished silver skin and blood-red and jet-black stripes radiating out from the one round light, above the Southern Spirits logo, and back along the entire train. The engine was a massive and beautiful thing, all cylinders and pipes, rails and rivets and gears, fronted with a cowcatcher that looked like claws and topped with a stack that bellowed smoke above the closed driver's cab. She was beautiful. She was elegant. She looked more like she'd been nurtured than manufactured. And as she came to a stop, she made a low sharp sound like a grunt. Behind her, she pulled cars carrying the identical colour schemes as the locomotive, most of them warmly lit from within.

Behind her, Cat heard Nathan whisper, 'I thought they were all painted black for some reason.'

Before she could respond, she heard Ben Oliver say, 'They were originally painted many colours, but eventually most companies moved to basic black because it cut down on cleaning costs.'

The door to the car nearest the engine clicked and slid open, revealing a large silhouette filling the entrance. Cat watched the figure reach up above the doorway and, a heartbeat later, a small metal ladder unfolded to touch the ground, and a miniature light illuminated him. He was a tall slim man with neatly trimmed dirty blond hair, moustache and beard, and eyes that sparkled with showmanship and promise. He was clad in an old-fashioned, neatly pressed white linen suit and black tie.

His voice completed the Southern barker's image as he addressed those assembled. 'Ladies and gentlemen, dear friends all. I am Jonathan Wheeler, your humble host for this weekend.' He leapt from the doorway, ignoring the steps to easily land in the gravel with a crunch beneath his shiny shoes as he extended his arms wide. 'And this sweet swift lady here is the Silver Belle!'

The Olivers applauded, at least. Others looked bemused, reserved or impatient. Cat, however, focused on Wheeler; like the photos of his train, the reality of the man seemed so much grander. He was larger than life, even as he began greeting people individually, shaking their hands with enthusiasm. 'Welcome, welcome, one and all! If you get your bags, we can be on our way.'

Nathan, carrying their cases, leant in beside her. 'Shall we board?'

'Why not?' Cat led him towards the steep steps, along with the rest of the passengers.

* * *

The interior of the reception carriage was an opulent display: rich red velvet and polished brass fittings, plush one- and two-seater chairs, ceiling lights designed to look like gas lamps, ornately framed black and white photographs of locomotives mounted on the walls between the shuttered windows, verdant potted plants in the corners and a bookcase at one end beneath some glass display. A woman tended a small bar at the other end. Cat could easily imagine Phileas Fogg making himself at home here during his travels.

Wheeler stood in the centre of the carriage, smiling and silently motioning for the passengers to draw closer. 'Fellow travellers, before we carry on, I wish to remind you of the safety and indemnity provisos you agreed to upon purchasing your tickets. The rules as described on the website are basic, but non-negotiable: no weapons, no drugs, no illegal business ventures conducted, smoking only in designated areas and we are not liable for losses from any onboard gambling. There are locks on your doors, but we will not be held responsible for anything going missing, so if you have any valuables, please bring them to me for safekeeping.

'Speaking of safekeeping –' he paused as a young man in a smart black vest, trousers and white shirt appeared with a metal strongbox, set it down and opened it to reveal compartmented shelves like a toolbox, filled with electronic items '– the instructions also state that cameras, recorders and cellphones are not permitted while onboard, for reasons of confidentiality. But experience has taught me that not everybody reads these, or believes that the rules apply to them. So here's your chance to redeem yourselves, because if you're caught with any of these following this announcement, they will be confiscated, you will be thrown off Belle – I might even slow her down – and you will not be refunded.'

Nathan glanced at Cat, who nodded to him to give up his

phone, but made no move to indicate she had one of her own. It would appear more realistic to have one phone between them than none.

The young man took Nathan's phone and moved on. But Wheeler seemed to take notice, and drew closer. 'Is there a problem, Ms Montoya?'

Cat smiled up at him, laying on the charm to distract him. Which wasn't too difficult; he was handsome, in a classic rogue's manner, with those dynamic eyes. 'No problem, Mr Wheeler. I just don't have a phone.'

An eyebrow rose. 'Really? That seems incredulous.'

'Why, because I'm a woman, and must live to gab?'

'No, because you don't seem the type to depend on anyone else for anything.'

Cat's gaze narrowed, and she let her voice drop to a whisper. 'You can't do everything alone, Mr Wheeler. As it is, my phone's in the shop for repairs. You can search me, if you like.'

Wheeler chuckled. 'Tempting, but judging from the quite understandable expression on your partner's face, I'd rather remain ambulatory.' Then he turned to watch the young man secure the phones and depart with the strongbox. 'I want to also point out the various safety notices near the access ways between carriages. This carriage has the only door to the outside, except for one at the rear. Should an emergency arise, proceed directly to the very rear, if possible.' He beamed now. 'And with that execrable legal business out of the way ... Faye?'

From the open doorway behind him, a woman entered, dressed in an elegant black silk evening gown and carrying a silver tray of tall, filled champagne flutes. She was a statuesque beauty, a chestnut-haired, chestnut-eyed woman in her thirties, with a Mediterranean Romany look in her expression, lingering with each new arrival as she offered the drinks.

'This is my associate and your hostess, Faye Scott,' he introduced with a glimmer of pride. 'She is an accomplished medium and expert on the occult, and during the course of the weekend will help acquaint us with the residents of the Other Side.' He accepted the last glass on the tray, raising it as Faye stepped aside. 'And if I may offer this toast: to Belle, who knows that travel, like passion, finds its true pleasure in the journey, not the destination.'

'To Belle!' the Olivers echoed loudly. Cat looked around: Richard Newholme was already sitting down and back to his book, his champagne set aside. Tara was staring intently at Wheeler, or maybe she was just trying to ignore Donnie.

'The Silver Belle,' Wheeler began, pointing to the photographs with his glass, 'was born in the years immediately following World War Two. And one of the last of the steam locomotives. From the beginning, she stood out as something special. Maybe it was her birthplace, in the Lafayette yards outside of New Orleans, coincidently the birthplace of many noted practitioners of *voudon*, what non-professionals call voodoo. Maybe it was the materials used, some unique and unrepeatable mixture of alloys. Whatever the case, Belle has served faithfully on the Southern Rail Express for over five decades, an unprecedented period, when she should have been retired long before.

'But Dame Fortune could not smile upon her forever, and she found herself abandoned in a railroad graveyard outside of Baton Rouge. It was there that I found her, and promptly fell in love.' He spoke the last with a subtle change of tone, an unexpected note of sincerity. 'And I spent the following two years restoring her to life again, and purchasing and restoring the carriages she now carries.'

Something from the corner of her eye caught Cat's attention, and she looked behind to see that the train had already started moving. In fact it was picking up some speed, and only now could she notice the gentle rocking of the carriage and the clack of the wheels on the rails.

'There are twelve carriages attached to the locomotive and her support car,' Wheeler was saying. 'This, the reception carriage, serves as a place of private discussion, as well as for the séances and the more worldly pursuit of cards. Occasionally one or two dollars have been known to exchange hands during the latter activities.' He paused for laughter from his audience. 'The next is our observation carriage, used for dining and the sale of snacks, condoms, toys and other souvenirs and, as its name suggests, it also boasts an observation suite upstairs, one of the few remaining in operation on the rails.

'Beyond it is the kitchen and pantry carriage, out of bounds but with through-access to the rest of the train. Our games carriages are especially designed for Southern Spirits, complete with a spa, Dungeon, private rooms, dance areas and other features I encourage you to discover and enjoy. Then there are the two sleeper carriages. And beyond these, the final carriage contains my office, private quarters, staff quarters –'

'Where do you keep your hookers?' Donnie asked.

Wheeler's face tightened, but he still offered a polite smile to the younger man. 'You seem to be labouring under a misapprehension. This is not a bordello.'

'Yeah, yeah, yeah. All these people spend all their money to ride around in the backwoods, sure. When does the fucking start?'

The tension in the room rose, just a little and, though no one made an effort to back away from Donnie, Cat had the feeling that they would have if they could get away with it and not be noticed.

Wheeler, for his part, maintained a cool demeanour. 'Our itinerary this weekend is jam-packed with activities, Mr Kolchak:

live music, a séance and tarot readings from Ms Scott tonight, a stop by a haunted church and a refreshing lake for a buffet on Saturday, a costume party on Saturday night. Anything else is at your fellow passengers' discretion – including the "fucking".'

Then Faye Scott spoke up, smiling enticingly at Donnie, 'I'm sure a man with your obvious qualities won't be without offers tonight.'

The man winked at her, his posture one of an alpha male being gracious in dropping any further contention. The tension seemed to hang in the air, however, until Tara spoke up, 'A séance, Mr Wheeler? I'd be interested in participating.'

Wheeler beamed, looking grateful for the change in conversation. 'And you'd be more than welcome, Miss Gilbrand, there's still a few places left at the table. Until then, I would suggest that you find your suites – your names are on the doors – unpack and unwind.' He set his glass aside. 'And once more, welcome aboard.'

Cat nudged Nathan. 'Let's get to our room.'

He grinned playfully as he lifted up their cases. 'Been waiting all day to hear you say that, Wildcat.'

Their 'suite' turned out to be smaller than the promotional photos on Wheeler's website had suggested. The berths in the first-class carriage were said to be larger, and themed, but Cat couldn't justify the additional expense for one of those. This was a snug enclosure of plain polished wood interior, the double bed dominating the room, with a two-seater facing the foot of the bed. There was a fold-down table next to a wooden chair and overhead storage cabinets. The windows were rectangular with rounded corners, and had fixed opaque horizontal shutters. The room, the colours of which reflected the red and black colours outside, had a more modern feel than the reception carriage, perhaps something from the 1950s.

Cat entered and went straight for the door beside the head of the bed, opening it to find the bathroom, an even more cramped area with barely enough room for a toilet, sink and a shower stall with a glass accordion door. 'Intimate', the promotional items had described it. No argument there.

She turned to see Nathan enter, set their cases down and plump onto the seater, putting his feet up on the bed. 'What, no mints on the pillows? I like mints.'

Cat reached down, touched the tight skin of white sheets. 'I like Egyptian cotton even more.' She fluffed up the pillow and propped it against the wall, then set herself down on the bed and kicked off her shoes. 'First impressions?'

He leant back. 'Jack Wheeler could probably sell porn to the Pope. Oozes charisma. His associate seemed interesting. What was her name again?'

'Don't pretend you don't remember, *pajiero*. What about the others?'

He shrugged. 'The Olivers seem genuine enough. Newholme looks so out of place here, he has to be a courier or agent from an outside party.'

'Donnie Kolchak gave me a bullshit story about being a watch salesman. He definitely smells of small-time Mob. The fact that Wheeler allowed Newholme and him alone, against the rules, supports that. What about Tara?'

Nathan folded his hands behind his head. 'She talked a lot about spirits and visions. She seems a bit of a flake.'

Cat found herself momentarily distracted by seeing how attractive he looked. Damn, this bed was going to be small with the both of them in it, being professional about everything. 'Bet you wouldn't kick her out of bed, though.'

'Bet *you* wouldn't either.'

Cat smiled. 'Maybe.'

He grinned back. 'And with that lovely Sapphic image in my

head, how about you call Gordy and get some checks on our fellow passengers?'

'Later. Do you mind if I have some time, lie down for a bit? Didn't sleep well last night.'

'Sure. I'll have a look around.' He rose, stretched, seeing and taking a key from a hook on the door. 'I'll be back in an hour, OK? I'll knock before I come in.'

'*Gracias.*'

She appeared sleepy as she watched him leave, heard him lock the door from the outside, before she quickly rose to her feet and moved to her case. She opened it up on the chair and fished through the contents for her small black toilet kit. She took it back with her and set it on the bed, this time lying down fully rather than sitting up. She watched the rise and fall of her chest for a moment, before closing her eyes and settling back. The gentle rhythm of the train was steady, hypnotic, enticing, like resting her head on the chest of a lover. She imagined feeling the heat from his skin, catching his scent, maybe shifting her mouth to dart her tongue out and taste his bare flesh again. She loved tasting a man after they'd had sex, especially after a good, hard fuck.

Dios, this was going to be hard. She'd been feeling hot since the night before, had almost masturbated in the shower that morning, but foolishly changed her mind. She'd hardly find many opportunities this weekend for self-gratification.

She ached inside her panties, but resisted the urge to respond immediately. Her hands moved over her T-shirt, fingertips trailing over the outline of the bra beneath, past the firmer underwire to the softer, frillier borders of the cups. She felt the slow peaking of her nipples within the lace material, the goose-bumps rising on the surrounding soft skin as if caressed by a cool breeze rather than her own touch.

Cat closed her eyes and wet her lips; the gentle rhythm of

the train seemed to seep into her body even more now. She also felt the pull of drowsiness, like the steadily encroaching waves of a rising tide as it engulfed more and more of her. Her mention of lack of sleep was no lie. But she had more immediate concerns.

She pulled her T-shirt out of her jeans, bared some of her bronzed belly as her fingertips stroked her flesh. A moment's decision, and she rose up on one elbow, reaching under herself to unclasp her bra. Then with a practised manoeuvre admired by more than one past lover who'd witnessed it, she quickly extricated herself from the offending garment and cast it aside without removing her shirt.

Cat settled down again, her hands moving under her T-shirt to trail her fingertips in wide lazy figure of eights, moving up along her stomach. Her breasts lay flat on her chest, and her fingertips reached the undercurves, then drew outwards to the sides, her mind's eye noting every detail, good or bad, real or imagined. She pictured they were Nathan's hands, his strong fingers exploring her, his eyes lighting up with delight and desire, his lips whispering words of appreciation and determination.

When her touch lingered around one of her nipples, making it pucker further, her sex cried out once more for attention. 'Sorry,' she murmured breathlessly to herself – and to Nathan. Apologising for not being able to chance having what they both wanted. Their one and only fuck together had been far from ideal. Wonderful, yes, but not ideal. Another one . . . would be far too risky. But she could fantasise. And did. Her fingers quickened, as her other hand moved to her other breast from outside her T-shirt, caressing more forcefully.

As she felt the familiar, welcome responses between her legs, she stopped, undid the belt and brass tabs on her jeans, one after the other, approving of how quickly and easily they responded to her touch. With both hands now, she slid her jeans and black satin panties down, down over her hips and buttocks, lifting the latter up off the bed to accommodate the movement.

With her feet flat on the mattress and her knees pointed up, Cat drew her jeans and panties down to just below her knees, leaving them there. She knew she could pull them back up again in a hurry if she had to – but she also knew that it looked and felt twice as rude to leave them there like that than if she just removed them entirely. She regarded the trimmed wedge of her bush, her steepled bronzed thighs and the outline of her pussy barely concealed beneath.

She felt hot, wet and pliant, and her nerve endings seemed charged. And when her hands moved over the tops of her thighs, fingertips sliding together as if trying to force her thighs apart, she twisted in place. She imagined Nathan doing this, unable to contain himself, forcing her jeans and panties down like this to get at her. She touched her pussy, pressed against it, feeling the bristly hairs against her palm, and pushed back with her hips.

Her body was slipping into this rhythm, and when she was ready her other hand reached out to her toilet kit, withdrew the short silver cylinder that at first glance looked like an electric toothbrush in a case – at least until she slipped the cover off, revealing the thin silver rod with the angled, coin-shaped tip. Even out of its cover, it wasn't immediately recognisable to people who believed that sex toys for women all had to resemble monstrous phalluses.

Never taking her hand from between her legs, she deftly twisted the control at the base of her favourite travel vibrator to life, feeling it buzz awake, grinning to herself with satisfaction; even on its lowest setting, it had all the delicious potential that a set of fresh batteries could provide.

The hand at her pussy grew insistent, and she parted her thighs to let her fingertips brush over her silky lips. As they lingered, stroked and teased her to open, she smiled again as she felt her wetness, abundant and slick, and she spread that wetness, up towards her clit, then down again.

The hand that held her vibrator approached as well, the instrument of pleasure still vibrating, almost sounding impatient to do its work, but she kept it back as the finger of her other hand continued to stroke her sex. Moving a fingertip upwards again, she circled her hardening clit slowly. A broad smile spread across her face as she imagined Nathan's tongue toying there. Then her hand left, replaced by the tip of her vibrator, sending bullets of pleasure through her. She worked the tip with practised, circular motions, raising her desire to a fever pitch.

'*Puta!*' she cursed between ragged breaths.

Brushing the tip of the vibrator against her clit caused more shock waves of pleasure to skyrocket through her body as she reintroduced her other hand into her playtime. Slipping a finger into her velvet folds, she curled the slender digit upwards, found and stroked her G-spot softly, then increased the pressure. Sounds of pleasure filled the room as she humped her hips towards the ceiling in an effort to milk more bliss from her touch.

Cat grew hotter, wetter, and the thumb on the hand that held her vibrator swivelled up and increased its speed, without it having to leave her clit. It sounded hungrier now and, as she also increased the pressure on her nub, she gasped as a mini-orgasm rocked her body. The finger at her pussy lowered, the slick finger brushing over her sensitive rear entrance, sending another shock of delight straight up her spine.

Shocked and pleased at the response, Cat let it linger down there, pivoting her thumb up to her pussy and stroking, then entering. The flat tip of the vibrator was sending more jolts through her, even as she had it orbit around her clit, ease off now and then. As it happened, she realised that she had fully adopted the steady, satisfying rhythm of the train, not racing towards her climax as she usually did, but forcing herself to pace her actions, relish the journey, relish the feelings building within her.

Cat cursed and blessed the tempo she had adopted, her supple body writhing and twisting on the bed as her vibrator and fingers drove her higher and higher. She teased the entrance to her ass again, then pressed down hard with her vibrator and held it there.

That was all it took. Fireworks exploded behind her closed eyelids and she yelped out as a new sensation raced through her body. She rode the wave of passion for as long as she could until, finally, she was spent, and her body demanded relief of a different sort. Easing her hands away from her sex, she dropped and straightened out her legs, aware of how wet she felt between her thighs and hoping, albeit with little power, that she didn't leave any patches on the sheets. Her vibrator still buzzed in her weakened grip and she feebly switched it off, promising herself a moment of rest before straightening and cleaning herself up. Just a moment . . .

4

In another part of the train, Faye Scott was lying down on a bed, watching the scene unfold via hidden cameras and microphones onto a PC screen, before it haemorrhaged into static and white sound once more. She cursed again, but never took her hand out of her briefs, her dress rucked up to her waist, feeling the garters holding up her stockings tighten as she closed her eyes and writhed. Damn, the Spanish woman was hot . . .

The office was a clutter of boxes and equipment, with the computer workstation and swivel chair sitting beside an old-fashioned roll-top desk and matching chair, beneath a well-marked railway route map of the Southern States. It was cramped, especially as there was also a low single bed, a Spartan frame with a thin pillow. But it served its purpose, and from here, she could watch and listen to nearly every point on the train.

She started as she heard someone work the office door lock. Seconds later, Jack Wheeler entered. 'A little early to be indulging, isn't it, my dear?'

'Fuck you. I'm entitled.'

'You should be welcoming the new guests.'

'Like who, Old Man Newholme? That black chick? The Olivers? Motley bunch this time.'

'They're not our only passengers.' He slipped out of his jacket, hung it up and loosened his tie. 'And what about Mr Ames? You obviously had your eye on him.'

Faye made a purring sound of agreement, her fingers stroking her outer lips. 'I came back here when he and his little spic piece went to their room.'

'Please, let's not add racism to your many, many faults.'

'Then he left her, and she was at it on her own.'

'Oh?' He sat down, checked the settings. 'Damn it, Belle.'

Faye rolled her eyes. 'Play it back, Jack.'

He tapped away at the keyboard, calling up the digital replay of the recording, and sat back, watching with obvious interest. 'You're right. She wrote she was an accountant. Love those types, all strait-laced during the day, wild fuckers at night.' He reached into the desk drawer and withdrew his Jack Daniels, then drank from the bottle. 'I'm sick of champagne. All bubbly shit.'

'You're a crabby bastard today.'

'To employ your own eloquent phrase, "Fuck you, I'm entitled."' He took another swig still watching Cat. At a sound from Faye, he added, 'Aren't you capable of controlling your own urges for even a little while?'

She smiled, but never took her eyes off Cat's image either, finding herself adopting the same position on the bed. 'If you were a real man, you wouldn't let me get to the point where I needed to satisfy my own urges.'

He grunted, recognised the taunt for what it really was, and rose. He stood over her at her right side, watching the gentle motion of the hand beneath the briefs. 'You annoy the hell out of me. I should –'

'You won't do shit,' she grunted, her face flushed as her hand changed rhythm slightly. 'You're a weak fish, a limp noodle –'

Wheeler was upon her, taking her hands from her briefs and forcing them into the leather cuffs fitted to the wall behind her, straddling her right thigh as she struggled and snarled. 'Get off me, you fucking pig! Scumbag! Faggot!'

'Shut up,' he replied calmly, his free hand reaching down between her legs. He touched her through her briefs and sharply slapped the inner thigh of her other leg when she continued to move, before returning to her sex, ripping at her silk briefs to touch her pussy, even as he began undoing his trousers – while still watching Cat's recording.

Unoffended, Faye's eyes followed his, as they fucked and watched.

Ben Oliver could barely hold onto the clothes he carried from the open suitcase to the drawers. 'Did you see the lines on her? Beautiful example of the Imperial III. Remember riding one as a boy.'

'I know,' Hannah Oliver agreed. 'So powerful and sleek. That GM D-78 engine runs through you like a . . .' She trailed off, stretched out as she was on the plush bed, but then sat up on her elbows, her face sobering as she looked at her husband. 'Ben . . . we're going to be OK, aren't we?'

He swallowed, knowing what she meant. It had been a rough year, the company laying him off, being unable to find successive employment, both of them forced to survive on what she earned behind the bar, and keeping the wolves and their final notices at the door. His grandmother's favourite phrase may have been 'The truly rich are those enjoy what they have', but for Hannah and Ben what they had nowadays was precious little. It was perhaps a terrible mistake to spend what savings they had on a weekend on the Silver Belle, but it was so welcome to get away from their house and their problems.

But the problems seemed to have followed them like cabooses.

He drew close, stroked her face. 'We'll be fine. We'll be back on our feet before you know it.' He pushed down the sensible part of him, the one that saw the mounting debts which didn't go away, and dropped to her lips to kiss her, determined to at least make this weekend an unforgettable one.

Tara was sitting on the edge of the bed, unbuckling her black leather ankle boots, grinning widely to herself. It was incredible! The energies onboard, thick, flowing like blood through veins! She'd never felt such a concentrated source before!

And the people she'd met: that sad Mr Newholme, the odious Mr Kolchak, the animated Mr and Mrs Oliver, and that new couple, with their secrets and dances ...

She needed to strip off, shake off the distracting impressions she received from wearing fabrics, even ones made from natural fibres. She rose to her feet and undid her jeans, wriggling out of them even as her thumbs slipped into the waistband of her white panties and made them follow. Lifting her short brown legs from the clothing at her feet, she pulled her T-shirt over her head and cast it beside her. Then she lay back and ran her hands briskly over herself. A vibration ran through her, as if the train had an extra engine with a frequency aligned with hers.

She was going to enjoy being onboard.

Richard Newholme took his time unpacking. He was never in any hurry, feeling no need to join in any of the carnal activities. He would be content to spend most of his time in his private berth – with his lover ... He sat down, closed his eyes and relaxed, waiting for her ...

... 'Ten minutes to Willoughby. Ten minutes to Willoughby.'

The conductor's voice barely carried through the berth door, announcing the train's final stop.

Their final stop too. There wasn't much time.

Enrique was in Val's arms, looking so handsome in his army

uniform, his smooth, sunburnt skin glistening with youth and excitement.

The room they'd found was bare, the single bed bereft of sheets or pillows, the drawn shutters letting only a few strands of sunlight in, and the air smelt of disinfectant. None of which meant anything to her as she pulled Enrique into an almost feral kiss, their lips grinding, parting, their tongues meeting, Enrique's shock at her boldness quickly melted first into acceptance, then boiled into a desire that matched her own. His cap fell off his head, ignored. He pushed her back against the wall, then his hands moved over her hips, around to her back, touching her through her navy-blue Sunday best dress, the erection in his trousers pressing against her side. Blindly she reached down between him to touch him.

She wanted him to know, clearly, that she would be doing more to send him off for two years to an army base in Germany than just kiss him. She knew she could get pregnant, but didn't rightly care. Everyone would know it was Enrique's anyway; they had been together since they were nine, half a lifetime ago, and they'd be married once his Selective Service finished.

Still kissing her, Enrique reached up between them, squeezed and stroked her aching breasts until they felt as if they would pop out of her underwear. Her head spinning, Val reached behind her and fumbled with the buttons to her dress, moaning into his mouth to give her a moment to manage this and not waste any more time. He obliged, never drawing away from her as she slipped her dress off her shoulders and wiggled it to her feet, leaving her in her all-constricting bra, slip, panties, stockings and shoes.

She felt herself blush seven shades. Though Enrique had seen her in the flesh when they'd been skinny-dipping in the lake behind their houses, this was different. And Daddy was nearby, sitting in the next carriage, waiting for her to return from her alleged trip to the lavatory. Damn him. Damn him for accompanying Enrique and her to Willoughby to see him off, and not giving them one final moment together alone. If they hadn't found this empty berth...

'Val,' he breathed, reaching up to touch her charm, the round brass charm that had been in her mother's family for generations. She hoped he wasn't going to waste time asking her to remove it.

Then his touch dropped, as if drained by the power of the charm, to her bared midriff, for a moment, slowly and delicately. He gasped, his breath quickening as his lips returned to hers, and his hand lingered, then descended between her legs, touching her through her panties.

Oh sweet God, it was so intense... she pushed against his fingers, reminded of those few furtive times when she had guiltily touched herself down there. This was far more immoral.

And it would get even more immoral in the next few minutes, if she had her way. The Christian discipline her father had imprinted on her warned of damnation for acts like this.

But she also knew, with equal fervent resolve, that she could live a long regretful life if something happened to him and she didn't take this chance, here and now. He was the only thing that gave her life meaning, the only thing to make her get up in the morning.

To want him. So much.

Val drew down her panties, keeping his eyes on hers so as not to exacerbate her modesty, not needing to prompt Enrique now to be bold and touch her, to go further than they ever dared in the past. He cupped her mound, feeling her hairs press into his palm as his middle finger settled into her groove, feeling how wet she was at her entrance. A moment's gathering of more courage, and she pushed herself down on him, letting him pierce her, enter her with his finger.

She gasped and clung to him, unbelieving of the sensations it produced, and she shamelessly wanted more, grinding against him, arching her head to one side to let him kiss and suckle on her neck, uncaring if he left marks. Her fingers fumbled with the buttons on his trousers, reached inside and grasped him, drew him out and stroked his hard length. Oh Lord, Val wanted to do this for hours, days, take time to explore each other fully, completely.

But they couldn't!

Driven by hunger as well as desperation, Val pulled back from his kisses, gasping, 'Bed . . . bed . . .'

Enrique grunted, understanding, then gently released her as they made their way to the bare bed. Val lay back, keeping her eyes on Enrique's to avoid further bursts of modesty as she spread her legs beneath him.

Enrique smiled, slipping out of his shoes, his trousers and underwear, and then positioned himself above her and lowered himself until his shaft pressed at her sex. Val lifted her rear, opening her flesh to the thick hardness, the bristly hair at his groin rubbing against her inflamed wetness. He slid in, thankfully slowly, filling her up, more and more, pushing overpowering sensations from her, with none of the pain she'd heard would come from her first time. Val let her eyes roll in the back of her head and her mouth open in a staggered gasp, her fingers digging into his biceps.

They lay joined together, looking into each other's eyes with such wonder, such lust and disbelief.

And then Enrique began thrusting into her, supporting her legs. She felt every inch of him, every contour as he plunged deep into her, ripples of delight running across her skin like water. He moaned, sounding lost to the pleasure, and began withdrawing slowly until only a part of him was inside Val, before sliding back in again. It was exquisite.

Her hands on his shoulders now, her excitement building, she slapped him lightly. 'Faster! N– No time now –'

Enrique, breathing more rapidly, quickened his rhythm to an urgent gallop.

Suddenly, outside the door, she heard her papa. 'Valentina? Where are you, girl?'

Enrique looked to the door, his pace slowing, but Val slapped his shoulder again, her voice low. 'Never mind him! Keep going!'

He pumped into her with abandon; she felt herself on the edge, wanting to feel those thunderclaps of pleasure inside her, wanting to feel it because of this man. He gave a strangled cry, spurring her on, her cries mingling with his as she came, her back arching beneath him, her legs wrapping around him, clinging to him fiercely, the sweat making her stick to her new lover . . .

. . . Cat sat up sharply, confused, unsure of where she was, sweat beading down her face. Then her mind focused as she glanced about the room, then at herself – lying there with her bra and shirt off, her jeans and thong around her knees, her vibrator beside her.

There was a knock at the door. Adolescent memories of being caught in similar situations resurfaced as she quickly returned her vibrator to her bag, slipped back into her T-shirt and pulled up her clothes, thankful that Nathan had kept his promise to knock before using the key. 'Wait, goddammit!'

Dios, she thought her scent was thick in the close confines of the berth.

Her head spun as she made her unsteady way to the door, ignoring the welcome hot glow between her legs. Damn, that dream was so vivid ... She was blushing again as she worked the door lock with trembling fingers. 'You can come in now.'

However, the man who stood there, Jack Wheeler, remained where he was, smiling. 'Thanks for the offer, but I'd better not.'

Cat stiffened, forcing down her ardent feelings. 'Can I help you, Mr Wheeler?'

Wheeler folded his hands behind him, letting his eyes seem to do all the work. 'I wanted to invite you, and Mr Ames, of course, to my table for a late dinner. Most of the other passengers have already eaten, but I always wait until the final ones have boarded.'

She saw his eyes flash down, for a second, and she realised her nipples were peaking beneath her T-shirt. Embarrassed but also amused, she leant against the doorframe. '*Gracias*. And what did we do to earn this honour?'

Wheeler leant back on the opposite side, mimicking, perhaps unconsciously, her own stance. 'In your case, the honour would be mine.'

Cat smiled back. 'Me? I'm just an ordinary accountant.'

'One who happens to have boarded a very extraordinary train, for what I hope will be a very special weekend for you. In fact,' he continued, shifting in place and looking as if he could read her mind, 'I believe you've been enjoying yourself already.' He nodded his head towards the bed, and his voice grew more confidential. 'I'll bet every dollar in my safe you've just experienced a refreshing rest. Belle possesses a special somniferous cadence that no one can resist, a lullaby of wheels on rails that takes you places you've never been before.'

Cat let her arms wrap around herself, lifting up her breasts slightly and distracting him momentarily. 'One should expect a train to take you places, Mr Wheeler. As it is, though, you're right. It *was* very restful.'

'Call me Jack.'

'You come here for anything in particular, "Jack"?'

Cat and Wheeler turned as one to the approach of a wary-looking Nathan.

Wheeler made a conscious move out of the doorway and back into the corridor. 'Yes, Mr Ames. I came to extend an invitation to dinner at my table tonight.'

Nathan nodded at this, moving closer and slipping an arm around Cat's waist. 'Much obliged. Now, if you'll excuse us, I'd like to spend some time with my woman before then, OK?'

Cat smiled, leaning into Nathan. 'I'm sure you understand ...'

Wheeler smiled back as he stepped away. 'Of course. See you both in an hour.'

Cat kept up her smile as she playfully drew Nathan into the berth, moving up as if to kiss him, but waiting until the door closed before pushing him away. 'You were rude out there, *pajiero.*'

Nathan grunted, before moving to the wardrobe, lifting up his suitcase and opening it on the table. 'It was for Wheeler's benefit.' His eyes fixed on the bed.

'And you'd act that way if we were going together, then?' Cat followed his gaze, saw her open toilet kit and reached for it, zipping up the bag and sticking it under her arm as she retrieved and pocketed her bra. 'Well, try not to get too protective, he has an interest in me.'

Nathan started unfolding and hanging up his shirts and trousers. 'That's obvious. But you're still new to fieldwork. You need back-up.'

'Not to keep a man's attention, *pajiero.* We're here to get information on Wheeler and his operations, after all. And if you want to make yourself useful, how about getting to know his partner Faye?'

'If you want. But I'll be thinking of you.' He grinned. 'I don't suppose you've called Gordy?'

'Are you kidding?' She reached into her pocket, withdrew and unlocked her mobile, hit the correct speed dial then, after a second's thought, put it on loudspeaker and tossed it to the bed between Nathan and her. 'You talk to him. I'm going for a wash.'

Before Nathan could say anything further, the ringing was replaced by a young and ebullient young man's voice. 'Ah, Agent Montoya. I know you couldn't bear to go long without calling me.'

Cat remained silent as Nathan sat down on the sofa, staring in her direction with some amusement. 'It's me on Cat's phone, Gordy, so keep it in your pants. She's . . . in the shower.'

'Aww, don't tease me like that, Hound.'

'No, no, it's true. Saw her strip down right in front of me and pad her cute little ass into the bathroom. But never mind that.'

'What do you mean, "never mind that"? That sweet little *chica*'s just a few feet away from you, naked and lathering herself up! How can you just talk normally?'

'Because unlike you, Gordy, I have a measure of, ah, sophistication . . .'

Nathan's words failed as Cat unbuttoned her jeans and shimmied them down, revealing her black thong. She stepped out of them, and then made a show of looking back at him as if she'd forgotten he was there. She mouthed the word 'sorry', with almost some sincerity.

Oblivious, Gordy's voice rose an octave. 'At least tell me what her underwear's like!'

Nathan recovered, but didn't take his eyes from her as he replied, 'She favours black lace. And as little as possible of it, too. Now, I have some names for you to run checks on. You ready to listen, or shall I call back after you're done having a good hard think about Cat in the shower?' He made some shooing gestures at her, looking unashamedly distracted.

Cat laughed softly as she entered the bathroom. She finished her undressing, switched on the shower and tested the water. It was a strong, forceful blast, and it invigorated her as she stepped under it.

But then she adjusted it to a softer caress. Closing her eyes, she reached out for the bottle of her favourite lavender liquid soap, then sculpted snake suds over her body, remembering the dream. Fucking hell, that dream! So strong and clear! And stimulating, far more than her own first time had been. She could have had another vibrator session when she woke up, if she'd had the time and opportunity.

Her nipples were firming again beneath her soapy hands. The look on Nathan's face when she dropped her jeans was priceless. But she knew it had been for more than just to tease him while on the phone to that horndog Gordy. She pictured him getting hard sitting there, watching.

Her hand found its way between her legs again . . .

The observation carriage was as elegant as the reception one, with white linen cloth-clad tables lined up in rows, topped with polished silverware and glassware reflecting light from brass ceiling fixtures, and staffed by young women in imprac-tical, skimpy black French maid uniforms.

Wheeler had changed into an old-fashioned billowy white shirt and black trousers, and sat at the head of one table, leading his dining companions through a sumptuous meal of grilled sole or steak, with toasts and tales of his travels.

Cat, dressed in a black satin camisole with white trim and a matching knee-length pinstripe skirt and with her hair pinned back, sat at Wheeler's right hand. Nathan, opposite her, played the charming guest, particularly with Faye, sitting next to him, looking regal in a rich red gown which contrasted with her dark features. With them also was Benjamin and Hannah, both looking unceasingly delighted to be there, and Donnie, who was busy alternating between vainly trying to keep Tara's attention, and flirting with the staff.

Dinner wound down, most of the diners had moved off to other parts of the train, as the staff efficiently transformed the dining carriage into something different, folding up and hiding the tables and chairs, setting up curtains and large cushions. A musician was hooking up his guitar to some equipment at the far end, and soon easy blues flowed from hidden speakers as the staff swiftly vanished.

Cat watched it all from one cushion, sandwiched between Nathan and Wheeler, with Faye opposite Nathan. The woman's interest in Nathan had been obvious from the start, though she refrained from being too forward. Cat for her part watched with amusement Nathan's attempt to balance showing devotion to his 'partner' and his reciprocal interest in Faye.

As for Wheeler, he rarely strayed far from Cat, without being too intrusive. He made it easy for Cat to set aside what she knew about him and treat him like someone she'd just met.

Faye set aside her glass. 'I need to walk around, clear my mind for the séance. But I can't do it without some chivalrous accompaniment.' She reached out and touched Nathan's arm. 'I sense you'd make an ideal knight errant, Mr Ames.'

'*Si*,' Cat agreed, smiling. 'He's into protecting damsels in distress, whether they need it or not.'

'Whereas some damsels are simply asking for a dragon to bite them on their gorgeous little asses.' He rose to his feet, took Faye's hand and helped her up. 'Shall we?'

'I'd be delighted.'

Cat watched them depart, turning back when Wheeler

noted, 'She's a talented partner. Says she's heard the spirits all her life. Her family grew up near an old Confederate graveyard, where she used to go out and talk with the ghosts.'

Cat bit back her initial reply about spirits and other bullshit. 'Is she just a business partner, or is there more to it?'

'There's more, but we're not exclusive. What about you and Mr Ames?'

Cat considered the best answer to the question. 'I've ... been with men since Nate and I first got together. I think he's been with other women. It's not something we've talked about.'

He leant forwards on his cushion. 'Maybe you should have before now. He seems the possessive type. Does he satisfy you?'

She almost affected a coy response, settling instead for something more honest. 'Every time we've been together, he has. And I think I do the same for him. I suppose it makes you wonder why we come onboard looking for other people?'

'Not at all. In fact, only people in secure relationships should try this lifestyle. They shouldn't come looking for alternatives to their partners, to try to fix something that's not working. They should be here for adventure, enjoyment, the opportunity to explore their sexualities, trying out things you couldn't risk in the real world.'

His eyes focused on some passengers, scantily clad, laughing and walking past them. 'You can wear whatever you want, or nothing at all. You can watch others, be watched, and join in if invited, or have others join you. Take it as far as you want to go – and then at the end return to your normal life. And best of all, it's a safe environment. Nobody will force you into anything you don't want.' He tilted his head. 'May I be bold and ask what you might want to get out of this weekend?'

'May I be stubborn and ask why you want to know?'

'Because I'm your host. It's both my task and my pleasure to endeavour to provide what I can for my guests.' He smiled. 'Well? What are you after?'

Enough evidence to initiate a full investigation on you, some distinction at the office... a chance to be closer to Nathan without risk... 'I... don't know what I want, Jack. Maybe not until I see it.'

He nodded, seeming to understand. 'Have you visited the games carriages yet?'

She smiled. Nathan had described it when they were getting dressed, but she hadn't been impressed with his account.

She revised her opinion when Wheeler escorted her there. She supposed it was different now, with the raunchy music in the background, and the lights above suffusing the air in glows of magenta and aquamarine. And, of course, the people.

It was like a labyrinth, narrow, twisting passageways within the carriage, opening up into niches and alcoves, some with padded benches, other areas larger with beds and armless chairs. These had spaces for spectators, to stand or sit, or even watch from behind one-way partitions. Another section contained a small theatre with an erotic movie playing on one wall, where couples watched and kissed and caressed each other. Other places had seats and tables with padding and fixtures for securing wrists and ankles, or raised platforms for dancing and displaying.

With Wheeler nearby, Cat moved through the light and darkness like a fish swimming through unfamiliar waters. People milled about, dressed in ordinary clothes, in leather gear, in lingerie or in nothing at all. They were talking or kissing or going further, some looking invitingly at her and their mutual host. Cat felt claustrophobic, but couldn't ignore the buzz of excitement. People brushed past, close without intrusion or unwanted touching, acting more civilised than many clubs she'd frequented in Miami.

She paused as she felt Wheeler's hand on her side, squeezing gently. She turned, looked up at him and saw him nod towards one area. Cat followed. It was one with a raised dais and pinky-orange spotlights trained on a woman swaying to the music. She was a middle-aged brunette, curving at the hips, with striking cheekbones and dark rosebud lips, clad in a black full-cup bra that barely contained her full breasts, suspender slips, stockings and high heels. Sensually she ran her hands down the sides of her body, then back up again, over her navel and her breasts, stroking the soft gathered chiffon and the bow in the centre. Her hair swung across her back, as she swayed her head in time to the music. Around her, men and women watched with clear enjoyment.

'That's ... Well, let's call her Bonnie,' Wheeler whispered, his lips close to Cat's ear. 'One of my regulars, and popular. In the real world, she's an ordinary wife and mother, an anonymous cleaner in some office building. Here, for a couple of days and nights, she's a goddess. Worshipped. Admired. Desired.'

Cat half-listened. The body of the woman and the sinuous movements she was making with it were hypnotic. She couldn't take her eyes away, and she felt her pulse quickening. The air was thick with scents that mingled with the heat and the colours. The woman brought her hands over her waist, unhooked her suspender straps and then slipped her thumbs into the narrow black sides of her beautiful silk briefs. She smiled at Cat and Wheeler, then turned in place on the dais so her buttocks were facing them, slowly inching the silk over her hips and down her legs, giving them a view of the long slit of her sex, pursed between her thighs, hairless. With the briefs at her feet, she kicked them away with the rest of her clothes.

Cat's senses were charged and, when Wheeler pressed up

behind her, she took her eyes away from Bonnie to look at him. His eyes sought her assurance that it wasn't too much for her. She gave it, her arousal obviously written on her face. He smiled and then turned back to the scene.

Bonnie, kneeling on all fours now, spread her thighs apart. Cat watched as her right arm snaked between her legs and began to caress her cheeks, her hips swaying from side to side in time to the music, her head hanging down so her dark hair brushed the dais. Gradually working lower, her fingers parted the folds of her sex, deliberately exposing herself, the flesh wet and glistening under the lights. Around her, some of the men were unzipping their trousers and drawing out their erections, stroking them. One woman dropped to her knees before a man – perhaps someone she knew, perhaps not – and took him full into her mouth.

Cat felt the excitement around her building, as in a graceful motion Bonnie removed her fingers, twisted and lay flat on her back, raising her knees and spreading her legs. And then, with her eyes still on Cat, she motioned for some of those around her to approach. They did, then knelt on either side of Bonnie. One man bent down to kiss her lips, another to kiss and lick her breasts, one woman joined in to stroke her inner thighs, slender fingers sliding up to the hairless pussy.

Cat wanted to move closer – not to join in, but to see Bonnie's face, see the bliss and exhilaration she knew would be there. Wheeler was right. The woman *was* the object of lust and adoration here. There was nothing sordid or degrading. Cat wondered if her husband was one of the men at her side now, or if he was watching, or even present.

Wheeler's hands had somehow found themselves on Cat's hips, as if to steady her, or restrain her. She barely registered it, until one hand slid across her stomach, as if admiring the silk of her camisole top, and his subsequent words in her ear made it seem as if he'd read her mind. 'That's her husband, moving between her legs now.' He nodded to the tall, thin, dark-skinned man with a shaved head, kneeling down, his legs and buttocks muscular and sweat beaded, his erection thick and bobbing. 'He's the only one she has penetration with. Everyone has their own rules and boundaries, and we agree to respect them.' His hands moved down to Cat's outer thighs. 'So long as you make them known.'

She understood exactly what he meant. She pressed her ass back against him, felt his erection, and watched as Bonnie's husband lowered himself onto her, entered her. Cat watched the muscles in his ass and thighs squeeze as he slowly fucked her.

'Are you ready?' Wheeler whispered.

It had all felt unbelievably wicked and wanton, and Cat's pussy mewled for attention. She tilted her head back, brushing against his beard. 'I'm always ready.'

His lips brushed against her cheek, as his hands returned to her sides. 'Good. Faye should be ready to conduct the séance.'

Cat swallowed, surprised at how much she'd wanted Wheeler to say something else.

5

'Forge a circle, with only the tips of your little fingers touching. No talking, and especially no laughing, for the dead can no longer feel joy and will be offended. Be receptive to everything around you. Open your eyes, your ears and in particular your minds.'

Cat could only promise Faye the first two. She'd remained aroused and distracted as Wheeler led her to the reception carriage, where they'd moved the chairs away from the centre to accommodate a large oval table draped in immaculate white linen. Thin black candles in brass sticks sat on the table, surrounding a clear glass bowl clouded with drops of blood from a volunteer. The carriage lamps were off, and the candles cast light and shadow around them.

Faye sat at one end of the table, the other participants alternating by gender on either side, with Nathan, Hannah Oliver and Wheeler on her right side, and Ben Oliver, Tara Gilbrand and Richard Newholme on her left. Cat sat opposite her, between Wheeler and Newholme. Nearby sat a smaller table with a collection of items such as a Bible and brass bells, to be employed should any malevolent forces visit.

'Contact may occur in various ways,' Faye was intoning, her voice smooth as glass. 'Perceived in various ways. A scent, a cold draft, whispers, the candle flames brightening, flashing with spectral coruscation. We may even see lights, apparitions.'

Cat glanced around, bored but fully aware of the coolness of the linen beneath her hands and the heat from the meagre touch of the men on either side of her. Newholme was staring intently into the candles. Wheeler was watching Faye, but occasionally glancing at Cat.

'We are here,' Faye was saying now, her expression focused. 'Come to us. We await you, your pleas, your wisdom and your warnings. Come to us. Come to us. Come . . .'

The woman's words seemed to blend with the clack-clack of the train rails, and Cat let her eyes flutter and her attention waver, even after seeing shadows dance around her, seemingly of their own volition.

The candles burst with light, quick flashes, as if sparks danced between the flames. There was a scent like burnt rubber in the air.

Then there were the voices: laughter, curses, music and conversation, as if a party was ongoing behind her. No, closer.

Cat sat there, startled at first as she saw people milling about in the darkness: train staff, perhaps, or passengers who'd wandered into the séance. They'd better be. If Wheeler and Faye Scott expected her to believe they were ghosts, then they weren't as professional as she might have expected. These didn't go 'boo' or rattle chains. They didn't even seem to notice the people at the table, as they drifted about, nursed drinks, played cards.

Cat swayed on her heels, gripping the piano behind her for support as the train took a sharp bend. She felt immersed in how clear, vivid, everything was becoming: the lights above brightening, the frost framing the windows, the tinkle of Pullman on the piano keys, the autumn-leaf smell of the Cuban cigars threatening to dry out her voice before she completed her set.

Still, Cat was enjoying herself, despite the circumstances . . .

* * *

... Still, Valentina was enjoying herself, despite the circumstances. She always loved singing, always had a good reception at her father's club, and not just because it was her father's club. Beside her, Pullman, the young coloured player they'd hired for her, knew all her songs. And they'd even given her some money to buy herself a new dress before they'd left New Orleans, a gorgeous silk chiffon Christian Dior evening dress with a side sash, waist-defining criss-cross of shirred material and a low neckline that her father wouldn't have approved of, the wine-red colour of the material matching her mane of hair. It'd be the best thing she'd take away from this experience.

She fitted on another smile as Pullman started into another number, one she'd recognised right away, and she returned to doing what she did best:

Well, I'm going back to Memphis, onboard the 9.03
I'm gonna see my sugar, cos that's where I wanna be
I've got the night train blues, got the night train blues
Got the night train blues
Cos I've paid my dues
Got the night train blues ...

Yeah, she was good tonight. Too bad no one was paying any attention to her.

Most of the men were huddled around the large green card table, black silk jackets hanging on hooks on either wall, sleeves rolled up, hands casually tossing twenties and fifties into the pot, or flicking cigar ash onto the floor. Women hung around the periphery, smoking, drinking and talking with each other, looking bored. A few looked over at Val as she sang, their disdain blatant. Val suspected they gave such looks to everyone outside their tight little circle, let alone anyone non-Italian.

To hell with them.

She finished the song, thanked Pullman, lifted up her glass from the piano top and sipped at her gin and tonic, determined to moderate her drinking and not leave herself vulnerable. She turned away, having learnt by now not to expect any response from them.

Until one of them broke the pattern. 'You know anything besides those fucking *moolie* numbers?'

Val's face reddened, and she glanced in embarrassment at Pullman, who had the good grace to pretend not to recognise the insult. She bit back her initial reply to turn around again, addressing the crowd, not knowing which of them spoke. 'If you don't like Billie Holiday, I know more modern numbers: Rosie Clooney, Doris Day. I'm here to please.'

From the table, the speaker, a ringer for Orson Welles, made himself known, though he never looked up from the cards he kept tightly in his podgy fingers as his voice rose. 'You hear that, Mickey? She's here to please.'

No one at the table, or immediately surrounding it, responded. Val looked past them. An ornate wall-to-ceiling screen, decorated in a narrow grid pattern, opaque glass decorated with Gothic swirls, divided the carriage. It offered at least visual privacy to those on the other side. The man she knew sat behind there never responded, having disappeared back there almost from the time that the train had pulled out of town. She was both relieved at this, and disappointed...

She started as Baldy's hand roughly squeezed her rear. 'You're wasting your time standing there singing. You can earn more on your back.'

Her reaction was instinctive, danger or not, as she slapped his hand away. 'You don't have enough money for that, you bastard!'

That elicited oohs and ahhs from the others, albeit laced with the arrogance of bullies who knew they'd always have the advantage. It was a swagger they had displayed from the day they'd come south, looking to acquire legitimate businesses as criminal fronts. Businesses like her father's club. Daddy was a good man, but a bad gambler, and the takeover had been as swift as it had been merciless. And though technically he still owned the club, he ran it in their name – on the condition that Val accompanied them back north for the weekend, singing for them.

She wasn't naive enough to think that was all that they might want from her.

In fact, with regard to the capo, the man in charge of this crew, she was counting on it.

Then a new voice spoke up from behind the screen, a man's voice, low but dampening the noise around the card table like a bucket of iced water. 'Send our guest in here.'

Baldy grunted, puffed his cigar back to consciousness. 'Well? You heard.' His words were poisoned with that petty, now-you're-gonna-get-it tone most people left behind in the schoolyard.

So she left him with a final, 'Good luck with that pair of deuces,' then slid the door aside and entered the private area, as Baldy lost his hand. The door, now shut, muted the sounds from the other side. It was a darker, more intimate area in here, with leather-backed chairs grouped in pairs around tiny round tables, and thick verdant potted plants providing token cover. It was a place for private conversations, for making deals.

This suited Val just fine.

'At the end.'

She walked along, seeing his polished black shoes and the legs of his immaculate black silk trousers. Her heart was fluttering and her legs were turning to jelly. She was afraid. She was excited. She adjusted her breasts inside her dress, her hands shaking.

Mickey was there, on his own, reclining in a chair, a brandy snifter at his side, studying a small chessboard. His hand reached out, almost touched a knight, but then withdrew again. The image had thrown her; she'd expected to see him counting his ill-gotten gains or polishing guns.

He didn't look up, and Val took the opportunity to compose herself, study him again. He was a young man, shockingly young for someone in his position, a man of distracting good looks, dark and smooth, with swept-back jet-black hair, an aquiline nose and chiselled chin which seemed to dare the world to take a swing at it. His jacket was off, and the cuffs of his white silk shirt were undone, the gold cufflinks sitting on the edge of the table.

This man had overturned her life, hung a sword of Damocles over it.

Sweet God, she wanted him.

'I hate cigar smoke,' he said suddenly, softly, as if she'd asked him something. He never raised his voice, ever, hence his crew's nickname for him: Mickey Whisper. He indicated the board. 'And I can't study this in front of them without getting ribbed.'

She nodded, in lieu of any other response, loving the surprisingly cultured, educated smoothness of his voice. She'd had a plan – sort of – but on standing here, it seemed to have deserted her. She kept staring at him, and it was melting her insides more than she'd wanted.

He reached out suddenly, almost impulsively, moved a white knight forward, and then turned the board around so that now he could see it from the black side. Except that now he leant back, regarding her directly as he reached for his snifter. 'What's that around your neck?'

Val's hand reached up to her charm. 'It's a family talisman for our Guédé loa.'

'"Gay-day lawa?" You mean voodoo? You believe in that stuff?'

She'd asked herself that, more than once. Her mother's family had, for generations, and her mother herself had been a mambo, a priestess. When Mama died, Papa had tried to raise Val as strictly Christian, but she had learnt on her own. And though she still didn't quite know if she believed, she was prepared to respect the beliefs of the maternal side of her heritage. 'I don't know if I believe, but I ... I won't take any chances.'

He smiled and, for a moment, she expected him to say something insulting. He wouldn't have been the first person outside of New Orleans to do that. Instead, he surprised her with, 'I said something similar once. My mother wanted me to be a priest, but the thought of saying prayers to saints and stuff with no guarantee of delivery seemed like such a scam. Why do you think you were invited to accompany us?'

When his eyes fixed on hers, Val swallowed, felt dizzy. She hated her body. Hated how it reacted to a man her mind saw as an enemy, even as she realised how it could make her intentions less unpalatable. Slipping on a mask of nonchalance, of flirtatiousness, she smiled. 'I think we both know.'

'Humour me; I prefer the direct approach.' He loosened the knot on his burgundy silk tie, smiling as he watched Val's eyes follow.

'So do I. I think we're much alike, Mister –'

He held up a hand, cutting her off gently. 'Call me Mickey. I think we need to be on a first-name basis.'

Val drew closer, one hand idly rising to play with some rebellious strands of hair near her right ear. 'Mickey. As I was saying, I think we're much alike.'

'In some ways.' Now he rose to his feet, standing a head taller than her, close but not too close – yet. 'Though I bet if

I stripped you to the skin I could find some interesting differences.'

'I'd ... I'd certainly hope so.' Val felt a shiver of excitement run through her at his words, his proximity, the heady scent of his cologne. She worked up the courage to reach out, as if genuinely interested in adjusting his tie. 'You should be careful. I might hold you to that.'

Mickey smiled again, with that mixture of amusement and desire that seemed to come so easily to him. 'Being careful isn't one of my stronger suits. And what makes you think I might be interested in ... being held?'

Val pursed her lips as if in thought rather than in anticipation of a kiss. 'The looks you've been giving me since you first came to the club. The looks you're giving me now.'

Mickey's expression never wavered as he drew in closer. 'Tell me more about these looks.'

Val swallowed, finding this equally more difficult and easy than she'd expected, her anxiety and arousal keeping her off guard. The room felt almost uncomfortably warm despite the cold weather outside, but she pressed on. She had him. She had him now. 'The looks of a man that wants to fuck me.' She swallowed; just hearing herself say That Word was arousing.

Mickey chuckled. 'You should be careful, such brashness could get that sweet little ass of yours smacked.'

Val smiled back, the heat in her groin flaring up as if in response to her embarrassment at using such language. 'I thought you said you preferred the direct approach?'

'I do.' He reached up, touched her face with his fingertips, making her shiver. His touch drew across her lips, before descending to the soft downy skin of her throat, threatening to continue down into her cleavage. 'And so, to be direct: turn around.'

Val started, the frisson of desire that had already ignited

within her now sparking and spreading to the rest of her body, forcing her to turn in place until she faced away from him, staring at some old sepia photograph of a steam train on the wall. 'L– Like this?'

'Bend forwards.'

She paused, leant forwards over a table until her breasts touched the smooth, polished wooden surface, followed by her charm, and she was resting almost totally on her elbows, her hair draping either side of her face. She heard Mickey move closely behind her, his voice touched her like his hands. 'Are you a virgin?'

'Does that matter –' Then she yelped at the hand that suddenly slapped her left buttock, more teasing than rough, sending a pulse straight to her pussy.

His hand remained there, stroking her through her dress. 'Well?'

Val swallowed, her head spinning. 'N– No. I'm not.' She didn't want to go into detail, didn't want to think about Enrique, away in Europe, and open up the floodgates of guilt. He knew nothing about what this mob had done, and certainly didn't know about her intentions now. He definitely wouldn't understand, but she promised herself she'd make it up to him when his tour of duty was over and he returned home.

'Not that I mind,' Mickey was saying, still stroking her.

She squeezed her thighs together. There was something undeniably dynamic and exciting about the man behind her: that air of authority, that voice, that gaze – and that touch, oh God . . .

Another slap recaptured her awareness, as did the question, 'Why did you come here?'

Val's mouth had dried, even as other parts of her grew wet, and sweat beaded down the curves of her suspended breasts in her dress. 'I . . . You asked me.'

'Yes. But you had your own agenda, too.' Now Mickey pressed his groin up against Val's proffered backside, his erection obvious, his hands moving up and down the her hips and thighs. 'You came to have me do this?'

Val felt her nostrils flare with her quickening breath as she eased her upper half further down onto the table, until her aching breasts rested fully on the surface, threatening to spill out, and her fingertips pressed hard onto the polished wood. 'Y– Yes.'

Mickey's crotch ground against Val's ass, and his voice retained that air of composure, of command, laced with a wantonness that fed Val's own hungers. 'And this?' He pulled back enough to let one hand move down over her other cheek, then gave her another slap. 'Open.'

Val obeyed, lowering her head onto her crossed arms on the table, experiencing both sheer arousal and embarrassment at how quickly, easily she responded to this man's voice, touch, very presence, forgetting her reasons for being here, feeling utterly and shamelessly selfish and self-indulgent.

Mickey moved against her again, this time his hands snaking down and lifting up the hem of her dress, raising it past the tops of her stockings, her garters, revealing her dark-red satin panties. Val wanted to protest, but that part of her had scurried into a far corner to wait, swathed and silenced by an ever-dominating lust. She bit her lip as she felt Mickey pull down her panties, down over her rear to the tops of her stockings.

The cool air failed to overcome the overpowering heat Val felt emanating from her naked, trembling flesh. Mickey's feather-light touch returned, trailing fingertips up over the contours of her ass, along the undercurves and up towards the dimples steepling her cheeks, as his other hand pressed down against her lower back, keeping her dress raised and out of the way.

Val trembled at his touch, his alternating waves of rough and gentle behaviour keeping her dizzy and wanting, made a sound like a whimper as she heard him undoing his trousers. Oh God, he was going to take her here and now, with his crew only a short distance away ...

Then Val heard his trousers drop, felt him, his shaft, the velvety hot tip of it, touch the apex of the sweet valley between her buttocks, sliding down. And it descended, pausing to tease at the tightened opening to her rear. As it continued further, Mickey leant in closely as if to whisper in Val's ear: 'And what about ... *this*?'

Mickey's cock reached the puffed, wet, waiting entrance to Val's pussy.

And entered.

Val moaned sharply, shamelessly, twisting like a worm on a hook as Mickey slowly filled her up, his hands gripping her hips. He kept still as she squirmed, and then flexed it inside her, making her start and curse into her arms.

He began to move, slowly driving into her, again and again. Val's hot wet flesh moulded itself around the hard member as it repeatedly, rhythmically filled her up and released clusters of lovely sensations.

'Yes, you came for this,' Mickey purred, still gripping Val by the hips, steadying her against the table, his broad hairy thighs brushing against her stockinged legs. 'But I think you came for more.' Almost imperceptibly, his left hand released its hold on her hip and moved up along Val's cambered spine, gripping the loose material of her dress and holding onto it, his cock still thrusting relentlessly into her.

And as the sweet assault continued, Mickey leant in still closer, until Val felt the man's breath on her neck. 'I think you came to try to seduce me, to win me over and convince me to free your father from his obligations. I think you were naive enough to believe you might be worth the investment we'd lose doing something like that.'

Val was lost, unable to deny, acknowledge, or make any coherent response. And when she felt Mickey's hand move around from her hip to her groin, touch her bush, stroking her as his middle finger sought out the top of her slit, found her clit, stroked it while still driving into her from behind, she cried out, uncaring of who heard her.

'Well, that's not gonna happen,' he informed her coolly, never raising his voice, even though he seemed as lost in the sensations as she was. 'What's gonna happen is that we're getting married.'

The words struck her and she briefly lost the rhythm she had adopted. She glanced behind her through a tangle of red hair. 'Wha– married – no –'

He drove into her harder now, roughly, forcing her down again. '*Si*. We're getting married, as soon as we get into Chicago. Your papa knows all about it. You see, a man in my position needs a wife, or people will think he's some limp-wristed *fanook*. Don't worry, we'll be making plenty of visits back home, perfectly legitimate trips, as far as everyone's concerned – especially the Feds.' He reached up with his free hand and took a handful of her hair, drawing it aside so she could look at him as they fucked. 'If it helps, just remember that I'm less likely to do anything bad to your papa if he's my father-in-law.'

Even as the sensations built within her, like a volcano about to erupt, Val tried to grasp what he was saying. Marriage? To *him*? Giving up her life down south? Leaving Daddy? *Enrique*? How could she do that? How could ...

Her thoughts jumbled as she came, bent forwards wantonly over the table ...

* * *

83

. . . As Cat, bent forwards wantonly over the table, released her grip and fell backwards into her chair, the chair tipped back until the back of her head hit the floor.

Dimly she heard someone racing for the carriage lights, and then finding them. Heartbeats later, Nathan was kneeling at her side, opening her eyes to peer into them. Concern etched in his expression. 'Catalina, what the hell –'

Behind him, Richard Newholme whispered, 'Cher?' before quickly looking away.

On her other side, Hannah Oliver asked, 'Is she OK?'

Cat tried to close her eyes again, found Nathan was still holding her lids open, and slapped his hand away. '*Besame el culo, pajiero.*'

Nathan let go and knelt back. 'She's OK.'

But his disquiet returned as the séance broke up, and he pulled her into a private alcove in the neighbouring carriage, glancing behind to ensure their privacy. 'Cat, what the hell was that about?'

Cat remained embarrassed, trying to shake off the residual feelings of arousal and confusion generated by that dream – weirdly, a dream featuring the same female character as the one she'd had in her berth, a woman she'd never seen before. It was stupid. She was obviously tired and wound up over this assignment. And over being close to Nathan.

Like now. He was up against her, his hands on her waist, holding her. 'I . . . I fell asleep, that's all.' *Dios*, she could still feel Mickey's hands on her hips as he drove into her from behind . . . only now it was Nathan's hands, and from the front. A hot wave enveloped her again, and she became acutely aware of Nathan's closeness, the intensity in his eyes as she looked up at him. 'We have to get back to the room.'

'The berth?' he asked, grinning.

'The séance room, *cabrón*. I want to look for the tricks that they'd obviously used.'

'What does that have to do with why we're here?'

She didn't answer, just led him back to the carriage – only to find someone had beaten them to it. They watched as Tara Gilbrand inspected the table and chairs with a professional scrutiny that belied her earlier easy-going persona.

She had her back to them when she invited, 'Come in and help.'

Cat and Nathan exchanged glances, but entered, Nathan's arm still around her, Cat allowing the continued contact – for the cover, of course. 'Help, with what?'

'With finding out the truth. That's why you're here, isn't it?'

Cat began to reply, but then felt Nathan slip behind her, snaking both arms around her waist and squeezing her gently as he replied, 'Actually, we came looking for you. We wanted to know if you'd be interested in coming to our berth for some . . . midnight refreshments.' He leant in closer, brushing the side of his face against Cat's as she felt his erection press shamelessly between her cheeks. 'Isn't that right, Wildcat?'

Cat couldn't help but react, but fought her flush of excitement to quip, 'Funny how your suggestions for threesomes never involve another man.'

Then Tara smiled at Cat in that multilayered way, as if she saw through their story but played along – or maybe recognised how much truth was there. 'Maybe later. Now, you two can help me look for the tricks our hosts used tonight.'

Cat frowned, reluctantly pulling out of Nathan's grasp as she realised she'd been unconsciously grinding her ass against his hard-on. 'Why would that interest us? We're just boring old accountants on vacation.'

'Of course.' Tara moved to the wall and dropped to all fours, scrutinising an electrical socket near the floor. 'Check this out.'

When Cat joined her, she examined the socket. 'It's fake.'

Tara nodded. 'You smell that? Odours, mixed with compound neutralisers.'

'A chemical emitter?'

'Produces scents of lilies, animal musk, whatever, at pre-programmed times. Seen it used at other so-called séances, to simulate olfactory manifestations.'

'I love this dirty talk,' Nathan joked, moving to the glass display by the bookcase. 'What's in here?'

Tara looked over at him, her contempt clear. 'Voodoo para-phernalia: amulets, beads.' She indicated a small black cloth bag tied up with string at the neck. 'A gris-gris bag, filled with all the necessary items to bring good luck or protection.'

'Do you practise?' Nathan asked.

'Yes, and believe it or not I and the millions of other decent, law-abiding devotees in the world do it without curses or zombies.'

'Sorry, didn't mean to offend.'

Tara breathed out. 'No, *I'm* sorry, for biting at you. My grand-parents abandoned their ancestors' faith when they left New Orleans – and they disowned me when I re-embraced it.'

Cat had moved away at the talk of the spiritual, finding something behind the curtains. 'Here.'

Nathan and Tara approached; Cat was frowning at the narrow gridlike strips around the windows. 'Air vents?'

'Speakers,' Nathan corrected. 'Using the windows them-selves as sounding boards. But it wouldn't be powerful enough for normal sounds like music.'

'Infrasound,' Tara said. 'Subsonic vibrations, producing goosebumps, unease –'

'Hallucinations?' Cat asked suddenly.

'Not that I'm aware of. Why?'

'Never mind.' Cat stepped away from the window.

'Do you make a living debunking mediums?' Nathan asked.

'Investigating them, for fraud claims, news programmes. The debunking is a sad after-effect.'

'Sad?' Cat asked, finally curious.

'I've spent my life looking for genuine psychic phenomena. And until I came onboard this train – a train I've dreamt of all my life – I hadn't found any.' Now she seemed to be embarrassed, as if having revealed too much of herself, and moved to the table. 'Pity Mr Wheeler has to resort to deception in here –'

'Not deception, Ms Gilbrand. Entertainment.'

The three of them turned to see Wheeler enter and approach, appearing nonchalant despite being caught out. 'Gimmicks, smoke and mirrors for the tourists. I readily admit to it. It doesn't detract from how special Belle is, however.' He looked to Cat. 'I hope you're feeling better after your ... episode, Ms Montoya.'

She ignored his apparent concern, but was aware of how Nathan drew closer to her in Wheeler's presence, a protective, possessive reaction she had initially found denigrating – but now found more ... arousing. 'You said before that this train was special, Mr Wheeler. You didn't explain. Care to now?'

Wheeler paused, and then shook his head, smiling teasingly. 'I fear someone of your ... stolid temperament ... isn't prepared for the full truth, my dear.'

He was baiting her, and she knew it. 'Sounds like a challenge, Jack. One you'd better have the *cojones* to back up.' Now she turned to face Nathan, fighting back the heat she felt at his proximity, how easily their bodies fitted together. 'I'm going off with our host for a while. Think you can keep yourself busy, Hound?'

Nathan smiled, and then leant in, pulling her into an

embrace. He began kissing her neck, sending potent flares shooting through her body, flares that still burnt as he whispered, 'You sure about this?'

Cat moaned audibly – and sincerely – and moved to his own neck, whispering back, 'Check out his office while I keep him away.'

Nathan pulled back, nodding almost imperceptibly.

And then he kissed her on the mouth.

Cat felt her head spin and her pussy clench as their lips moved together, parted, their tongues meeting, swirling and dancing together.

All part of the cover, of course.

6

Nathan worked his universal key on the door to Wheeler's office, having already knocked and determined no one was present. He heard and felt the lock surrender to his touch, and then he entered, pocketing his key.

The facilities were cramped, as if the place served as much for storage as administration: there were boxes piled in one corner, books and papers on trains, business administration and – coin collecting? – in another, an old-fashioned roll-top desk at one side beneath a US rail network wall map, and a single bed opposite. A PC monitor and hard drive sat on an adjacent table to the desk, left running. Nathan checked it out, pleased at Wheeler's carelessness in leaving it unattended and without measures like password-protected screensavers. He slipped in the memory stick, let its invasive program bypass any security measures Wheeler might utilise and then quickly sought out and copied as many documents, spreadsheets and emails as it could find and fill.

Meanwhile he opened the desktop and rifled through some pages, hoping Cat was safe in Wheeler's company. Yes, he was certain she could handle herself. But still . . .

But still, what?

He paused, checked himself. Cat had been right. He was too protective, too territorial when he had no real claim on her. Yes, she brought it out in him, but that was no excuse.

A thick black leather-bound notebook caught his attention; he flipped it open, found diagrams of the train, its carriages and berths, with copious amounts of notes written in various places: names, dates, events – focusing on sexual events. A history of occurrences on the train dating back over fifty years, though Nathan knew Wheeler's operation wasn't that old.

He sat down in the chair and peered through it more closely: secret affairs, honeymoons, orgies ... moments of soft slow lovemaking, or hard fast fucking ... Wheeler seemed obsessed with sex, beyond his business interests.

And Nathan's concern for Cat grew. She'd seemed disoriented at the séance. What if Wheeler was somehow drugging her?

No, no, she seemed clear-headed enough, if distracted. He could hardly blame her for that, being onboard a train where one could witness all manner of acts – or participate in them ...

He was fingering through the back pages of the notebook when he heard a key in the office door. Quickly he set down the book, retrieved his stick and put his feet up on the desk, folding his hands onto his waist. He took a heartbeat to whisper a calming mantra, to establish the placid, easy-going demeanour that he so rarely felt inside these days.

The door opened, and Faye Scott entered – with Donnie Kolchak. The woman's laughter died away on seeing Nathan, but then her smile quickly returned. 'Now this is what I call room service.'

Nathan smiled and tipped an imaginary hat to her. 'I hope I haven't intruded.'

Donnie stepped around from behind Faye. 'As a matter of fact you have, so why don't you fuck off outta here?'

Nathan rose to his feet, glad the man reacted in this way, giving Nathan an excuse to leave quickly. 'Sure, we've no problem here.'

He started out, until Donnie couldn't resist the urge to add, 'Go teach that smart-mouthed bitch of yours some manners.'

Nathan paused, ignored the voice that told him this dick wasn't worth the effort, and drew closer to him. 'Oh, *now* we've got a problem, kid.'

Donnie's lip twitched, as if realising that he was provoking someone physically stronger than himself. 'Ah, hey, pal, I was just joking.'

'Really? Make me laugh some more: insult my woman again.'

And then Faye took a symbolic step between them, still smiling, one hand on Donnie's chest as she purred, 'Boys, boys, don't waste that testosterone on each other. Save it.' She reached out with her other hand and closed the office door, before stepping over to a cabinet, which she opened to reveal racks of bottles and glasses. She retrieved a whiskey bottle and some shot glasses and started pouring. 'I stopped here with Mr Kolchak on our way to my suite for a drink. Instead, I find you. I'm not complaining, but why are you here?'

He smiled, never taking his eyes off Donnie as he replied to her. 'I liked playing your knight errant earlier this evening. And I thought you might need me to escort you back to your castle. But as you already have someone –'

'Don't go, Mr Ames.' Faye handed them each a shot glass, then retrieved her own, regarding them both with obvious interest. 'And I'm telling you that you don't have to fight over me. Not when I can have you both.'

'What?' Donnie exclaimed. 'No fucking way.'

Nathan smiled again. 'What's wrong, kid, afraid it might make you gay if we accidentally touch?' For his part, Nathan's arousal grew. Not that he'd go through with it. But Faye had a dynamic quality to her, a heady, exotic lust – and it had been a long time since his last lover.

'Hey, fuck you! I mean . . .' Donnie turned to Faye now. 'I don't share my women with any man. Ever.'

'Fair enough.' Faye approached him, retrieving the glass. 'Go.'

'What?'

'Do I whisper, Donnie? I said go. I'm not your woman. I'm not anybody's woman.' She downed his shot in one, then her own. Then she looked at him again, indicating the door. 'Well?'

Donnie stared in sheer disbelief, his mouth opening once, then again. He glared at Nathan, but cursed under his breath as he stormed out, slamming the door.

Nathan cursed as well, inside. He'd hoped to make his escape, but now he found himself sliding deeper into a situation he didn't want. 'Ms Scott, I apologise, I didn't mean –'

'Didn't mean what? Didn't mean to leave me earlier, force me to find a poor substitute for a more experienced man like yourself? You're forgiven.' She drew closer, her perfume something attractive if unidentifiable; strands of dark hair framed her cheekbones and her hazel eyes gleamed. She reminded Nathan of paintings of Morgana Le Fay from the Arthur stories: the powerful, predatory woman of magic. 'Donnie has his charms, but you remain a definite improvement.'

'Thanks.' Nathan swallowed as Faye drew even closer, casually slipping an arm around him. 'But to be honest, I don't think I should be here.'

'No?' She feigned shock, though her expression was more amused, as her free hand rested on his chest, played with the top button on his shirt, tugging it open. 'Don't you find me attractive, Nathan?'

He felt his face flush. 'That's hardly the issue, Ms Scott.'

'Call me Faye. And I think it's entirely the issue.' Her eyes meeting his, her hand drifted down over his shirt, then suddenly ripped it open. 'Because we've only got a weekend onboard, and we've already brushed over the small talk earlier. I've expressed an attraction to you.' Her hand reached his belt, then the bulge in his trousers. 'And you obviously have one for me.'

Nathan should have been extricating himself from her growing presence, her influence. Yes, definitely. Instead, he relished the warmth and fullness of her breasts on his bare chest as she pressed herself against him. 'Oh?'

'Well, you *did* talk about being honest. And since we're being honest, what I would like is for you to bury that hard shaft inside me in this room, and then again back in my suite.' She stepped away, still watching him as she shrugged off her dress, leaving her pale fit figure clad in royal-blue lace: a very revealing bra and stockings, and nothing else. Her bush was a dark, trimmed arrowhead that Nathan missed as she moved to the bed. She reclined on the mattress and looked up at him. 'Well? Get over here.'

Nathan found himself following. 'I don't know about this. What about Cat?'

Faye smiled, one knee raised, the foot flat on the mattress, lost in her own hunger. 'Don't worry, stud. She doesn't have to know.' She reached up to wrap her hands around his neck, then pulled him close to kiss him.

He stared for a moment at the woman, then glanced up over her, saw the metal frame of the headboard, the leather wrist cuffs attached there. He reached up, took her wrists gently but firmly in his hands.

Faye's eyes followed. She let him bind her wrists to the leather, grinning. 'Hey, you should wait, I've got better restraints in my suite.'

'I was ready to hit Donnie for insulting Cat.' He rose to his feet. 'I won't hit a woman. But I won't tolerate insults from one, either.'

'Excuse me?'

'Suggesting Cat should be deceived is disrespectful. She deserves better.'

It took a moment for the penny to drop, and for her hunger

to give way to shock, and then a quickly growing anger. She tugged uselessly at her bonds, her serene faux-European accent gone. 'Hey! Hey! Get me out of these fucking things, you asshole!'

'I'll see if I can find someone else to do that, Ms Scott.'

Her curse-suffused voice rose as he departed, but he found that her voice hardly carried out once he closed the door and walked down the corridor.

Good. But his words – about Cat deserving honesty – followed him ...

... Sharon was alone upstairs, and she was taking advantage of it. Not the scenery, though with the roof and upper sides of the observation deck almost entirely made of glass, it afforded a magnificent view of lush foliage surrounding the mighty Mississippi, bright with the midday sun. No, it was the isolation, and the chance to test out her new cellphone's reception.

Which was clear, to judge from the caller's next demand. 'Open your trousers now.'

A wave of thrilling excitement made her shiver, and her hands almost fumbled with the thin black leather belt, then the large round button, her waist breathing a sigh of relief.

'Have you done it?' he asked eagerly.

'Almost,' she whispered. Looking behind her once more at the spiral staircase, she worked the tiny strip of clenched metal of her zipper, locked together as if in an elaborate embrace. Her fingers moved to it, lowered the zipper and peeled the front of her trousers open, revealing a delta of brocaded blue lace obscuring the trimmed thatch of crimson hair. After a moment, she lifted her ass off the seat to slide her trousers further down, until they were almost at her knees. She'd not gone this far before. 'Oh God.'

'Are you all right?'

'Yes.' She felt the air on her thighs as she pushed her ass to the edge of the seat and parted her knees. 'This feels so rude.' Without thinking, her own flattened palm snaked down and over her thong, pressing down against her mound.

'Are you touching yourself?'

Her hand caressed her sex, the middle finger running along the indent in the lace made by the furrow of her pussy, feeling moistness in the fabric. 'Yes, outside my panties.'

'Are you wet?'

She felt her face burn, in an incredibly delicious way. 'Yes. I can feel it inside me, seeping out my slit.'

He moaned, and she smiled, enjoying pushing him further and further, enjoying his surprise that she would say that now, when he was ready to keep talking. But this was not monologue, this was dialogue, there were two people here. The hand at her crotch drew back, enough to slip under the waistband of her panties, touching her pubic hair. She combed through it with her fingers before reaching her hot puffy flesh, the tip of her thumb brushing over . . . 'Oh fuck . . . my clit . . .'

With her thumb working at her clitoris, her middle finger curved downwards until it slipped between her folds, found the entrance to her sex, stroked the brim, thrust sharply, shallowly, repeatedly.

Her caller's voice had taken on an urgent monotone, punctuated with gasps and grunts. 'My fingers are keeping you open, as my tongue dives in and out of you, lapping at you . . . my thumb is stroking you further down.'

Sharon cursed as she suddenly leant forwards, her legs parted as much as she was able, and the waistband of her panties ripped as she continued to masturbate furiously, her ass still on the edge of her seat. 'I'm taking . . . I'm taking your come . . . in me.'

'I . . . feel . . . I feel you coming . . . Oh God, Sharon, I'm losing it . . .'

So was she. She listened to him listening to her listening to him, listened and touched, their words devolving into primal sounds. She called out without shame as her whole body shuddered and spasmed and, in vain, she squeezed her eyes shut to the white light that permeated her . . .

. . . Cat opened her eyes wide, blinking in the darkness of the observation deck, suddenly aware of the sky full of stars on all sides, aware of the couples in the seats behind her, in various stages of fucking. Aware of her pussy, crying out for attendance, and her hand, nearly fully up her skirt to minister to it. She removed her hand, embarrassed.

Wheeler still sat beside her, his voice low, his eyes stayed fixed on her, though seemingly not out of prurient interest. 'Belle likes you. You slipped into that easily.'

'Slipped into what?' Cat slid away from him, embarrassed at falling asleep like that – again – and she thought her voice was too low over the background sounds of the train. 'A hypnotic trance?'

'You weren't hypnotised. You're sitting in what I call a hotspot, one of many places on Belle where, under the right conditions, one can make contact with the ghosts of those who've ridden onboard. You, for instance, were in communion with a young woman named Sharon, from about fifteen years ago, who apparently made a habit of masturbating in public with her boyfriend on the phone.'

Cat felt her jaw drop; whatever she'd expected from him, this wasn't it. 'What the fuck are you talking about?'

'I said Belle was special. This is how: she carries the dead as well as the living. And certain people, under the right conditions, can channel them. You see what they saw, feel what they felt. As you did just now. And as you did, during the séance.'

Cat's face tightened. 'Nothing happened to me.'

'Oh, so you weren't at the séance table, bent forwards, talking to someone named Mickey?'

The memories – no, dreams – about Valentina came back to her, as vivid as her own thoughts, but Cat pushed them aside, glaring at him. '*Besame el culo.*' She rose to unsteady feet, pushing down the arousal that had grown within her, and stormed away, nearly falling at the top of the spiral staircase. It was insane, the idea of possession, of being other people.

She stopped, remembering Richard Newholme's reaction during the séance. Who did he think Cat was?

'My Cher.'

The old man was sitting alone in the downstairs, nursing a brandy. 'She died in an accident onboard this train, years ago. The way you spoke at the table ... reminded me of her.'

Cat sat opposite him, studying, trying to remain sympathetic. 'Did Jack Wheeler tell you that her spirit was onboard?' She frowned; if Wheeler had tricked this poor old man into paying to ride this train based on that notion, she'd personally hand him his *cojones* for breakfast.

Newholme's gaze dropped to the table, as if distracted by the swirled patterns in the dark polished wood. 'He didn't have to. I *felt* her, heard her, when I first boarded, a year ago, while supplying Wheeler with authentic train memorabilia. I've come back as often as I could. You're young. You don't know what it's like to miss someone for longer than most people around you have been alive.' Then he added with a self-deprecating smile, 'And yes, I *have* been tested for dementia. I remain sadly rational, in an utterly irrational world.'

She couldn't help but smile back sympathetically. 'I know the feeling.'

'Hey, JLo!'

Cat glanced behind her, grunted at the approach of Donnie Kolchak. 'What do you want, *idiota*?'

The man marched in like he owned the place. 'I want to know where your boyfriend gets off stealing my woman!'

'Your ... woman?' Then she made the connection, though she found herself strangely disquieted at the thought of Nathan with Faye, even though she had ordered him to see her. 'You mean Faye? *Muy malo, cabrón*. Why are you bothering me?'

Donnie seemed to work up a swagger as he approached. 'Well, I'm thinking that, well, if your man steals from me, then I get –'

Cat burst out laughing before he finished. 'You've got to be fucking kidding! You expect me to put out because you're not man enough to stand up to my partner? *Veta al Infierno.*'

Donnie tensed with anger. 'Don't cross me, bitch. You don't know who's behind me.'

'Watch how you address this lady,' Newholme suddenly warned. Around them, people had begun quickly and quietly shifting away.

Donnie responded with a smirk. 'You should mind your own business, old man, or you'll be going back to the home in a coffin.'

Newholme rose to his feet more quickly than anyone had expected. 'You wanna give it a try, punk?'

But Cat stood as well, standing between them and glaring at Donnie. 'You can stick your wounded pride up your cuckolded ass, and take a flying fuck while you're doing it. Just stay the hell out of my way.'

It wasn't a prime example of defusing a hostile situation as per training, but she had no patience now. Nevertheless, she made a deliberately wide circle around him as she tried to depart the carriage.

Until he suddenly made a move to grab her forearm.

Two seconds later, he was on the floor, crying out as Cat twisted his arm behind him and placed her full weight onto his lower back. She ignored his cries and curses of pain and protest.

She heard someone approaching from behind, and drew back her free hand to defend herself.

It was Wheeler, looking anxious, confused and angry. 'What's going on?'

'He grabbed her first,' Newholme explained before Cat could.

Wheeler looked to him, then back to Cat. 'Let him go.' When she didn't move, he added, 'Please.'

Finally, she complied, her heart racing despite her attempt at a cool demeanour, and stepped back, ready to take him down again.

But when Donnie helped himself up, he avoided looking over at her, clutching his arm and making sounds of self-pity, as Wheeler turned on him, his face red. 'Mr Kolchak, you boarded this train with the understanding that you were bound by the rules of decorum. I will not tolerate physical assaults. Is that clear?'

Donnie was dusting himself off, still avoiding looking at Cat to focus on the host. 'When Leo hears about this, you're gonna wake up wishing you were dead.'

'It wouldn't be the first time. As for your uncle, I will inform him of your disreputable behaviour.'

Donnie sneered. 'Like the word of a cheap lowlife redneck hustler is gonna matter to him.'

Wheeler now looked as angry as Cat had ever seen in the

normally genial man, even as he recollected his composure. 'Why don't you repair to the games carriage? There's an amateur lap-dancing contest ongoing, and they could use some judges.'

Donnie sneered again, but grunted and departed, pushing past Wheeler for no good reason. Wheeler said and did nothing, until he turned to Cat. 'I must apologise for that unprecedented incident.' He glanced at Newholme. 'Apologies to you both.'

Newholme just shrugged, retrieved the chair he had kicked away and sat down again, nursing his brandy. Cat absently rubbed at her knuckles, having grazed them when she'd brought Donnie to the floor.

Wheeler nodded at her hand. 'Let me see to that.'

The kitchen was unoccupied, closed up for the night. The spot-less counters smelt of disinfectant, the stainless steel doors on the freezers and refrigerators gleamed, and the huge pots and pans hanging together on the rack over the sink rocked slightly with the rhythm of the train, occasionally clanging against each other.

Wheeler walked around the stand-alone stove, then returned from the refrigerator with a dark, unmarked bottle in one hand and a bag of frozen peas in the other. He handed the latter to Cat. 'Try this.'

Cat accepted it and pressed it against her knuckles. 'Your bedside manner could use some improvement.'

'Care to help me with that?' he teased, some of the man's good humour returning to him. He set the bottle down on the chopping board beside her, then went fishing for some glasses. 'After that unpleasant encounter, I think we could both use some special libation.'

Cat reached out and lifted the bottle, noting the Japanese script, recognising the word sake and the high alcohol proof. 'What, no moonshine brewed in a tin tub?'

'Left at home, with all the other hillbilly stereotypes.' He started up one of the stove hobs, selecting a small pot. 'It's Shinkansen sake, a taste for which I acquired while I was stationed at the army base in Sagamihara. Named after their bullet train, and goes through you just as quickly when it's served hot and straight. And as it has no sugars or impurities, you don't get hangovers.' He smiled. 'Well, hardly any.'

Cat grunted, believing she could handle a shot or two of it – and if it helped loosen Wheeler's tongue a little, then so much the better. 'Hoping to take advantage of me, Jack?'

He watched the contents of the pot heat up, but glanced over his shoulder at her. 'Maybe you're hoping to do the same.'

'I don't think it'd take much to get the advantage of you.'

'No?' He switched off the gas and poured the liquid into two waiting glasses. 'Of course, if you've had enough for the night, I might be able to make you some hot cocoa, or whatever it is that boring old accountants like to take to bed.'

'*Besame el culo.*' She took the glass from him, raised it in salute and downed her shot in one. She'd recognised the puerile challenge for what it was, but she'd be damned if she'd . . .

It struck her like a hammer as it hit her stomach. *Jesus!*

He grinned. 'Shall I kiss your ass now?'

Wheeler stretched out the subsequent rounds over the following hour. Cat was perched up on the counter now and gripped the edge as though ready to fall off it at any moment, as if the train ride was bumpier than it really was. Her face felt flushed and her vision went in and out of focus on her drinking partner. 'Twins, huh? Horndog. How many times did you have them?'

'No, you've had your Truth.' Wheeler was leaning against the stove, avoiding banging his head on the overhead exhaust vent again. 'My turn now. Where'd you learn martial arts?'

'Easy: paid for by my employers. Miami can be a dangerous place for accountants. You suck at this game.'

'Oh, I'm learning everything I need to know.'

'My turn. What the hell's the business with Kolchak? What's a nice guy like you mixing with the Mob?' She smiled teasingly, proud of how well she was coping with the alcohol in her system and, despite herself, excited by his reaction to her. 'Well?'

'When I found Belle, I had only three hundred dollars to my name. I needed money to get her and the carriages fixed up and furnished, not to mention the various licences, staff hire, etc. The banks were less than charitable. Mr Kolchak's uncle helped out.'

'Sounds dangerous.'

'Not really; Leo's a businessman. I make my payments on time, he treats some of his wise guys to free weekends.'

'So you're not a captive business, then? You don't launder money?'

He smiled back. 'My turn again. Have you experienced any other hotspots onboard?'

Mention of the hotspots again made her frown. She pushed her feelings down and shook her head, immediately regretting it. 'Sorry, not answering that one.'

Wheeler's smile lifted the corners of his beard. 'Fine, then, a Dare: a kiss.'

Cat felt her face on fire, with a similar heat between her legs. Despite her attempts to remain casual, in control, she could feel her breathing grow heavier. She could handle this easily. 'That's it? All you want?'

'For now.'

She smiled, motioning him to her with her finger. 'Right, let's get it over with.'

Wheeler set aside his glass and approached her. She swallowed, fought and failed to control her pulse as he reached up, gently touched her face, placing the palm flat against her hot cheek. His other hand cupped her other cheek, his eyes staring into hers.

Cat felt her head spinning despite his touch. 'Well? Aren't you gonna go ahead?'

'One doesn't just jump into these things,' he replied softly. 'It's the journey, not the destination.' The thumb of one hand swivelled out, brushing against her full lips. She parted them slightly, feeling the moistness and breath escape. Her pussy called to her, and she gripped his forearms for support.

He pushed his thumb in slightly, barely penetrating Cat's mouth, as she let the tip of her tongue brush against the tip of the digit. It was insane, an insane desire that she had to keep under control.

Seconds later, her thoughts were lost as he pulled her in, found her mouth with his lips and kissed her, hard and hot and with an unleashed hunger. Cat responded, moaning into his mouth...

...as Mickey slipped his tongue into her, then making him moan in return as Val slid her tongue over his, mixing their saliva. Sweet God, this was heavenly!

Val pulled back, perched on the stool, her feet resting on the first rung, her thighs parted and her hands resting between them. She watched him unwrap the cellophane from the tray he'd retrieved from the icebox. 'How'd you manage this?'

'You asked for a late-night dessert, I deliver. I can be persuasive.' He set a tray on the counter beside her: the feast of the world before her eyes, selections of a dozen chocolate desserts from tonight's meal. 'Nothing's too good for my new wife.'

Wife. Val had struggled enough to come to terms with that, to meet with Mickey's request to be at least outwardly happy, though to his credit he acknowledged how difficult it was for her.

Now Val's mouth was shamelessly watering in classic Pavlovian style at the desserts. 'Where do we start?'

He sectioned a gooey piece of pudding with a fork and lifted it up invitingly towards her mouth. 'We start with you opening your mouth.'

She did. And it was scrumptious, the rush through her body as she tasted and swallowed like a leap from a cliff. She crooned to herself, licking her lips, realising that her situation could have been far less palatable with any other man than Mickey, who proved devoted and at times even gentle. It didn't take away her guilt, especially when she thought of Enrique, who had stopped writing and calling following a terrible long-distance argument she'd had with him when she broke the news of her marriage.

But Mickey, and the life he led, was at least distracting. 'Feed me some more.'

Mickey laughed, then continued with another sample, and then another, each taste satisfying her, and yet leaving her wanting more.

At some point he'd moved behind her – she could smell his cologne, feel the hairs on her neck rise at his proximity – and he reached around to continue feeding her, his other hand warm on her shoulder. There was a hard, tight knot in her stomach.

He started licking and nibbling on her ear, and she could feel his cock, pressing into her lower back. A wave of heat washed over her and she felt faint. She gripped the stool until she thought her nails would pierce the seat, her inner protests aborted.

Mickey set aside the fork now, and let the freed hand reach around and knead her left breast through her tight black silk blouse, making her gasp and shudder, even as his right hand, promising more, snaked down boldly beneath the waistbands of her slacks and panties. Still silent, he cupped her pubic mound, hot, wet and puffy, gently squeezing, feeling her curls press back.

Val gasped aloud and shivered in place, pressing her head against his as his middle finger extended, tracing the groove of her outer lips down, then back again, lubricating with her dew.

His finger pierced her, diving and withdrawing, his thumb massaged her stiffened clitoris with a circular motion which drove her mad with pleasure. She drank in her own strong musk from between her legs, letting the pressure build further and further, as Mickey drew her to the inevitable, drew her . . .

And took her there, her pussy clamping onto Mickey's fingers, refusing release – how lovely! Waves of dizzying heat ran through her like lightning, and she clutched her face, as if fighting to tame her breathing, her fingertips gathering sweat from her brow. She leant back onto the counter . . .

. . . Cat leant back onto the counter, staring up as she felt the mouth travel higher and higher between her parted legs; her clit throbbed as it reached her upper thighs. Come on, come on, Cat silently urged, even as a part of her acknowledged what had gone on in the here and now, how their game had progressed to this, with her panties on the floor and her shirt opened to reveal her full breasts inside her frilly black bra.

This was a dream, she decided, as the bearded face gently nibbled away, teasingly, tantalisingly close to Cat's aching pussy, knowing what Cat was waiting for. Cat pushed her pussy up against the face. *Hurry*, she urged, before she returned to her senses. She was so close, so close.

Wheeler parted Cat's thighs further, dropping a brief kiss on her bush, before trailing his tongue along her clitoris. Cat sighed with immense satisfaction. *Dios!* Wheeler's tongue continued its long, teasing course, painting the outline of Cat's open, throbbing sex.

Cat was very aware of the heat radiating from her pussy onto his face. She imagined the taste of herself on Wheeler's lips, and felt giddy from the sheer pleasure. The world beyond Wheeler's tongue and her own sensations seemed both a distant, ignorable thing, yet also acutely perceptible, her senses charged.

Then suddenly Wheeler's tongue teased no longer, entering Cat's slippery, receptive sex, the penetration making Cat bite her lip to keep from crying out. Wheeler's nose nuzzled at Cat's clitoris, tormenting it simultaneously.

Cat's mouth had dried, and her breathing grew ragged, staccato through her nostrils, punctuated with muffled gasps, as Wheeler's tongue expertly moved in time to the throbs its ministrations produced. On and on, unrelenting, Cat's buttocks rising from the hard countertop, rising and falling to the rhythm of the thrusting tongue. Fuck, how sweet!

The man brought her to a shuddering climax, making Cat tighten her sweaty thighs around his head, refusing release, wanting to keep him there forever.

7

'Mr Ames?'

Nathan had returned to the berth, changed his shirt, texted Gordy and waited for Cat to follow. And waited. He shouldn't have gone out looking for her, but he had, and searched the public portions of the train, trying not to interrupt anyone. There was no sign of her, and his concern grew, especially after finding Newholme and hearing about the incident with Donnie Kolchak.

Now he froze at the voice, heard over the raunchy blues music from the speakers above, and turned. 'Where's Cat?'

A flushed-looking Wheeler drew up to him, looking thoroughly embarrassed. 'I was hoping you might wish to collect her from the kitchens. I fear that, like me, she's some- what in her cups.'

Nathan started to reply, but didn't trust himself to remain civil, forcing his anger down as he followed Wheeler out of the carriage, his ire returning however as he found Cat in the kitchen, sitting on the floor with her back against one of the chrome refrigerator doors, her clothes dishevelled. She looked up with a broad, silly grin. 'Hound! *Qué tal, mi grande pajiero?*'

Nathan knelt and examined her, noting the buttons done up wrong on her blouse as he opened her eyes and checked her pupils. His voice was tight as he addressed Wheeler. 'You make a habit of getting your female passengers drunk and vulnerable?'

'I can assure you otherwise, Mr Ames. I had intended only one or two shots each, but Ms Montoya kept . . . provoking me.'

'I know the feeling.' He leant back as Cat slapped his hands away. 'You OK, darlin'?'

Cat focused on him – and shot him a killer smile that, coupled with the fact her blouse was revealing her bronzed, sweat-jewelled cleavage, made his cock throb awake. 'Oh yes, Nate.' She drew closer as if to impart a confidence. 'But I'm afraid I've given up some of my secrets.'

Nathan's heart leapt into his throat, but he affected a casual acknowledgement of the woman's obvious drunken state. 'Now, now, Catalina –'

Then she grabbed his shirt and informed him gravely, 'He knows I've taken it *por el culo*.' She slapped her rear for unnecessary emphasis, adding, 'But I don't do it any more. Feels way too good.'

'We'll all keep that in mind.' Nathan blushed over that revelation, helping her to her feet, glancing at Wheeler. 'I'll ask you not to get my partner into such a state again, otherwise our next conversation won't be as civil. Understood?'

The man held up his hands in surrender. 'Fully, sir. I apologise.'

Eager to get her out of there, Nathan turned back to Cat. 'Come on, let's get you to bed.'

She grinned. 'Horny bastard.'

The walk back to their berth took ages. Partly because Nathan had to steer Cat and himself around passengers more interested in making love than making way. Partly because Cat would sometimes grow alert enough to try to steer him here and there for a dance.

Mostly it was because since taking her in his arms, feeling the heat from her body, he had an erection that refused to die down. It was distracting enough to swamp his anxiety that she might have unintentionally let slip anything about their mission onboard to their chief suspect.

The side of Cat's breast brushed against him again. Jesus . . .

He locked the berth door after setting her on the edge of the bed. It was hot, the air conditioner malfunctioning for no good reason. He pushed her back down as she started to rise again and retrieved her phone from its hiding place. There was a coded text message indicating their contact had information waiting.

He was in the process of calling Gordy back when Cat moaned, 'Nathan.'

He dropped the phone to the bed and knelt before her, grateful for the give in his trousers. 'What is it, Cat?'

Now she focused on him. 'I told Jack I thought he was as sexy as hell.' She held his face. 'But you're sexier, Hound. A hundred times sexier.'

Nathan wasn't sure how to respond, except with the regulation reply honed from nature and professionalism. 'Cat, you're drunk, we're on a mission. I made a promise –'

'*Dios*, I'm partnered with Dudley Do-Right.' She slumped forwards, burying his face in her hair. His nostrils flared as he caught the light fragrance of her shampoo, reminding him of when he saw her earlier stripping off for a shower, and the muscles clenched in his groin.

Just then, Gordy's voice manifested from the phone. 'Nate, you there? Or is it the delightful Catalina?'

Cat pulled back. 'It's both of us, studmuffin –' Nathan's finger on her lips cut her off.

'Hello?'

'It's just Nate.' He glared sternly at Cat, ignoring how she made a lick at his finger. It wouldn't do either of them any good to stoke the fires of rumour back at the office further. 'Cat's out having fun.'

Cat drew back, smiling wickedly and fumbling with the buttons on her blouse. Nathan looked away tactfully, hoping that fatigue and common sense would take over and she would stay silent, get herself undressed and go to bed. 'Well? What have you got?'

'Donnie Kolchak is the nephew of Leonid Kolchak, head of a splinter of the Russian Mob working out of Tampa, but intelligence suggests Donnie's little better than a delivery boy, has some minor convictions. Ben Oliver worked as a train driver with Atlanta South Rail, but got laid off a year ago. Hannah Oliver has a manager's job in a bar in Plainsboro. Neither have any record to speak of, and no obvious connections with Wheeler.'

'Hound,' Cat whispered.

He looked to her. She seemed to be having trouble managing her buttons and appeared embarrassed about it. It was a vulnerability, coupled with her innate attractiveness, that made it harder for him – on many levels. He would help undress her – just down to her underwear – and put her to bed, and that was it. Nothing more. She'd thank him in the morning.

'Nate, you still there?'

Nathan watched Cat now as he undid the buttons on her blouse. 'Yeah, Gordy. Keep talking.'

'Tara Gilbrand's family is one of the wealthier in Atlanta. Various local authorities have hired Tara as a psychic investigator and consultant, with some apparent success. Richard Newholme runs an antiques business in Boston, specialising in railroad memorabilia. Clean record, pays his taxes religiously, and the last return included the business dealings he had with Wheeler.'

Nathan nearly fully listened. He was focused on the way

Cat's breasts heaved within her black lace bra, ellipses of sweat framing the darker skin of her cleavage, and her nipples pursing behind the arabesque-patterned cups. And when he looked up, she fed his reaction further with a hungry gaze and a lick of those full lips of hers, as she slipped out of her blouse with a grace she hadn't displayed moments before, her hands clinging to the edge of the mattress as she cambered her back, pushing her breasts out.

Good Lord. 'What about Faye Scott, Gordy?'

'Oh yeah. String of petty fraud convictions, some civil suits from people swindled in fake exorcisms, all dropped. Nothing outstanding. I'll send you the full details on them all.'

'Uh huh.' Nathan's head swam as Cat took his hands and moved them purposefully, undeniably, to the waistband of her skirt, smiling impishly.

He'd get her shoes and skirt off, and put her to bed. And that would be it. His fingers fumbled, as Cat kicked off her shoes and lifted her rear up, enough to let him slide her skirt down over her bronzed thighs and shins. Now his eyes fixed, unashamedly, on her panties, on their black lace caress of her sex. His hands moved over her warm thighs, relishing the smooth touch, and his head spun as his cock strained further inside his clothes.

No. He had to be the responsible one, had to pull back and put her to bed. Even as he acknowledged how much he was enjoying this.

He was rising to his knees when Cat pulled him into a kiss, swooping on him and pulling him so that he practically fell on top of her. They struggled, until he pinned her arms above her head. 'Damn it, Cat, stop this right now or –'

'Or what, you fucking *puta*?'

He kissed her, ostensibly just to shut her up, though still savouring the feel of his lips on hers and the heat of her mouth as his tongue explored it. She moaned into his mouth, and ground her thigh against the lust-stiffened cock still restrained within his clothes. He tasted her desire, as strong as the alcohol on her breath.

It was that reminder that made him pull from her mouth, though he still kept her wrists pinned. 'Ca– Cat, no.'

She looked up at him from under heavy lids, her dark hair spread out on the mattress like black flames. 'Damn it Nathan, say *yes*. I am as horny as you. I think maybe we just need to fuck and get it out of our system. Otherwise we won't be able to do our jobs.'

'Uh, you guys know I'm still on the line, don't you?'

Grimacing, Nathan reached out, lifted the phone long enough to say, 'Call you in the morning,' before hanging up and tossing it to the nearby couch. 'Awww, Lord.' He glared at her as she giggled. 'Hey, at least you're drunk, you have an excuse.'

Her giggles blossomed into a smile. 'Oh my, you know, I think I probably *am* a little drunk. Who knows what could happen next ...'

'What? Next? *No!* I couldn't do anything, Cat. I'd regret it in the morning.'

'Hmm, such a dilemma.' The playfulness in her voice was obvious and hugely endearing 'So, if you did do anything, you'd feel guilty for taking advantage ... and yet if I let you waste this opportunity, you'll have nothing to remember on this trip of a lifetime. I can't let that happen, Nathan.' Her voice was like honey, kittenish and deliberately vulnerable. 'So, really, you're gonna regret it either way, *hombre*. At least if you give in we'll both get some relief. Think about it. Either I'm so drunk that I won't remember any of this, or I'm not that drunk and I know precisely what I'm saying. It's the perfect opt out.' She smiled again. 'What was it you told me during the Christmas

Incident? "The one thing you can know about me is that if I go to hell, it won't be for not trying..."'

He took in her words, then caught her as she swayed a little and fell forwards. She threw her arms around his neck and giggled playfully as Nathan lowered her onto the bed. She refused to let go of him and pulled him down on top of her. 'OK, Cat, OK. How about we just lie here a while and get some much-needed rest, all right?'

She pouted. 'OK. But get those trousers off. They're rough against my legs.'

He doubted that, but relented, kicking off his shoes and socks and removing his trousers, hoping that as soon as she relaxed and the rhythm of the train took over, she'd drift off with her dignity intact, and he could take care of himself while she slept.

It seemed to be going well; he stroked her hair and whispered encouragements to her. Cat closed her eyes, pulled him in close to her, nuzzled into his chest. Until lazily, half-dozing there, her soft fingers tracing small circles on his chest, she gently undid the buttons of his shirt and planted soft kisses on his shoulder.

Somehow, his hands wandered too, along the small of her back, feeling the soft downy skin and relishing her hips pushing closer to his as he cupped her sweet ass. An imperceptibly small shift left them face to face, Nathan acutely aware that his hard-on was pressing insistently against her tummy. Without a word, Cat reached behind and unclipped her bra, removing it with a minimum of effort, then gently slipped back resting against his bared chest. Her breasts felt soft, warm and heavenly against him...

Finally, the last reserves of his resistance melted away, and he embraced her, hungrily kissing her open mouth, the heat of her body penetrating him through his briefs. As if reading his mind, Cat's hands were there, slipping under the band and rolling them down.

'Wait. Cat, are you sure?' Nathan breathed.

She didn't answer, but took his hand and guided it under her own panties, letting his fingers dance over her wetness, giving him his answer and punctuating it with a wry smile as he gazed at her flushed face.

'Mmm, I guess you are,' he whispered, removing his briefs and releasing his cock. Pulling him back next to her, Cat took his hands back to her sex, lifting her hips as his fingers grazed her moist folds. He felt her push against his fingers, squirming with delight as he left light, tantalising kisses on her neck and throat, and then her nipples, driving her wild. Relentlessly he brushed over her bush and continued working her pussy, his fingers slipping into the sensitive wet niche.

As Nathan caressed her, his lips still on her breasts, Cat moaned and throbbed to his attentions, grinding her sex shamelessly against his hand. He felt her building, building, then cascading over as she let out a sharp, 'Puta!' She spasmed beneath him, then collapsed, trying to catch her breath. When she recovered, she looked wide-eyed up at him and asked breathlessly, 'What are you waiting for, Nathan?'

He wondered that himself, and he watched as she made her way up to the head of the bed, even as he followed, moving like a predator cornering his prey.

Cat's eyes locked with his, strengthening his resolve that this was the right thing to do, as she parted her thighs and raised her knees up. Nathan held her legs and guided himself into her until he filled her up. Cat's mouth opened and she let out a groan of intense satisfaction, one he echoed as he rocked back and forth, withdrawing and then plunging back into her silky depths, repeatedly, fighting to control his need for release.

A fight he lost when Cat wrapped her arms and legs around him, biting his neck and swearing in full Cuban, and he rode her with a faster, harder pace. He was losing control, and for once didn't mind, pumping into her, in and out, as if racing the unending rhythm of the train.

He felt her climax again, on the heels of the one he'd given her moments before with his fingers, until he too gasped and grunted as his orgasm roared through him, filling her up.

They lay locked together until he slipped from her. He lay back and Cat resumed her place resting on his chest, Nathan stroking her hair once again, unable to believe what had just happened.

'I can't believe this is happening,' Wheeler muttered, more sober than he had played to his passengers, as he tried once more to adjust the settings and make the webcam and microphone planted in Cat and Nathan's berth work. And once more, it refused to do what he wanted. 'Goddammit, Belle, stop being an obstreperous bitch and behave!'

Nothing but snow and white noise.

'If you're quite through,' prompted the voice behind him.

Wheeler turned, stared at an almost-naked Faye, still bound to the bed in his office for the past hour, her fury at his ignoring her predicament and protests now passed.

He regarded her for a moment, smiled as he recalled her tale of Ames leaving her tied and unfulfilled, considered fucking her as she was, and settled for rising and freeing her. He then returned to the monitor, putting his erstwhile partner out of his mind again. 'Come on, Belle, play nice.'

Suddenly the picture appeared, and Wheeler watched, intrigued, as Nathan talked on a cellphone he shouldn't have, while his delectable partner was undressing. Interesting . . .

Faye slipped back into her dress, reached for the whiskey

bottle still on the desk. 'I want him thrown off the train, right now!'

He kept watching as Ames finally tossed the phone aside and attended to his partner. Wheeler kept his tone deliberately measured and calm, to infuriate her. 'I'll give your request all the consideration it deserves. And here's my answer: no.'

'Just get your prick into her and get your infatuation over with already. Or are you losing your faculties down there as well?'

'There's more to her than just her pussy, as appetising as it was. Belle senses it as well.'

An emptied bottle of whiskey shattered against the wall overhead, making him duck. He shook any pieces out of his hair, spinning around to her. 'What the hell –'

With that out of her system, she seemed to calm down, if only a little. 'Save that supernatural bullshit for the rubes! I grew up getting that fed to me, which doesn't mean I swallow it now! Who do you think you're fooling here? I know you, Jack. You have a talent for lying to everybody, including yourself. It was funny the first few times, listening to you talk about this shitty train. It's not funny any more.'

Wheeler seemed to regard her words.

Before turning back to the monitor and keyboard. 'Go find yourself a stray passenger to keep you amused. And don't insult Belle again, or you can go back to fleecing rich old widows in fake séances.'

He felt her eyes on the back of his head, was ready for another attack.

But not for her dropping to a squat beside him. 'Sorry, Jack.' When she caught his attention, she continued, 'I didn't mean to lose it like that.' She grunted, offering a slight, self-deprecating smile. 'Guess I got a nasty streak in me.'

'No shit.' But then Wheeler smiled back as well. 'Good thing

I like that in a woman.' He pulled her into a kiss, hot and leisurely, fuelling his own growing lust. Then he pulled back, licking his lips. 'I have some work to do. Why don't you go make an appearance among our guests? I'll join you in a bit.'

'Are you sure?'

He nodded. 'Have some fun.'

He watched her leave, relaxing once more – at least until his thoughts returned to Cat, seeing her begin to fuck the ineffably unworthy Ames. Wheeler's thoughts touched on the image of her on the kitchen counter, bucking against his face as he licked and teased her pussy to climax. His cock throbbed with the memory as well.

He hadn't been lying to Faye. There was something more to the woman than just the sex and how easily she accepted Val's memories. Something that had raised his hackles as well as his cock. She was guarded, too guarded. And there was that business with the cellphone ...

Still, she could be the one Belle and he had been waiting for all this time.

Or the one who could destroy everything.

He lifted his own phone to make some urgent calls. He performed a cursory identity check on all passengers before boarding, but if he spent a little more, he could dig a little deeper ...

... Wilma yelped when she felt Zhen's lips at her breast, nipping at her, drawing her nipple into his mouth and sucking hard, while his sister Ling lay further below, shamelessly nuzzling into Wilma's bush, her fingers stroking. Wilma spoke again, not knowing why; it wasn't as if they'd absorbed each other's languages since undressing. 'Guys, this is groovy, but maybe we should ...'

She stopped herself. But maybe we should ... what? Her boss

had sent her to Chicago to collect Zhen and Ling, the twins of his potential new partner from Hong Kong, and his orders were simple: 'Keep them happy and out of the way for a day or two.' He'd left out a few minor details, like that they were in their twenties, had a negligible grasp of English, and were as playful and mercurial as a pair of kittens. They wanted to see 'the big shark', so she took them to that new movie *Jaws*, though they didn't understand any of the dialogue. They wanted to visit a disco, so she obliged, stuffing cotton in her ears to protect hearing more accustomed to Neil Diamond. And they wanted to go back with her to New Orleans by train rather than plane, even though it would take ages rather than just a couple of hours.

She had initially ignored their advances. It wasn't as if she was in a position to complain; she was creeping into her forties now, back in the workplace after Steve had left her for his therapist's secretary, for God's sake, and her boss had given her a chance at this job. Was she going to get heavy if some VIPs got a little grabby? She'd planned on putting up with it, letting them have fun, and then escorting them to their berth to sleep off the rest of the night.

What she didn't plan on, though, was how she had started responding positively to them. But then why not? They were attractive: lean, fit, with infectious grins and, despite their youthfulness, well mannered. Also, it had been a long, long time since any hands but her own had touched her. And what woman wouldn't be turned on by the thought of a man – and a woman! – nearly half her age, desiring her? And, judging from their actions, they did desire her.

Zhen moved up the bed, drawing his cock closer.

She breathed in his scent, guiding his shaft into her mouth. Her tongue licked the length of him, tasting him, salty male-ness flooding her senses, sensations which doubled as she felt strings of tiny climaxes burst from her at Ling's touch below her, especially as one finger had moved up to the entrance to her rear, playing with her there as well.

She pulled back from Zhen's cock and gasped, 'Jesus!' as Ling removed her fingers, replacing them with her tongue, suddenly darting into her wet sex with short, rapid bursts ...

... Tara jerked at the touch, laughing, glad the beds provided in the games carriages were big; as cosy as the berth beds were, sharing one with a couple would have been awkward at best.

Even a couple as lovely and inviting as the Olivers, whom she'd grown to know better over the course of the evening. They were a friendly, attractive pair, who hadn't let a recent run of financial bad luck dampen their *joie de vivre*. The three of them talked, laughed, kissed and petted each other for ages, before finding a spare bed in a 'private' room, where spectators could watch them from behind a trick mirror without disturbing them – and one with a hotspot, one that they could all share. This train was magnificent!

But now they were back, aware once again, as Hannah moved behind her now, kneading Tara's aching breasts and cupping her furry mound. Tara made her own groaning sounds, feeling her body move once again towards climax, wondering how long she could endure this.

Not long, as it turned out, as Hannah pulled her off Ben, making the man moan; Tara could sense how close he'd been to his own zenith. But Tara, her senses ablaze, felt hypnotised, turning as Hannah was leaning back on a pillow, leaving Tara kneeling. Hannah parted her thighs, revealing a pussy of delicate flesh; Tara drank in her sweet and heady fragrance.

As if from a distance, Tara could feel Ben behind her, lifting her up and parting her thighs. Warm fluid seeped from within, and she desperately craved attention. Ben kindly obliged; the lips of her sex swallowed the tips of his fingers as he reached between her thighs and stroked her pussy lips, dipping into her before seeking out her clit. His rhythm was slow at first, considerate, able to support himself without disturbing Tara and Hannah's own love-making; she felt his erection press against her outer thigh, while his hands gripped her sides. But soon he was coaxing the rhythm into a lovely gallop.

Tara let the thrusts draw her down, down Hannah's body, until she buried her face between the woman's thighs, lapping at the soaking folds of her moist pocket, finally delighting in the exquisite tastes. Hannah's thighs reflexively closed against the sides of Tara's head, her pussy wavering between taut reaction and supple submission to her bliss, ultimately becoming impotent to fight the exquisite sensations, the same sensations Tara herself felt.

Fuck, girl, I could bend you over now and take you up the ass...

The thought hit her like a pungent odour and, with a sudden feeling of being exposed and dirty, Tara looked up and over at the mirrored glass, knowing who was behind it, getting off on watching.

'Tara?'

Her attention returned to a concerned Hannah, looking down at her, wondering what had happened. The woman was more worried about Tara than about her own interrupted pleasure.

Tara smiled in reassurance and returned to the woman's sex, regretting letting herself be distracted by the asshole behind the glass. She set up an internal mantra to block out the external thoughts and feelings around her, and continued to kiss and lick the woman until she grew wild, the cries from her mouth inarticulate pleas and demands, her fingernails digging into the sides of Tara's head. Suddenly Hannah stiffened, her muscles contracting sharply against Tara's face, indeed her whole body shaking with release. Before she even realised it, Tara's own climax from Ben's touch followed, and her throttled cry was muffled into the sex of her new lover, as wave after wave of pleasure swept through her body, making her dig her nails into Hannah's soft hot thighs.

The women reclined together, Ben with them, his own erection waiting, but he seemed content to take his time.

Come on, babe, give us more of that brown sugar ...

Tara frowned, unable to block the thoughts from her mind. She kissed Hannah, letting her taste her own sex. 'I need to use the toilet. You two don't mind carrying on?'

Their disappointment was evident, but they remained good-natured, Ben replying, 'Only if you promise to find us again before this weekend's out.'

Tara grinned. 'I promise.' She kissed him too, before rising and dressing, leaving them alone to continue for the benefit of their unseen audience.

Her post-climax warmth was fading quickly as she made her way out into the corridor, hoping to avoid the author of her distraction.

And failing. 'Hey, nice show.' Donnie leant against a corridor wall and smiled at her. 'How's about a private session?'

From an early age, Tara had the gifts: second sight, prophetic dreams, clairvoyance. For a long while, they had been curses, when she could perceive things she'd rather not have: what some supposed friends really thought of her, her mother's secrets and her father's scandals, casual bigoted and cruel thoughts from seemingly the most saintly. She had ventured into adulthood, gradually accepting what she possessed, and seeking a place where she felt at home. Here, she felt that way. It was paradise.

Only this man made her feel like he was the serpent in it. And the train's innate energies were amplifying her own perceptions. Thoughts and images flooded her now from him, drenching her earlier satisfaction and leaving her feeling mortified. 'Who's April?'

He blinked. 'Huh? No one. I don't know anyone named April.'

'Is she onboard?'

'No. I mean, who?'

Then the truth hit Tara like a punch, and she glared with sudden disgust. 'You stupid prick. You've no idea what you've done.'

Before he could respond to her cryptic condemnation, Faye stepped into view, barely glancing at Tara before fixing on Donnie, taking him by the arm. 'Come on.'

Tara said nothing as the pair disappeared, glad to see the back of both of them. They deserved each other.

Without ceremony, Faye guided him into an unoccupied alcove, one with a waist-high padded platform like a doctor's examining couch and one she knew had no microphones or cameras. She pushed him back against the platform and dropped to her knees, the swelling in his baggy linen trousers prominent but not indicative of a full erection. Her hands reached up along his sides, before moving to his belt and zipper, undoing them. She drew out his penis: long and thick and dark, with a flaring head glistening with moisture.

'Told ya you shouldn't have sent me away,' he swaggered.

'Shut up.' She drew in first his odour, musky and salty, and then parted her lips and drew in the rest of him. He made a sound of intense approval above her as she ran her tongue along the rim of the head, tasting him.

She kept it up for a while, but then pulled back and looked up at him in the deep pink light in the alcove, knowing she now had his full attention. 'I've been thinking... this train needs new management. How'd you like to run it with me?'

8

Mickey gripped Val tightly by the hips as he drove into her. 'Him? That's Frenchie, some big Cajun slab of beef from deep in the bayou. Not much upstairs, but strong. Why? You know him?'

'No,' Val lied, adjusting the pillow beneath her as her husband fucked her from above. Her family charm dropped to the right side of her neck. Outside their berth window, the retreating Louisiana wilderness was a blur of speed and darkness broken by the odd flash of light as the train passed a house near the tracks. 'Risky, isn't it? Hiring someone you hardly know, and he's not even Italian.'

'Riskier recruiting in Chicago; the Feds know us up there. Besides, he knows Spanish, and I want someone who does when I deal with those *cacasodo* Cubans again.'

Val understood. In the year they had been married, she had made many rail journeys between Louisiana and Illinois, sometimes with Mickey, other times with one or more of his men. Never alone. And always carrying money from Chicago, either to launder through their clubs in New Orleans, or to transfer to Cuba to help keep the government casino-friendly. But there was trouble brewing from revolutionaries in the hills, though Val doubted if that bearded mumbler Castro and his bunch of hairy rebels would get far.

She stroked his face, while squeezing his shaft with her pussy. 'I don't like the look of him.'

Mickey grunted, quickening his pace. 'I didn't hire Frenchie for you to like, but to keep an eye on you and our investments in my absence. Keep that in mind.'

'Yes, Mickey.' She let him go faster, kept her grip on him to increase the friction, while her mind drifted back to twenty minutes before, before they'd gone to bed for a quick fuck, when some of Mickey's men – including his latest recruit – came to the berth to check in with him. She could still see the heavy-framed figure standing respectfully in the rear, clad in an ill-fitting new pinstriped suit, the square jaw and aquiline nose and short-cropped chocolate hair. Their eyes had met, for only a moment.

You stupid bastard.

She willed Mickey to finish up and to shut up. Not that he did. 'The Fratellis' anniversary party is this weekend. Think we can improve relations this time?'

Val didn't answer, having given up arguing about that as well. The Mob wives hadn't exactly accepted her into their collective bosom, seeing her as some unsophisticated Southern rube, though Mickey's standing within the organisation precluded them from saying so aloud, to her face. She found herself less hypocritical, however, more than once berating the beehive-haired bitches for their obsession with Tupperware parties and self-denial about their husbands' jobs and girl-friends on the side.

Of course, it was little better when she visited New Orleans. Her father remained the same, but her old friends now looked on her as a traitor, a whore who literally climbed into bed with outsiders.

She'd never felt so isolated.

So Val rode at his pace, made all the right sounds that pleased him, until he finished.

After a while, he regained his senses, rose and began cleaning himself up and dressing. 'Gonna go meet up with the boys.'

She nodded, pulling the sheets up around her. 'Whatever.'

He wasn't long out the door when she was moving her hands under the sheets, lightly stroking her breasts, letting the nipples stir and pucker and her skin tingle, even as she squeezed her thighs together, grinding against the mattress as if fighting an intruder. She had to do a lot of this lately too, Mickey having grown too busy to put much effort into fucking. She watched her body move beneath the sheets, catching glimpses of herself as she lifted a knee and raised the covers, seeing her soft light skin and dark delta . . .

There was a knock at the door and she cursed, the spell broken. She rose and slipped into one of Mickey's shirts, half-buttoning it, expecting the porter or maid . . .

'Hello, *ma chère*.'

Enrique, large as life. Larger; he seemed to fill up the doorway.

Immediately she reached out and pulled him inside, slamming the door, the emotion she'd had pent up inside her since seeing him unleashed. 'What the fuck are you doing here, you asshole?'

He blinked at her unexpected use of profanity and then recovered. 'It's Frenchie now. Their idea.' He shrugged, smiling.

'It's not funny! If he finds out who you were – *are* –'

'How? I wasn't around on previous visits, and I had my friends give me a good story.' He drew closer, giving her that smile that made her ache more than once. 'What, did you think I'd take "no" for an answer? Just leave you –'

'Leave me what? Protecting my father's life, our business? Didn't those letters I sent explain clearly enough for you? Is that why you're doing this? Some stupid romantic gesture? The soldier boy come back to kill the bad guy and rescue the damsel? What then? Have you thought *any* of this through?'

Enrique's expression sobered now. 'I promised I'd look after you. Everyone said you were fine. I didn't believe them.'

Val was torn between holding him tight and never letting him go, and throwing him off the train in order to protect him. She settled for: 'You should have listened to everybody. I am fine. Mickey doesn't hurt me. He treats me OK.'

His face hardened at her words, and his eyes moved past her to the bed and its crumpled sheets. 'I'll bet he does.'

The anger and fear boiled over at him, and Val swung up and slapped him across the face. She winced in pain but determined to repeat it, until he grabbed both her hands and pinned them behind her, pulling her up against him. Her blood boiling, she struggled in his grip, feeling the air in the berth touch her rear as her shirt rucked up. She felt overwhelmed by his closeness, the heat of his body and his male scent. So close again, so familiar, a reassuring presence in her life once more.

This was insane. She had to have Mickey fire him or reassign him. Anything to save his life – both their lives.

He held her tightly with one arm, the hand of the other reaching up and touching her face, drawing her tousled hair back, his fingers tracing along her ears. 'I've missed you, Val,' he whispered in that husky, captivating way of his. Then he leant in and tongued and nipped the rim of her ear. Val moaned, her nipples aching as she felt the warmth and quickness of his breath, and the solid flesh pressing against her thigh through his trousers, as solid as the rest of him after two years in the army.

His mouth was soft, though, working its way across her cheek to the corner of her lips. She relished the gentle, seductive warmth and manner, then opened her mouth to his, her tongue a hot arrow winging its way to meet his.

Val began melting from his kisses, feeling stimulated in a way that Mickey had stopped doing for her. Her lips ached and her pussy ached more – but this remained a very, very dangerous gambit. 'N– No, we can't.'

Val turned in place to escape him. But Enrique gripped her again, this time from behind, one arm gripping her beneath her hot needy breasts, the other hand unbuttoning her shirt enough to reach inside and cup one breast, his thumb brushing against the tip. Val jerked, feeling her pussy thicken and heat up, thrumming in sweet response. She whispered a prayer of help to Mamselle Belagrís, for strength . . . 'N– No,' she moaned weakly.

He slipped his hand out, as if genuinely listening to her.

And brought it down between her legs, jolting her . . .

. . . awake, Cat blinking in the strong morning light streaming in through the slats on the berth window; the train had stopped, as per schedule. She was resting her head in the hollow of Nathan's arm, her breath caressing his skin, her eyes seeing the outline move underneath the cotton sheet. Cat made a soft sound to herself as she recalled the events of last night. *Dios*, that was such a luscious fuck! To feel Nathan succumbing to her suggestions, his body against hers, tasting him . . . And when his hand dived down between her legs as he held her from behind . . .

No, that was the dream! Damn! What the fuck were those about anyway? Damn Wheeler and his mystical bullshit . . .

She pushed it out of her mind for a while, gently lifted the sheet and moved it aside to look at their naked bodies. His cock was soft and curved in its flaccid state until the russet head, collared by dark-tipped foreskin, rested against one ball, almost hidden beneath black curly hair. Its musk was strong, and it looked so peaceful, sleeping like its master.

But not for long . . . She reached down and playfully stroked the head. There was a twitch, one that repeated as she repeated, running the tip of her thumb around the head, again and again. Cat felt the shaft pulse in response, though Nathan himself didn't stir.

Bolstered by the reaction, Cat softly engulfed the thickening shaft in her hand, feeling his pubic curls as she slowly drew the sheath of skin up and down, feeling it grow harder. She smiled mischievously to herself.

Nathan stirred, and she released him, drew the sheet back over them, pretending to have just awakened herself. He stared groggily at her. 'Wha– What are you doing?'

'Me? Nothing. Just felt something stabbing me in the side, thought you might have brought your gun to bed.'

He seemed to waken more now, blushed crimson as he slid out from under the sheet and turned away from her, searching and finding his boxers. 'Sorry, I don't know what I was doing.'

'I do. I was cold last night, you agreed to lie beside me. Share your warmth, as any good partner would do.' She regarded the lean, smooth line of his back and buttocks, smiling as he deliberately kept his back to her, his erection still obvious. 'Remember?'

He glanced behind him. 'Yeah. Yeah, that was it. Hope you . . . slept well.'

She smiled. 'Oh, *si*. And I had this wonderful dream.' Cat moved in place, twisting around to lie on her belly with her head at the foot of the bed. 'It was so erotic. I was drunk, and in trouble, and this cowboy took care of me, kissing me, undressing me, being so tender, so giving and satisfying.'

'Uh-huh. Sounds like quite a guy.'

She rested her chin on her hand, grinning. 'Pity he wasn't real.'

'Pity. You hung over?'

'Just hungry. How about you go out and bring back some breakfast?'

'Me?'

'Of course. You: big hunter-gatherer, me: helpless female.' She glanced down, just enough to reveal the upper halves of her breasts. 'I can't go out. Look at me.'

'Yeah, look at you.' He grunted, rising. '"Helpless female", my ass.' Then he stopped at the knock on the door. He looked to Cat, who quickly sat up, securing the sheet around her before he answered it. 'Yes?'

A buxom young redhead, one of the train staff, stood there in a skimpy black uniform. 'Ms Montoya, Mr Ames, Mr Wheeler requests your urgent presence this morning.'

Nathan frowned. 'Urgent? Does he know what time it is?'

'I expect so, sir, but all he ordered me to do was escort you there as soon as possible. And to inform you that dress was very casual.'

'"Very casual"?'

The woman smiled, taking a moment to look Nathan over. 'That usually means whatever you wear to bed.'

Nathan nodded. 'Wait out here, please.' He closed the door as the woman departed, and fixed his gaze on Cat, his voice low. 'Well?'

Cat swallowed, her thoughts racing. '"Well" what? You think I gave something away, don't you?'

'Well, you *were* drunk.'

'I think if something had gone wrong he'd be asking us to pack our bags. And not show up in our skivvies.' Still, her mind raced back to last night, to the kitchen, and Wheeler down between her legs ... *Dios*, that had been satisfying, though not as much as the time she had with Nate after ...

'Perhaps. Best be ready regardless.'

'I'm always ready, Hound.'

'I'll bet. Well, I don't run when Wheeler snaps his fingers,

I'm gonna shower first. Don't suppose you wanna join me before you go? Just to save time and hot water?'

'Just hurry up.' She smiled as he disappeared into the bathroom, listened to the water running, remembered with delight the weight of him on her, how Enrique – *puta*! What the fuck was going on in her head? The dreams again. They had to mean something. Perhaps some half-remembered, subconscious facts about this case, ones her memory was bidding her recollect?

She rose, keeping the sheet wrapped around her, and retrieved her phone. '*Buenos dias*, Gordy.'

A groggy voice replied, 'Mmm? Catalina? Is that you, *chica*?' Then the familiar lasciviousness returned. 'Oh my God! What happened last night with you and Hound? I want details, figures, videos!'

'And I want you to do some searching for me, regarding an Italian mobster from Chicago, active in the 1950s, known as Mickey Whisper.' Her brain struggled to recall the other facts from her dreams. 'He married a girl from New Orleans called Valentina. There was also a local man he hired as a bodyguard, Enrique, nicknamed Frenchie.'

'Some wiseguy, his squeeze and his muscle from fifty years ago? Are you serious? Talk about a waste of my considerable talents.'

'Also, find me everything you can about someone named...Mamselle Belagrís. No matter how ridiculous it sounds.'

'Oh sure, anything else?'

She dropped her sheet. 'Would it motivate you if you knew I was naked right now?'

'Bullshit.' But he couldn't keep the interest from his voice.

She ignored her bra and reached for her panties. 'I swear, it's true. And I'm running my hands over my body even as we speak.'

'Send a photo to prove it.'

'Just get to work, Gordy.' She hung up, looked around to decide what might classify as 'very casual' to someone like Wheeler.

Cat chose a new royal-blue shoestring camisole top with embroidered lace along the edge and matching French panties, something she found she looked very distracting in, especially to judge from Nathan's reaction, who'd chosen a more modest, simple black T-shirt and cotton boxers for himself.

The woman had delivered them, not to Wheeler's office as Cat had expected, but to one of the games carriages, a private area labelled THE DUNGEON, bedecked with stocks, pillories, alcoves and furniture that looked more at home in a gym than here. Simulated stone covered the windowless walls, and torches on the walls were burning and crackling, though there was a smell of butane which confirmed they were gas-operated.

Wheeler sat on a raised high-backed chair like some fallen prince, dressed in an old-fashioned white silk shirt, half-opened to reveal curls of blond hair in the centre of an otherwise smooth-looking chest, black trousers and shiny leather boots. 'My friends, apologies for summoning you at this ungodly hour of the morning, but an urgent matter has arisen that simply couldn't wait.'

Beside Cat, Nathan stepped forwards, and she could almost feel his protective aura. 'I think I know what this is about. I left Ms Scott tied up in your office last night, after she insulted Cat. I should apologise.'

Cat turned to him, seeing an attempt to defuse a potential situation. And she took it, punching his arm, letting out her feelings in over-the-top fashion. '*Cabrón*! You do that to our hostess, after the courtesies they've extended to us?'

'I was defending you!' he replied, wincing at her attack.

'Please, no more violence,' Wheeler requested. 'I knew of this already. She deserved what she got. That's not why you're here. I possess an inherently suspicious nature, a nature that my questionable background has nurtured. And speaking of questionable backgrounds, let's talk about yours.'

Cat blinked, her stomach twisting. 'Excuse me?'

'Yours and Mr Ames', assuming those are your real names. I have access to outside resources with considerable IT experience and dubious ethics. He dug deep into your credit history and related information, and found enough discrepancies to endorse my suspicions. Further, my wireless internet network picked up a signal last night from a rogue cellphone. I narrowed the phone's signal to your berth.' He paused to sip at his champagne. 'Care to elucidate?'

Cat's stomach stopped twisting, preferring to simply plummet into her feet. They'd had peripheral false identities set up in their own names, given the low-level nature of their mission, and the risk of discovery, though slim, was present. And then there was the phone, which had also been risky, but seemingly worth the risk.

She looked to Nathan. 'Looks like we've been found out, Hound.'

He nodded, crossed his arms and grunted. 'You wanna fess up, or shall I?'

Cat breathed in, forcing herself to appear calm, if somewhat annoyed at being forced into this action. 'Nathan and I aren't ordinary passengers. We're . . . freelance operatives.'

Wheeler stared. 'Like Belle, that term can cover a lot of ground.'

'We work undercover, usually specialising in corporate espionage,' Nathan replied.

Now Wheeler smirked. 'Investigating or committing?'

'Both, when the price is right.' Cat moved in place, affecting her body language to project truthfulness. 'Certain parties hired us to board your train and ascertain your business's potential for concealed lateral investment.'

'In plain English, money laundering. And who are your supposed employers?'

Now Nathan piped up, 'If they'd wanted their identities revealed now, they would have approached you directly. We can say that if you're willing, and if it's worked right, it could net you a profit of up to a hundred grand a year.'

Wheeler took in the offer, drinking from a champagne flute on an adjacent table. But then he declared, 'I'm an honest businessman. How do I know you're not reporters or police officers?'

Cat rolled her eyes. 'We're not cops. If we were, then our denying it now will mean we can be accused of entrapment if we entice you to commit a crime.' That was a common urban legend, she knew, otherwise there'd never be any undercover operations, but she ran with it. 'And if we're reporters, we'd get a much better story from you by being open with you.' She paused, breathing in deeply. 'Contact your source, and have them confirm the stint I did in Alderson Prison Camp in West Virginia, three years ago. Nine months' stretch, industrial secrets theft.'

'A jailbird?' Wheeler teased. 'And in the wilds of West Virginia, too. It must have been an arduous experience.'

Cat shrugged, glad that the Department's IT people planted additional layers to their covers, enough to explain away any discrepancies found. It was a half-lie, something almost as strong as the truth. 'Only in the showers.'

Their host stared a moment longer. Then smiled with relief. 'Actually, that was already confirmed.' He finished his drink, set it back on the table, which also held bottles of massage oils and lubricants. 'Your story ... makes sense. Not that I'm saying

I'm interested in breaking the law, of course. But I'm glad I won't have to throw you out into the middle of the wilderness.' He rose to his feet, drew closer to them, his eyes moving with obvious interest over Cat in her underwear. 'However, you *did* break the rules by keeping your phone. You really should be punished for that.' He met her gaze. 'I suspected it's yours, Catalina.'

'So you think you should punish me? Now there's a surprise.' She folded her arms across her chest. '*Besame el culo.*'

He shrugged. 'Then you should pack your bags right now. We're about eight miles from the nearest town, it shouldn't take you more than a couple of hours in the August heat.'

Nathan drew up close behind her, putting his hands on her upper arms and staring at Wheeler. 'You're not punishing her, pal.' He turned her away from Wheeler, to face him. 'She's mine. That's *my* job.'

She looked up at him, confused. 'Excuse me?'

He kept staring into her eyes, his hand moving up to stroke her cheek, snaking along to the back of her head, cradling it, his expression deliciously confident and dominant as he stared back. 'She's always been a wildcat. But sometimes she needs to be reminded who's in charge.' Nathan was still speaking to Wheeler, but Cat knew the words were meant for her, a challenge to maintain their cover as long-time lovers and to keep Wheeler distracted and willing to let them stay onboard for a while longer.

It was a challenge she accepted. 'Hah! You think you're in charge? You can bite my ass after you kiss it.'

'Soon.' Then he was pulling her to him, possessing her lips hungrily, and she moaned into his mouth with a sudden rush of desire at the feel of his tongue as it moved, invaded her mouth, his lips hot and pliant and both sapping her token resistance and galvanising her. She pressed up against him, mindful not only of the growing hardness she felt in his boxers, but of Wheeler's proximity. From the corner of her eye, she saw him approach.

And, apparently, so did Nathan, because he suddenly pulled back from her mouth and made her face Wheeler. Nate was directly behind her, one arm wrapped around her, pinning her arms to her side and leaving her gasping for more of his lips. He looked over her shoulder at Wheeler. 'No. You may be our host and we may owe you a forfeit for breaking the rules, but you only get to watch, not touch. I told you she was mine.'

The craving in Nathan's words, so obvious and true beyond their cover identities, sent thrills through Cat, but she still kept up her side of it. 'I'm not anybody's, *cabrón*.'

Nathan's free hand slapped her right buttock, making a wonderfully audible slap to accompany the feelings it gave her. He still stared at Wheeler. 'Well, Jack? Agreed?'

Wheeler smiled. 'Agreed.' He moved to another chair by a wall, took it and swung it around so that he could sit on it backwards, arms folded over its back. 'Carry on.'

'I will.' The hand that had just slapped Cat's rear now moved around the front. The pair stood there, facing their audience of one, and Cat gasped as Nathan's free hand moved up, caressed her breasts through her camisole, fingers playing with her nipples as they began hardening, standing up beneath the silken material. Nathan's lips moved to her neck, kissing and nipping her as she arched her head to the other side, giving him more room. And her eyes stayed on Wheeler, who had to make obvious adjustments in his seating position. Having him there, watching, knowing how much he wanted her, added such spice to her already potent feelings. Nathan's hand slipped beneath the elastic waistband of her fluted French panties, down to her bush, stroking the hairs as he cupped her mound, his middle finger teasing her folds, steadily stroking.

He withdrew his hand, brought it up to her mouth. 'Moisten it.'

She caught her scent, then parted her lips and took his finger in her mouth, running her tongue along its length and coating it with her saliva.

He returned it to her pussy, this time opening her, piercing her.

The room had grown deathly quiet, especially with the train having stopped. Nathan's finger stroked her clit softly while she ground against him, still in his tight embrace, her nipples aching now inside her camisole, missing the attention they had been receiving before. She looked down to see his hand inside her panties, looking as obscenely rude and wonderful as it felt, as his middle finger penetrated her deeply, curving up to touch her G-spot, while the base of his hand pressed against her clit. His actions encouraged her sex to swell, carrying her closer to a climax. And she was rising, growing hotter and higher, like a rocket reaching its zenith.

Wheeler breathed in audibly, and Cat watched him watching her, glad he was there, glad he wasn't involved any further. She pushed her rear against Nathan's bulge, as he nipped at her lobe, letting his tongue dart inside her ear.

With a long moan, she reached the summit, punctuated with a sharp, '*Puta!*'

The strength briefly left her, but Nathan held her up, until he withdrew his hand from the front of her panties and carefully helped her over to a low metal stool with two padded areas, a narrow area lower to the ground, a larger area higher and angled away from the ground. 'Straddle it, bend forwards.'

Cat swayed there in post-coital bliss as if still drunk from last night, smirking and offering him her middle finger.

Nathan smirked back, and gently but firmly guided her down onto her knees on the smaller padded area, bending her forwards until she rested on the larger area. He knelt before her, taking her wrists and guiding them to the legs of the kneeling stool, watching her for some sign, any sign – a silent invitation to back out now.

Instead, she stared defiantly at him, to do his worst – or better yet, his best.

He slipped her wrists into leather hoops already positioned there; she watched, seeing how he ensured she could free herself with a simple twist of her wrists, if necessary. She heard him walk around, stand behind her. He stroked her bum through her panties and then peeled her panties down to her knees. Cat felt a flutter in her belly as she was exposed, feeling more naked like this than if he'd stripped her completely. Her ass felt cool, but her sex felt hot, her pussy lips pouting, especially as Nathan's hand drifted down between her cheeks and stroked her gently along her slit. She turned her head as she heard Wheeler rise and move his chair around to get a better view of her.

A sharp slap of Nathan's hand on her right buttock made her yelp loudly. 'Fucker! That hurt!'

'Good.' She felt his hand return, striking several times in succession, offering just the right amount of force in the right places, making deliciously rude sounds against her warming flesh and sending pleasurable sensations up her thighs and into her sex. Her belly pressed against the leather padding; she wasn't uncomfortable, but she was certainly helpless – at least, ostensibly. Cat was amazed by her own level of excitement at it.

And then Nathan stopped and reached once more between her burning cheeks to her pussy, thrusting deep inside and drawing out her juices, drawing them up along the strip of skin between her sex and her anus – and then massaging there as well. Cat was overcome by the intensity of the sensations there now.

He was teasing her. And it made her look up from beneath

her hair and snarl, 'Come on, Nathan, get that cock in my pussy!'

'Jack, can you get me some lube, please?'

'Certainly, Mr Ames.'

Cat gasped. 'I'm wet, *cabrón*, I don't need lube!'

'Yes, you do.' Nathan's hands held her buttocks, spreading them apart as Wheeler returned. As Cat dropped her head down again, she felt the cool viscous substance run down the cleft of her buttocks. Moments later, she felt his finger working at the tiny entrance to her rear.

'No,' she said sharply. She felt a shudder – though not from fear. That *pajiero* knew how intense it would be for her. 'No fucking way!'

'Oh, now I want it twice as much,' he said quietly, underlined with the sounds of him lowering his boxers, before lubricating the length of his shaft.

The desire in his voice, genuine and potent, excited her. It was the most exciting thing about fucking Nathan, how he obviously desired her so much. Their situation was forgotten. Wheeler was forgotten.

'Fucker,' was all she finally said, a soft surrender.

He pressed forwards. Cat felt the little ring of muscles at her entrance resist and, for an instant, she had the desire to pull away, but resisted. Those times she'd had anal sex, or used one of her vibrators there, there was always a little bit of pain, but she knew it would pass quickly.

Nathan pressed forwards again slowly sinking into her.

Cat felt a shock of sensation that almost took her breath away. She rode the initial scream of protest from her nerves, rode it until it translated into a wide, all-encompassing surge of pleasure that she rarely met. It was a pleasure on the same wavelength as pain, and of the same incredible intensity, one barely indistinguishable from the other.

Cat braced herself, as she realised that Nathan had barely penetrated her at all, and was ready for more.

His hands, smeared with lubricant, grasped her hips sharply, as he pushed further forwards, the breadth of him stretching her, the sensation furthered by the inclusion of a spectator, who looked barely able to contain his own excitement. Nathan's cock slid deeper and then, with another push, it was as deep as it could be.

Cat gasped, the blood racing to her head and making it spin, riding the waves of extraordinary delight. Tentatively, she pushed back against him, feeling his balls against her mound. His cock twitched inside her, translating into pulses of pleasure. She was able to feel every millimetre of him, and any initial pain of discomfort had been eclipsed by floods of passion. It was *muy bueno*, a wonderfully sexy sensation, and she wriggled her ass shamelessly from side to side to accentuate her thrills ...

Until Nathan slapped her again. 'No, no. You got us into trouble by wanting your own way. But not this time.'

Yeah, right.

As he drew in and out of her, he slapped her bum again, making her squirm and fight with the bonds around her wrists and curse and bless him in equal measures. Cat was plummeting into a deep pool of intense bliss, and her sex pulsed wildly, as if fed from the sensations radiating from her adjacent passage.

Then Nathan leant forwards, almost lying on top of her, his cock still driving in and out of her, but now he was reaching around her waist, between her skin and the bench, to find her pussy. Suspecting his intentions, she adjusted her position slightly, raising her hips and parting her thighs further, giving him access to her clit, though she doubted if he could actually reach. '*Puta!*'

Just as she thought she could feel no more, more came. Nathan couldn't do very much, not being a contortionist, but the presence of his fingertips, rigid little tips pressing against her clit, was enough to complete a circuit within her. And as quickly as a circuit delivering a signal, Cat felt herself coming, a huge snake of sensation slipping over her.

Nathan's cock began to twitch again, and it seemed to swell within the tight, unfamiliar confines surrounding it. Each tiny twitch was like a sweet kick inside, tempting her with the promise of another imminent orgasm.

That expectation hit her as her next orgasm did. Pleasure turned into a moment of pain as he surrendered to his own burgeoning release, and quickened his pace, his body hot and sweaty as he shot into her. But her pain passed, as if coated by his ejaculation. She felt every spurt inside her, her fingers digging uselessly into the bench, her final cry a short, sharp plea, which made her eyes roll into the back of her head and sapped her remaining strength.

Dimly she felt Nathan gently withdraw.

She lay there, clenching her buttocks to keep her received prize inside, and her throat felt raw. She was facing in Wheeler's direction, and she opened her eyes, silently challenging him to respond.

But he just sat there, keeping his obvious erection from view, his expression unreadable.

9

Wheeler returned to his suite, an opulent berth of drapes and huge plush pillows in the style of some clichéd nomadic tent, though the double bed dominating the room was more conventional. Light filtered through shutters onto the sleeping form of Faye, her nude body half-covered by wrinkled white Egyptian cotton sheets.

Wheeler stood there, staring at her while he undressed quickly, his hard-on seeming to sap any excess energy from him. She'd come to bed only a few hours before, when the last of the passengers had finally exhausted themselves and retired to their own or other people's berths. He hadn't expected, or particularly desired her return to his side – at least, not until now. Watching Ames take the luscious Catalina like that had been like injecting nitro into his libido.

Without waking Faye first, he pulled back the sheets, exposing her long hot frame. She lay on her left side, almost on her belly, and her right knee was curled up, hiding her pussy but leaving her rear deliciously exposed.

He carefully climbed onto the bed from behind, kissing and nipping her buttocks. Beneath him, Faye stirred, mumbling something, and finally yelping as he parted her cheeks with his hands and ran his tongue along the strip of skin between her pussy and her anus. From the corner of his eye, he saw her look over her shoulder from beneath her tangled hair. 'Oh. You. What's wrong, your little Cuban quim not satisfy – *oh fuck*!'

Wheeler smiled to himself with satisfaction as his tongue

entered her rear, probing gently and generating the desired reaction. She pushed back against his face, grinding her ass against him, even as she shifted her body into a familiar position, Wheeler following as Faye rose onto all fours, her hands moving to grasp the brass framework of the head-board.

Finally, he rose onto his knees behind her, then looked to the side table. 'Lube.'

Faye cursed and reached out for the tube, practically flinging it at him. 'Should have thought of that before, stupid.'

'Shut up.' He coated his shaft in the clear substance, and then her entrance. He wanted to fuck, not talk.

But Faye displayed the same obstreperous nature as just about every other woman he'd ever known. 'Your little accountant leave you with blue balls?'

He sighed; at least Faye seemed much more amenable now than last night. 'She's not one. Neither is Ames. They're industrial spies, working for potential investors.'

'What?'

He positioned his cockhead at her entrance. 'Yes. This is a business trip for them.' Now he looked up. 'You're tensing. If you're not ready ...'

'No.' The woman began relaxing. 'You sure know how to wake up a girl, Jack.'

Wheeler barely heard her, picturing another woman ready and eager to be taken by him.

Unsurprisingly, Cat slept for a few hours longer upon returning with Nathan to their berth. When she awoke, she saw him sitting by the table, still only his boxers, working on the phone. She cleared her throat. 'I hope you're not just playing games on that.'

'Well, those frogs don't get themselves across the highway.'

He glanced up. 'I'm just examining the downloaded records from Wheeler's PC. How are you feeling?'

Well and truly fucked, you gorgeous bastard, she thought, settling for, 'Hungry. So, you take total advantage of me, ravish me in front of witnesses, and then leave me to starve? Some partner.'

'We're parked by a lake for the afternoon, and the staff are setting up a Cajun buffet. How about we go out to eat, and get off this train for a while?'

'Good idea.' Not that she believed it. A part of her wanted to invite him back to bed. But, as tempting as that was, this time she could find no excuse for it – no maintaining their cover, no drink-fuelled need for release. To do anything like that otherwise would complicate their working relationship, more than it already was. 'Are you OK, Hound?'

He looked like he was almost going to supply a token answer, before he responded with, 'Were *you* OK with what happened in the Dungeon?'

She smiled; her pussy still throbbed delightfully, and she wriggled beneath the sheets. 'Well, you *were* put on the spot. And we had to maintain our cover. I suppose I could forgive you.'

'You're too kind.'

'This afternoon I want you to get closer to Faye, while I –'

'Get even closer to Wheeler. Why don't we switch targets? You do a little girl-on-girl with our hostess, and I'll take him?'

'Because Jack doesn't have a hard-on for you.' She eyed him suspiciously, sitting up again. 'Do you have a problem with this? I know the alpha male role you played for us this morning wasn't totally made up –'

'Catalina, this is your first field assignment. And, given the sexually charged atmosphere, and the obvious charms of our host –'

'And because I'm just a naive little girl swayed by the attentions of a dashing Southern rogue –'

'I'm not saying that. But if you compromise yourself with him, it could have repercussions later, for you and the Service.'

Cat scowled. 'Don't go there, Hound. Firstly, we both know this is a fact-finding mission, and that any subsequent investigation will base a prosecution on the evidence that they gather. Secondly, the criminal activities being investigated are not connected with sex, nor is sex being used to lure the subject into illegality, and therefore charges of facilitation would be groundless. Thirdly, given the "sexually charged atmosphere" of the environment, sexual behaviour can be legitimately employed to help the investigator fit into the setting, adding credibility and helping to avoid raising suspicion –'

Nathan raised a hand. 'OK, OK, so you know the undercover manual references verbatim. I withdraw my suggestion.' He leant back in his chair. 'Cat, if I offer my advice, or concerns or whatever, it's not because I don't think you can handle yourself. It's just to remind you that you don't *have* to. OK?'

His explanation deflated some of her anger, if not her own doubts about how she was managing Wheeler, and that was without even taking into account the weird dreams she was having, or the weirder explanation for them from Wheeler. '*Gracias*. But I'm still assigning you to Faye. Our secondary covers have given us greater freedom with them. Find out more about the deal they have with the Kolchaks.'

'Sure.'

She rose to her feet, pulled her camisole over her head and slipped out of her panties, offering him a view of her naked back and rear as she padded into the bathroom for a shower, delighting in his hungry expression. 'Eyes back in your head, Hound.'

'Spoilsport.'

* * *

It was in the latter half of the day. The train was parked by a dark oval lake, bordered by thick foliage and a wall of tall ancient cypresses tasselled with moss. They could have been hundreds of miles from civilisation or just a short walk. Most of the passengers were out skinny-dipping in the water or partaking of the sumptuous Cajun buffet set up, and the air buzzed with excited insects.

Cat had changed into a frilly black blouse and slacks, and sat on a rock at the edge of the water, finishing off the latest plate that Nathan had brought over, telling herself not to be so surprised at how famished she was. She nodded to a naked Tara, who was waving to Cat while chasing and being chased by an equally naked Ben and Hannah Oliver, kicking up water in the shallow end of the lake. It was an idyllic, sensual setting.

But it was not a time for relaxation. She watched as Nathan accompanied Faye across the tracks, to an abandoned church, where their hostess would regale them with bullshit ghost stories. And now Cat rose, looking for Wheeler.

She found him in the graveyard surrounding the church. Here, the air buzzed and chirped and chattered with life, defying the overgrown, forgotten rows of grave markers, from simple headstones to elaborate crypts. She trod carefully along the winding rows, noting the gathering clouds overhead, expecting a storm soon, which would certainly add to the atmosphere of Faye's ghost stories but would ruin the skinny-dippers' fun on the other side of the train.

She caught movement by one golden-brown marker, paused and watched secretly. Yes, it was Wheeler, kneeling down and trying to read an inscription, consulting a black notebook, occasionally scribbling into it. There was an intensity to his features and, without knowing what it was all about, Cat was reluctant to disturb him.

But as it turned out, she didn't have to worry. 'You thirsty?' He never looked up; he might have been addressing the dead.

Cat took a chance that he wasn't and stepped into view, approached him. 'How'd you know I was there?'

He smiled. 'The bayou is awash with many agreeable scents, but your perfume is not typically one of them.' When she stood beside him, he looked up, squinting with the light behind her. 'Why aren't you with the others?'

'I'm here on business, not pleasure.'

'Ironic, since for me, pleasure is my business.' He turned back to his notebook. 'If you're out to persuade me about your employer's offer, save your breath. I'm turning over a new leaf.'

'In an old graveyard?' Cat squatted beside him, feeling her skin prickle at his closeness, though he seemed to be ignoring her now. 'What is this really about, Jack?'

'Do you really want to know? Then you'd better start being honest with me.'

'I've already told you, Nathan and I are onboard on behalf of –'

'I mean about what you've experienced. I know you've been repeatedly channelling the spirit of a woman.'

Cat stiffened. 'You don't know –'

'Valentina Uscione, wife of mobster Mickey Uscione, lover of local boy Enrique Cazenove. Over fifty years ago, they rode this train, and Valentina and Enrique were killed on it. But their spirits remain and still ride with us. And you've seen them. As I have.'

'Bullshit. It's just…just memories from some gangster movie that this train ride has revived.'

He smiled, fishing through his notebook. 'This must be movie publicity then.' He handed her photocopies of fifty-year-old newspaper and magazine articles, not on movies mobsters but real ones, real crimes, and one on a Chicago wedding, complete with a photograph: Val and Mickey, just as she remembered them.

It was insane. Cat considered herself a rational person, able to focus her logic to reach plausible conclusions, and yet those same skills pointed her now towards an inherently implausible deduction.

Finally, she felt compelled to ask, 'How do you know about all this?'

Now it seemed his turn to react, and he settled back on a shattered stone grave marker beside him. 'Prior to forming Southern Spirits, I was . . .' He paused, and his whole body seemed to deflate, the ebullient, florid persona he presented to others set aside. 'I was a crook. A thief, a liar . . . How did Donnie describe me last night? "A cheap lowlife redneck hustler"? A painfully accurate assessment. Always moving, one step ahead of arrest warrants and civil suits. I was convinced I was a free spirit, living by my own rules, smarter than those nine-to-five idiots chained to mortgages and kids.' He pursed his lips at something only he saw. 'I was fooling myself.'

Now he looked up, past Cat to Belle. 'One night, though, circumstances had me sleeping in an abandoned railway depot and in a forgotten locomotive that had seen better days.' His face grew pale. 'That was the first time she talked to me, whispered her name. Oh, at first I dismissed it as a dream, the product of a vivid imagination. But I stuck around and felt more, in other abandoned carriages. I watched and listened and learnt.'

Cat's gaze followed his, to the great silver and red locomotive that sat nearby. 'Learnt what?'

'That spirits permeate the Deep South. The families have as many skeletons buried beneath them as do the antebellum mansions and the ruined mills, the battle sites and the abandoned graveyards. The past, and those from the past, are unignorable. And that Belle did more than just carry departed spirits. She could employ the living to help the dead. Valentina and Enrique were killed, and their bodies buried anonymously somewhere along one of these railway lines. Their spirits can't rest until they're found and identified. And that's ... where I came in.'

'And that's what this is all about? Then why not just go ahead and do that? Why renovate everything and go into the swingers' party business? Why not get a team of scientists onboard to investigate?'

'Because Belle didn't want to be studied. She wanted to be restored. And it made sense, as she needed people onboard, people who might be receptive enough to pick up on the vibrations.' He sighed. 'In case you hadn't noticed, there's a residing theme to the experiences: arousal and sex. The energies generated during sex are potent, used in magical ceremonies for millennia. They can touch us to our very core, strip us of our facades and leave us open, vulnerable.' He smiled. 'At least, if done right. And so, I observe and listen, and look for clues.'

'Uh-huh,' she replied finally, amazed at how much she was accepting.

'I know how it sounds,' he confessed. 'And I readily admit that the séances and ghost stories are fictitious. But this is real. And it's given me a chance.'

'A chance at what?'

He paused. 'Enrique was a better man than I've ever been. I've looked through his eyes, felt his deep abiding love and passion for Valentina, a love and passion that was more important to him than his own life. It's something I've never experienced myself.' His gaze dropped, embarrassment and honesty stark on his face. 'If I can do this for him, for both of them, then maybe I don't have to be ... what I am. I can be something better, too.' He smiled. 'This was meant to be. I was drawn to Belle, as you were.'

Cat stared. She'd been trying, almost desperately, to see the angle behind all this. Was it about money? He'd turned down hers and Nathan's offer from their 'employers'. Was it about getting into her pants? It seemed unnecessarily complicated for that. Was he simply delusional? If so, then how did he induce these incidents in her? 'What do you want from me, Jack?'

He smiled. 'I don't know if I should ask. I don't want to get into trouble with Mr Ames. He seems the possessive type.'

'He doesn't possess me,' she snorted. 'No one does.'

'Indeed?' He smiled at her. 'It's hot, and I'm going for a swim. Want to join me?'

She didn't answer, wordlessly following as he gathered his materials and walked around the outside of the graveyard to the edge of the lake, a cul-de-sac partly hidden from the rest of the passengers at the far end. A dark canopy of foliage hung over the water, a haven for a swarm of insects overhead, ignoring the two below as Wheeler sat on a moss-covered rock and began removing his shoes. 'Well? You never said if you were joining me.'

'No, I didn't. Is it safe here? No 'gators, I mean.'

He smiled, unbuttoning his shirt. 'No 'gators, no snakes. Just spirits.'

Cat watched as he cast aside the shirt, revealing the tanned compact chest with the curls in the centre and the tiny dark nipples, and then rose to his feet and unbuckled his belt. He slid his jeans off his legs, revealing tight white briefs that hugged his cock and balls.

Her hands moved to her blouse, pulling it over her head without unbuttoning it, even as she kicked off her pumps, feeling the soft wet earth beneath her feet. She slid out of her slacks as she watched him slip off his briefs, his cock emerging, alert and ready, seemingly thickening more as she stared boldly at it, but he made no move to get closer to her.

Suddenly, as if overcome by Old World courtesy, he announced, 'I'll let you follow when you're ready.' He turned and rushed into the water, making noises suggesting it was colder than he had expected.

Cat steeled herself, finding it a little more difficult to undress in the open, even if no one else could see them. But the air felt lovely on her exposed skin, and the water looked even more inviting. She slipped out of her panties and bra and followed him, feeling her feet sink into the silt beneath them as she rushed to reach a water level that would give her some cover. As she suspected, the water was cool, and her nipples scowled, but when she was waist high, she dipped down until she wet herself up to her throat.

Wheeler turned around, openly admiring her. 'If I were Mr Ames, I would never let you get out of my sight.'

Cat smiled, rising up until her breasts were exposed to the air, and his eyes. She was enjoying the reaction she was getting from him more than she had expected. 'You can't control cats. They do what they want.'

'So I've noticed.' He splashed her, making her curse and splash him back. They half-swam, half-played like that, occasionally acknowledging the people at the far end who waved to them. The smells of cooking were beginning to reach them, making Cat hungry despite the breakfast she'd had.

And whenever Wheeler touched her, ostensibly as part of their playing, she hungered for more, reminding herself of how she'd denied herself relief that morning. Damn, she should have come up with an excuse when she'd been with Nathan in the berth!

After a time, he made a show of pursuing her, and she half-stumbled to escape his clutches, shrieking and giggling as he chased her out of the water and onto the bank near their clothes, both of them collapsing, rolling over each other, Wheeler behind her.

Then she felt his hand around her, holding one of her breasts, squeezing it appreciatively. 'Hey.'

He whirled her around to face him, to look up at him as he kissed her lips. He didn't loosen his grip on her until he felt her soften beneath his kiss, felt her lips give way and part. He held her tightly until she mouthed something.

When he drew back, still holding her, Cat's head spun as she sought her voice. 'What the fuck do you think you're doing?'

'You want me to stop?' His hand reached up between them and touched her breast again, playing with the nipple.

She said nothing, feeling his cock throb again, against her thigh, as if reacting to the warmth she knew was building up down there. It was wearing her down like a hurricane wind against a flimsy cabin wall. He bent down and kissed her again, this time his tongue slipping in and brushing along hers. He moaned his pleasure before leaving her mouth to move his lips along the length of her throat, drawing her hair up and out of the way, using the gentle weight of his body on hers, as his hands moved to the front of her body, sliding up and down her breasts.

She didn't have to go this far, she told herself. She could still do her job and keep him at a proverbial arm's length. She swallowed as his hand rolled a nipple between his fingers. He shifted against her so that his erection now pressed between her legs, but he made no effort to get closer to penetration. But she parted her thighs a little wider to give him some space.

Her body was beginning to respond, a recipient to his attentions, swelling and moistening to complement his own desire.

As he ground his body, his shaft, against her sex, she could not deny the intense sensations of the touch against her clitoris. Her nipples burned beneath his tongue as he sucked on them, catching them between his teeth, his fingers stroking her body, moving downwards, as his lips moved back to hers. He was back on her mouth as he shifted off her body to lie close beside her, and his hand reached her bush, stroking downwards, downwards, letting Cat part her own thighs and raise her knees until her feet sunk into the mud for purchase.

Wheeler cupped her pussy with his hand as continued to kiss her. Cat's head spun like a dervish, and the heat seemed to radiate from her whole body as if she'd been set on fire. His tongue danced out and ran along her mouth, occasionally taking one of her lips between his and sucking gently, smiling as her pelvis thrust up against his hand, demanding attention. He pulled back and watched her face as his fingers stroked and parted her folds, bringing a wider smile to his face as he felt how wet she was.

Cat couldn't quite believe, or at least couldn't quite accept, that she was letting it happen. A finger slipped easily inside, and he drew it out slowly, taking obvious pleasure in the feeling of it and the sound it made. She sought out rationalisations – part of the cover, a means of distracting the target – but then wondered why she was bothering, as she wallowed indulgently and pushed her pelvis up automatically to meet his descending finger, repeatedly.

Wheeler worked his touch faster and faster, sometimes using two fingers, gently pinching and rubbing her clit, or a thumb once or twice. Cat's moans were louder, her hips shuddering as she rode tiny climaxes, but she tried to avoid the maximum sensation which could send her too quickly over the edge. She felt her juices seeping down her slit towards her rear. Her breasts rose and fell with the waves of bliss, faster and faster as the ripples ebbed out from her thighs, and her breath felt ragged. She closed her eyes and let herself be all sound, all touch, driving her conscience further from her body with every second his hand worshipped her sex. When she cried out in ecstasy, the sounds seemed to join the sounds of the bayou around them.

Afterwards, they lay side by side, Cat's head cradled in the crook of his arm. She stared down at his cock, which had softened and settled against his thigh, like an obedient dog awaiting the call of its master. The animal heat of her orgasm had faded, and her voice sounded strange. 'What do you really want, Jack?'

'I want to try an experiment.'

She sat up. 'Experiment?'

'There's a place in the games carriage that used to be a private berth where Val and Mickey stayed, and I think contains a pivotal moment in their history. We can recreate what she heard and felt, let you connect with her.'

'And give you a chance to "connect" with me?' she asked with a smirk.

'We won't actually have to fuck. Reaching a state of arousal can be sufficient, not actual sex; we both know that one can do the latter without ever attaining the former. However, should you actually want to fuck at any stage of the experiment, you have but to ask.'

It made sense – as much as any of this supernatural bullshit made sense. Still . . . 'Ask, eh?'

'Ask. Beg.'

Her smirk descended into a snort. 'I never beg, *pendejo*.'

The church near the graveyard was a gutted Gothic miniature, something suitable for whatever town had been nearby, but no longer. The passengers who had attended Faye's lectures and ghost stories now filed out to return to the food and the swimming.

Nathan waited until everyone had departed before returning inside. It was a dark, almost claustrophobic interior, the walls cracked and weed strewn from decades of surrender to the elements. Faye Scott stood on a raised step by the altar, cast in a Jacob's ladder of yellow light that shone through her dress. 'I thought you'd left, Mr Ames.'

'It's Nathan. And I wanted to apologise to you for last night.'

'Forget it.'

Her tone suggested that he shouldn't press further, so he didn't. 'And to compliment you on your performance. Very informative.'

She snorted. 'It was a crock of shit. We don't know anything about this place; I just made it all up when we were scouting for suitable locations for the tour.'

'Very entertaining, then.'

She smiled. 'I'll accept that.' She rested her hands on the edge of the altar behind her, looking him over. 'Let's fuck.'

Nathan stopped. 'You're not one for overtures, are you?'

'Who has time? Life's too short – and for that matter, so's the weekend, for the money we charge people. We know we're all onboard to fuck, or to watch others fuck. Indulge in everything, deny yourself nothing. Those are my rules.' She smirked. 'Of course, some of us are here for more than that, aren't we?'

Nathan continued approaching. 'Jack told you why we really boarded? And that he turned down our offer?'

Faye nodded, her expression turning serious. 'But before you leave, you should know that he won't be in charge for long. And you'll find you can deal more easily with me.'

Nathan was almost upon her, breathing in the blossom scent

of her hair, admiring those lips, while trying to remain casual and not to react to her words. 'Is Jack selling Southern Spirits?'

She smiled, her hands reaching out to touch his waist and hips. 'Yes. He just doesn't know it yet. You might want to keep the news to yourself until he's signed the papers.' Her hand reached the bulge in his trousers. 'You're almost as excited as I am about that, aren't you?'

Nathan swallowed. He had reluctantly agreed to go along as Cat had wanted, learning more from this woman about the operation. And it wasn't as if the woman wasn't attractive as hell, or that he couldn't respond to her. But his words to Cat about getting too intimately involved with the suspects of an operation came back to haunt him. 'I'm excited that I might get a bonus for securing this deal. But I want more information on any existing arrangements.'

Faye pouted coquettishly. 'Awww, I'm feeling neglected now. You have no interest in me? You sure know how to hurt a woman's feelings, Nathan.'

Suddenly he took a chance, grabbed Faye by the waist and lifted her up onto the edge of the altar, making her yelp, startled, but approving. His eyes still on hers, he reached down to her knees and parted them, parted them until he could step forwards. He lifted up the hem of her dress, having already seen that she wasn't wearing any underwear.

Then he let his eyes drift deliberately down to the silky brown triangle of her pubic hair, barely concealing the borders of her pussy. He caught her scent in the still, enclosed air of the church. His eyes returned to hers, as his fingers traced playfully around her sex, feeling her wet and open and ready.

Faye's hands went up to wrap around his neck, cooing and sighed indulgently, moving to pull him closer and kiss him.

But he reached up with his other hand and blocked her gently. 'No. I don't kiss anyone else. I don't fuck anyone else. Those are *my* rules. And we haven't begun talking business yet. You have a problem with any of that, speak now, or let me do this.' He slipped a finger straight inside and began taking her further along with long, deliberate thrusts. The knuckle of his thumb, meanwhile, moved up and pressed hard against her clitoris, massaging in a rough manner which Faye seemed to respond to appreciatively. The hands on his neck now gripped him for support, and her body rocked to the rhythm he had established, her breathing going shallow, ragged.

Nathan leant in to the side of her head, letting his tongue lick out, before he whispered, 'Tell me about the arrangement with the Kolchaks.' When she didn't respond, he stopped the hand at her pussy. 'Now.'

Faye talked. Quickly.

10

The room Wheeler had referred to was one of several semi-private enclosures in the games carriages, equipped with one-way glass which let players in the corridor watch, if the inner curtains weren't drawn. A large black leather-padded hammock-like sling in the centre dominated the room, suffused with apple-red light from strips built into the walls. It was suspended waist-high and supported by four sturdy-looking chains attached to the ceiling, with leather wrist cuffs and stirrups fixed in strategic places on the sling. 'People use this?'

'It's one of our most popular features.' Wheeler carried a cardboard box he'd collected from his office over to an adjacent table. 'A woman can relax in it and be treated for hours, without her or her partners requiring Olympic stamina.'

Catalina stood at the doorway, her arms crossed over her chest. 'Uh-huh. "Treated".' When she saw the top of a bottle in the box, and heard a distinctive rattle of glass, she added, 'You're not getting me drunk again.'

'You're not getting any alcohol. I want your mind unimpaired and your memory sharp. Close and lock the door, unless you want spectators.'

Cat stepped in and locked it. 'What exactly do you intend to do?'

'I'd rather not say; part of the atmosphere I wish to generate involves the unexpected.' He set out a small MP3 player with speakers. 'Take off your slacks and make yourself comfortable.'

His words sent an unexpected thrill running through Cat. But she didn't move. 'You expect me to trust you, Jack?' It seemed strange to ask, after all they'd been through already.

'Well, if at any stage you want me to stop, just say ... "gothic". It's what we call a safe word.'

'I know what a safe word is, you patronising *cabrón*.'

He sighed. 'Someday I'll meet a woman who's not an obstreperous smart-ass, and –'

'And she'll bore you to tears.' She stood watching him watching back, as she slipped out of her shoes and moved her fingers over the catches on her slacks, giving a little shimmy to send them to her feet and leaving her in her blouse and panties. The air felt cool on her bare legs, but the rest of her seemed to heat up as she stepped out of her discarded slacks and walked towards him, reaching out to her side to draw the curtains across the one-way glass, enjoying the look of unadulterated lust Wheeler was giving her. She turned and walked over to the sling, taking a moment to study it more closely before settling into it. She set her head back on the padded leather rest, playing with the edges of her blouse, keeping her feet on the floor. 'Ever had a girl in this?'

'A few. Nervous?'

'You wish.'

He drew closer, carrying a black silk scarf, and stepped behind her. Then he looked down at her. 'Raise your head.'

She did. Wheeler wrapped the scarf gently around her head twice, cutting off any light filtering through the material, before tying the ends at the left side of her head. Her pulse had begun to quicken, but she forced herself to try to appear calm, if not be calm, as Wheeler took her left hand, gently guided the wrist up and slipped it into the leather cuff on the nearest chain overhead. Moments later, he had secured the other wrist appropriately. Unlike her time on the bench that morning, she felt no means of escape.

A frisson immediately shot through her, an acknowledged excitement at this restraint, not quite knowing what this man would do. It wasn't a genuine fear – he had no prior record of violence, showed no inclination towards it in all the time she'd known him. She thought of telling Nathan, but knew that would open too many ...

She swallowed as she felt Jack take her left shin, then raise and set her leg at an elevated but comfortable angle, resting it against padding on one chain. He slipped her foot into a soft stirrup and secured a cuff around her ankle. Moments later, he secured her right leg too and she silently admitted that it was exceedingly cosy. She also became keenly aware of her spread thighs, imagined Jack gazing at her waiting sex, encased in the black brocaded silk of her panties.

With her sight cut off, Cat listened closely, listened to Jack lifting up and setting the table closer to her. Seconds later, music – some scratchy tenor – played at low volume. It wouldn't have been her first choice of music, but it did have a calming, almost hypnotic effect, even as a buzz began growing deep within her, an inner echo of the approaching storm outside.

She started as she felt something soft, willowy, brushing along her forearm. 'What the fuck?'

'Shh.' Wheeler had returned to her silently, and was drawing something along her. Cat tried to focus, to guess what it was – a strip of sable perhaps, wrapped around his fingers – but felt overwhelmed by the shivers running through her like a current. The touch ran up her arm towards the sleeve of her blouse, and then seemed to leap over the material to touch her throat, draw along her collarbone, before trailing slowly down to the upper curves of her breasts. It moved upwards as she began to smile, the smile blossoming as it drew across her lips. '*Dios*.'

She felt Jack draw closer to her face, seconds before his tongue lightly stroked her lips in pursuit. Her shivers increased despite the sweat-inducing heat in the room, and her breasts rose and fell within the meagre confines of her blouse; she wasn't sure if she was glad or not about not wearing a bra that morning.

The furry touch brushed across her cheeks, and then down again, dipping into her cleavage, and Cat felt as if her blouse had just spontaneously shrunk a size on her. She wished a hand was free to . . .

Suddenly, Jack deftly undid a button, then another, alternating with brushing along each part of newly exposed skin. Slowly, languidly, he opened her blouse, never just fully baring her breasts, but leaving it to whatever he was caressing her with to dip beneath the material, the tip slipping over hardened nipples. Her pulse quickened, pleasure rippling outwards from wherever she was touched, and she let out a sound like a sigh embracing a moan.

She felt Jack orbit around her, stop at her feet and draw closer again. He returned to her blouse, undoing the rest of the buttons and baring her midriff, leaving her breasts barely covered. The touch of sable returned to her skin, down from her breastbone and over her stomach, making her squirm within her bonds at the sensations. They vanished for a heartbeat, but then returned along her inner thighs, up along one, down along the other. It lingered, seeming to trace along the border to her panties, making her writhe and moan. '*Hijo de mil putas*.'

'What, a *thousand* bitches?' Jack chuckled, but then quickly returned to silence, continuing his teasing, obviously enjoying his chance to outdo Nathan's earlier performance.

Then he was gone, leaving Cat to contemplate. It was a rare opportunity for her to let go like this, something she hadn't expected to do for a long time, needing someone trustworthy enough. That she should feel that way about this man ...

'Fuck!' Cat felt something cold drip onto her, as Jack peeled away the covering on her left breast and touched her right nipple, circling something around it. He drew it away, she heard a slight crunch, and then it returned, this time to her right breast, drawing upwards to her throat, her chin, leaving snakes of moisture like trails of tears along the way. It brushed across her lips, and Cat recognised the scent: strawberries, chilled strawberries, kept in ice water. Jack let it linger, silently inviting her to consume it.

She did, even as she felt him produce another and return to running it back down her body, over her breasts and nipples once again. She could feel the cold trails of melted water and juices running along her curves, igniting her nerves like fireworks. Her skin felt hot, and the ice seemed to burn with delicious warmth now, as it circled round her nipples, pleasure shooting through her, ebbing out, spreading from her breasts.

He ran the strawberries down over her stomach, following the same path as the sable, circling her navel, then moving down over her pelvis and down the outside of her legs, always taking a bite from them and feeding the rest to her when they were nearly spent of cold and moisture.

Cat's body felt on fire, charged and sensitised, every touch making her squirm. She could feel Jack moving his attentions along the inside of her right leg, up her thigh, and she held her breath as she readied herself for his touching her sex – except that he didn't, instead hopping over to her left thigh. She was shivering with an acute expectation, hating and revelling in the sweet sensations, the agony twisting her in place, making the swing sway.

Then she felt his fingers at her panties, drawing the patch of fabric against her sex and gently holding it to one side. He touched the strands of her bush, almost imperceptibly stroking her folds, parting them slightly.

She yelped as she felt the icy drips of water from another strawberry patter onto her burning pussy. *Dios*, that was intense! She bit her lip as Jack brushed the whole strawberry along her pussy lips, up and around her clitoris, making her hips buck, making her want it to stop and go further.

But it was out of her hands. She felt him withdraw it. He took a bite and then offered the rest to her. She accepted it, tasting herself on the fruit, trying and failing to catch a stray trail of juice running down from the side of her mouth.

Jack chuckled at that.

'Fuck you and the horse you rode in on,' she replied huskily. She heard him draw back, popping a cork. She listened to the gurgling of fizzy liquid overflowing and dripping onto the floor, and hoped for a drink to quench her thirst, despite her earlier insistence on sobriety.

'Here's to you, Catalina,' Jack declared, as if toasting her. 'And what's to come.'

And then Cat gasped as she felt the champagne pour over her breasts, first one and then the other, felt it collect between her breasts and run down in fingers to pool around her navel, before pouring over her sex, soaking her panties. She panted at the fizzing bubbles tickling her skin, and listened to it trickle to the floor, her mind drifting.

Her attention drew to Jack's lips and tongue as they followed the champagne ...

... sucking and licking Val's nipples, her breasts. Val cried out loudly as Mickey continued to lick the liquid from her skin, his fingers teasing her elsewhere. She was naked but for her blindfold and the scarves binding her wrists to the headboard of their now-soaked berth bed, and she let herself be swept away by Mickey's touch, his voice murmuring filthy things in Italian as Mario Lanza crooned on the nearby radio.

As first anniversaries go, it was intense. Lately Mickey had shown a returned interest in her, and a taste for bondage, something that she couldn't help but respond to, despite her lingering guilt over Enrique, who was in his own berth, minding the latest money transfer. She felt Mickey's erection rub against her wet thighs, and ground her pussy against his hand. 'Come on, come on.'

Mickey froze.

Val froze too, smiling. 'Hey, you still there, you big mook?'

No answer.

Val's heart beat a little faster. These moments of creepy uncertainty were recent with him as well.

Then he began kissing and touching her again, as if nothing had happened to interrupt them. She knew that wasn't the case, but also knew that she couldn't do anything about it. Soon, she felt her desire rise once more. She yelped, more loudly now than in other circumstances, as Mickey nipped and sucked at her nipples, biting softly and making her squirm against the hard cock pressing between her thighs. 'Come on, Mickey, take me.'

He pulled away from her mouth, leant in towards her ear. 'You want me?'

'Oh God, yes,' she panted, being truthful as much as wanting this over as quickly as possible now. 'Untie me and let's fuck properly.'

His hands moved over her hips again. 'Have you any secrets?'

She froze again. 'What?'

'Secrets. You know what secrets are. Do you have any?'

Val swallowed, tried to shake off her instinctive fears. Stupid, stupid bitch! Had he found out about Enrique? It was a struggle to stay calm, but already she could feel the sweat running down the back of her neck like the champagne. 'W– What sort of secrets, Mickey?'

'Oh, I don't know.' His fingers toyed with her pubic hair. 'How about ... family secrets? Any skeletons in the closet I should know about?'

She gave him a laugh. 'Of course not. Now come on and untie me.'

Mickey laughed too, but his was as false as hers was. 'Not even that your mother was coloured?'

Val's fears about Mickey learning about Enrique vanished – replaced by something equally dangerous for her. Mickey's crew and their wives and girlfriends were hardly the most liberal of social circles, in fact little better than some backwoods crackers with Klan sheets. Mickey, however, had always seemed to be a cut above the rest, though she still hadn't risked informing him. Now, however, she couldn't, and wouldn't, deny it. 'H– How did you find out?'

'Did some checking. You didn't hide it too well.'

She breathed in, wishing like hell she wasn't blindfolded and tied up like this, wishing her heart didn't feel like it was about to burst from her chest. 'I wasn't out to hide it at all. It was an open secret in my parish, it wasn't as if my mama and papa were married.'

'So you're a *bastardo* as well.'

Val shivered, feeling like she was tumbling down into her own grave. 'My mother's family was respected for their abilities; no one ever gave us trouble. It just became habit not to say anything.'

'I understand,' he said simply.

She breathed out. 'Mickey ... Untie me. You can have –'

'But I don't have to untie you to have you.' He pulled back, tightening his grip on her and turning her over onto her stomach.

The arrangement of scarves that bound her wrists had enough give not to tighten further around them, but she had to turn her head away from the pillow to keep breathing. 'Mickey ... untie me ... it'd be better.'

'Oh, I don't think so.' She felt him pull back and get off the bed. 'Lift your ass up. I want to have a good look at you.'

Apprehension more than arousal gripped her now, and Val shifted in place, raising her rear end to him, feeling exposed. She wanted to be fucked. She wanted to be untied and be able to defend herself if things got nasty between them. The cool air in the berth touched her pussy lips.

Then he was back, kneeling behind her, his cock pressing between her cheeks, brushing across her hot, wet folds, one hand steadying her by the hip, the other gently working his shaft into her. Val forced herself not to tense any more. 'Mickey, I ... I do love you.'

'I know.' Then he began pumping into her, slowly, measuredly.

Val's eyes widened, as if she could burn away the scarf, her whole body shaking from the intensity of the feelings he was producing in her. Despite her fears, despite feeling as if he had a gun to her head now, she couldn't fight her returning arousal. Mamselle Belagrís, protect me. 'Mickey, please, let's talk.'

'If you mention this again to me,' he warned, his body slapping steadily against her rear as his cock pistoned in and out of her. 'To anyone –'

'I won't, Mickey, I promise.'

'I found a place, off Lake Tallacocha, where the fishing's *eccellente* – and the lake's bottomless. A great place to hide secrets.'

'N– No. Fuck me, please, Mickey.' And she was being truthful. Her arousal was as much a driving force as her need to get them away from this line of thought.

'Yes, Valentina. Always happy to oblige my wonderful wife. But first . . .'

She felt him leaning in and, for a terrible second, his hand was at the back of her neck. By the time she realised he was reaching for her charm, he'd already broken the chain as he yanked it off her. She heard it hitting the far wall of the berth. 'M– Mickey –'

'Don't ever wear that *moolie* voodoo shit again.' Mickey gripped her firmly, moving savagely, no longer gentle, but forcing her to come. Val buried her face in the pillow and let her tears flow freely, even as she realised that this would not be the end of it, no matter what he said now. And if not this, then maybe about Enrique. She had to do something, and soon.

She cried out in climax as Mickey drove his cock into her . . .

. . . Cat cried out in climax as Jack, kneeling between her bound, spread legs, drove his tongue into her, dipping up to circle around her clit. Beneath her ass, she felt the remnants of her panties, torn to pieces in his hunger to have unfettered access to her pussy. Her body shook within the swing, as if moved by the contractions deep within her, her body spasming, making her cry out, 'Fuck! Get it in me, Jack! Get it in me!'

His breath was cool on her inner flesh. 'Is that you begging me now?'

The blood was pounding in her head like waves. 'This is me demanding, you fucking *puta*, now get your cock in me!'

Dimly she became aware of him rising, and then reaching out and pulling the scarf from her eyes. She blinked in the pink light of the room, looked down at her bare thighs and pussy, and watched as Jack practically tore the clothes from his body, revealing his lean, hairy frame, and long thick erection. And she watched as he drew closer again, silent now, his face a picture of his overpowering hunger for her as he guided his cock into her, fast and deep, pumping furiously; she felt so wet that the level of friction was ideal. The sling was at the right height, allowing him to stand upright, making the chains rattle at the feral pace of the fucking, over the rapid slap of their bodies together.

Cat gasped at the waves of pleasure coursing through her, and she wondered distantly how long she had been wrapped up in the vision – and it had been a vision, they all were, all real, she had to acknowledge that now. A part of her wondered how she would explain it to Nathan.

Nathan. Oh *Dios* . . . Her voice felt parched and dry as she looked up at Jack and breathed, 'C– Come . . . outside me . . . want to see you shoot.'

Jack chuckled. 'I can do that.' And when it was time, he did, drawing out of her so quickly that she gasped, spasming herself as she watched him pump his glistening shaft with his fist, producing thick hot necklaces of milky-white come onto her stomach and bush. It triggered another mini-climax from her. She bit her lip.

He stood there, clutching one of the support chains, watching her still, a weary smile on his face. 'Didn't . . . Didn't know you'd be so dirty.'

Cat grunted, glad he'd listened to her, and not willing to explain that another revelation had come to her in here, that she didn't want any man's seed in her but Nathan's. That place was for him alone.

Nathan escorted Faye back to the train, but his mind was elsewhere. 'I'd better go find my partner.'

Faye kept an arm locked around his. 'No need. We can check the monitors from Jack's office.'

'Monitors?'

'Yes.' She glanced around, ensuring no one was there before explaining, 'Jack put cameras and mics in all the berths and the players' rooms.'

Nathan's heart skipped a beat. Jesus, they could have heard every detail of their investigation! Stupid amateur, he should have checked as soon as they'd boarded!

On the other hand, if Wheeler had heard anything of value, he would have exposed them by now. He wouldn't risk his operation by keeping undercover agents onboard. Not even for a chance at getting closer to Cat. 'He's very naughty. But if he was listening to us, why didn't he know who we were all along?'

'Because they barely function. Jack spouts some bullshit about it being the train's fault, but I think it was just crap work on his part. We could watch you, but not hear anything.' She stopped and faced him, wrapped her arms around him. 'Now, if you want to punish me for voyeurism.'

Nathan disentangled himself from her, his spirits lifted at the news that their cover might still be intact, but not in the mood for any more games. 'Not now.' He slapped her on the ass. 'Maybe later.'

Faye smiled. 'Maybe.'

On entering the berth, he looked around and quickly found the webcam and microphone hidden in a false smoke detector on the wall above the head of the bed. He quickly dismantled the unit, and then swept the room again, mentally kicking himself for not being more careful.

Once he was satisfied, he moved on to less satisfying duties. 'Afternoon, Gordy.'

The voice at the other end failed to hide his disappointment. 'Aww, I was expecting the grateful Catalina in all her naked glory.'

'Grateful? What for?'

'I have some information on those people she'd asked about.'

Nathan blinked, but hid his confusion. 'You can tell me, and I'll pass it on.'

'But then I won't be on the receiving end of her gratitude.'

'Gordy!'

'OK, OK. Mickey Uscione was a *capo* with the Moreno family in Chicago, from 1950 to 1958. He ran a money laundering operation, trafficking funds to the pre-Castro Cuban casinos and hotels, via Louisiana businesses. In 1957, he married Valentina Sauveterre, the illegitimate daughter of Nick Castille, a New Orleans club owner. On 16 August 1958, the couple and their bodyguard, one Enrique Cazenove, went missing while delivering a cash shipment south. No traces of the bodies or the money were found, but it was commonly believed that they were killed by members of the rival Lebowski family, in revenge for a recent robbery on one of their mansions.'

Nathan swallowed, recognising some of those names in Wheeler's office notes. 'Is that it?'

'No, give her a good spanking for wasting my time on the voodoo one.'

'Voodoo?'

'Yeah, that Mamselle Belagrís. I spent ages searching the criminal databases, and I find her in a mythological site.'

'What?'

'Yeah. Apparently, she's some Guédé loa, a voodoo spirit of the dead, one that families can employ for protection and stuff. I'll transmit all the files.'

Nathan's mind reeled. What the hell was going on? He had to find Cat and talk with her.

However, first things first. 'Thanks, Gordy. Open the voice-mail account.'

'OK.' He paused and added, 'Hound, aren't you gonna tell her about what you're doing?'

'Not yet, Gordy. Open the account.'

'Done.' Gordy's voice disappeared, replaced by the account access firewall. Nathan keyed in his security code and, when prompted, began speaking, determined to get the unpleasantness over with as quickly as quickly as possible. 'Continuation of report on agent Catalina Montoya: Despite her inexperience, and the atypical environment, Agent Montoya has managed to adapt to rapidly changing circumstances . . .'

11

'*Nothing*? You saw nothing?' Wheeler's voice was thick with incredulity as he dressed.

'That's right,' Cat lied, using tissues to wipe what remained of his seed from her belly. And the more he went on about it, the more she was glad she hadn't let him finish inside her. 'Sorry, Jack. Great fuck, but no vision.'

'Why are you lying?' A hitherto unheard hint of anger crept into his voice, and he drew closer, facing her again after she'd turned away. 'You saw her! You *were* her! And I was him!'

Cat buttoned up her blouse and turned away once more, looking for her slacks. He was right, right about everything, though she dared not admit it aloud. Until this weekend, her world view had been grounded in the concrete, in hard data. She based decisions and attitudes on substantial evidence. Now, she had been forced to expand on that.

Or deny it. She slipped back into her slacks. 'Sorry, sport. Better luck next time.'

She moved to the door, but Wheeler approached her once again, his frustration almost palpable. 'Damn it, there are two souls who can't rest until their remains are found. Don't you *see*?'

Cat looked him over, tensing. 'I see you losing your cool, Jack. Don't lose it with me, *comprende*?'

Wheeler made a visible effort to calm down. 'I'm sorry, Catalina. It's just that before you, no one had ever made such a close, sustained connection with Val's spirit. It's like I've – *we've*

– been waiting for you all this time. And now we're so close … so close …' He reached out tentatively, took her hand in his, none of the aggression she'd seen before present now. 'We've got to help them, Cat.'

He sounded so genuine. She almost relented.

Until the knock at the door distracted her, and she pulled out of his touch. 'I'll … think about it.' She strode to the door, grateful for the distraction, and opened it, expecting one of Wheeler's staff.

And finding Tara and Ben and Hannah Oliver instead. Tara looked determined as she announced, 'You have questions. I have answers. Let's go somewhere and talk.'

The observation deck was unoccupied that time of day, allowing the group to relax a little. Cat glanced around, better appreciating the view than she had the night before: a panorama of tree tops extending to all directions, beneath a sky of thickening, darkening clouds gathering to huddle and rumble like a mob.

Cat sat in a different place from the night before, at a collection of leather chairs around a glass coffee table, as Tara and the Olivers sat opposite. She relayed her accounts to date, glad to be able to open up to someone unlikely to judge her.

And when she was done, she looked to the younger woman. 'You were right, I have questions. Firstly, am I going loco?'

Tara smiled. 'Not at all. In fact, I commend your strength in dealing with these unprecedented experiences as well as you have. You've never been comfortable with matters beyond the concrete, have you?'

Cat pursed her lips, not certain why she felt so open with the girl, but taking advantage of it nevertheless. 'Only when the answers never satisfied me. My paternal grandfather used to smack my hand whenever he took me to church and I wouldn't stop asking questions that weren't getting any answers.'

'That's awful,' Hannah noted, appalled. 'Punishing a child for curiosity.'

'For stubbornness,' Cat conceded with a wry smile. 'And it outlasted Grandpa.' Back to Tara, she asked, 'These hotspots, are they ghosts possessing us, like Wheeler says?'

'No. These are not multiple hauntings, or loa spirits mounting devotees during voodoo ceremonies. These are psychometric echoes.' At Cat's expression, she elaborated: 'Think of them as psychic fingerprints, "vibes", recordings of thoughts and events left on objects and in places, by people at moments of emotional intensity, such as sex or fear. And other people with suitable psychic attunements or states can "read" these. But they're just fragments of energy, with no more intrinsic intelligence than characters in a movie.'

'And that's what's happening on this train?'

Tara nodded, barely able to contain her own excitement. 'I've been a middle-aged woman in 1976 having sex with Chinese twins, and a bridegroom in 1963.' She grinned with amazement. 'Belle contains the most potent collection of psychometric energy spots I've ever encountered. Her own energy seems to be amplifying the hotspots to incredible degrees.'

'"Her"? Then you're with Wheeler, in thinking that this train's . . . alive?'

Tara seemed to consider her reply before answering. 'Let's just say I believe that something more than the man in the locomotive cab is driving her. There's a definite consciousness present, manifesting itself for a reason – and you're being targeted with Valentina's memories for a purpose. I don't know more yet, but –' she leant forwards '– I know you were experimenting with Wheeler on deliberately sharing a vision. While you were there, did you manage to gain control?'

'Control? That's possible?'

'Oh yes. Have you ever heard of lucid dreaming? It's when someone in a dream is aware of being in a dream, and with this awareness can control elements within it. It's an established skill that psychiatrists teach to patients suffering from recurring nightmares. We can use it to control the visions we receive from Belle onboard, as they operate on the same hypnagogic level as dreams. Further, because the visions originate externally, two or more people involved in the same vision can be aware of each other.'

'Tara's already shown us how,' Ben informed her, smiling. 'It was like nothing we've ever experienced before.'

Tara smiled again. 'Belle likes them. I know of a place or two you might not have visited. We can both enter a mental state receptive to the visions, and I can guide you into maintaining lucidity.'

The suggestion intrigued Cat, especially without Jack Wheeler around to muddy up the proverbial waters. 'Why are you doing this?'

The black woman sat back again, looked up and about her, seeing things only she could. 'I've had the gifts all my life, perceiving things others didn't. As a result, I've always felt out of place, like I didn't belong anywhere. Until I got here. I feel at home. And something tells me that helping you and your partner will help me stay here.'

Cat considered her answer; she certainly trusted Tara more than Wheeler. Still . . . 'Jack said something about needing to be sexually aroused to experience the visions.'

Tara blushed now. 'Well, it helps. Magic rituals involving sex are among the most primal and powerful. But I think we can reach the required levels of perception through simple relaxation.' She looked to the Olivers. 'If anything goes wrong, you can wake us from it.'

Hannah grinned, presenting a mock salute. 'Here to serve.'

Cat considered the proposal. Tara seemed sincere enough in her offer to help Cat understand – and not try to get in her panties.

Not that the thought was entirely execrable to Cat. She was attractive.

Tara suddenly grinned, as if she'd heard her.

Puta.

Wheeler cursed again, knocking some files off his desk as he stared with impotent frustration at the PC screen. He'd been able to tune into the group on the observation deck, but not pick up any sound. Now they'd moved to the spa and looked ready to strip off and enter the sauna, where there was a hotspot – and a luscious little hotspot it was – but it had proved impractical to install cameras or microphones in there. At least the hotspot in there didn't involve Valentina, so Cat couldn't learn any more without him.

What was Tara Gilbrand about? He'd looked into her background, grew interested in her family's wealth and influence, but then grew uneasy about her purported psychic experience. Perhaps he should have focused on her instead of Cat.

Belle, what are you doing?

The spa was an area in one carriage with some token exercise equipment, where passengers could work up a different type of sweat than they might otherwise expect. But it was the nearby sauna that Tara had indicated to Cat and, as they stood in an adjacent changing area, and the younger woman had begun undressing, placing her clothes in a storage box provided, she noted, 'Everyone seems to be taking siestas at the moment, so we're alone.'

Cat glanced around anyway, before following Tara and the

Olivers in stripping down. Her trust hadn't yet wavered, but she remained self-conscious. Still, after a moment, she slipped out of her underwear and quickly wrapped one of the supplied thick white cotton towels around herself, grunting as she noted how tenuous the cover was on her.

A problem that didn't seem to bother the seemingly uninhibited Tara, who was standing there naked, tying her hair up. 'This carriage used to be a boxcar. It was interesting to see ...' Then she paused, slipping a towel around her. 'But I'd better not say anything further, in case you think I might influence what you experience.'

'*Gracias.*' Cat followed the trio into the sauna, a relatively small enclosure that could comfortably hold a dozen seated on the benches built into the walls. Slatted beech wood panelling ran from floor to ceiling, and steam emerged from between the slats, rising and collecting like, well, like ghosts. The effects of the heat were instant on Cat, and her lungs seemed to open up that much more even as sweat seemed to appear magically on her skin. 'What now?'

Tara slowly paced around, breathing in deeply, as Ben and Hannah sat opposite them, watching and staying quiet. 'Now, you relax. I know it's not easy for a woman like you to do that, even for a while. But you can – once you stop trying.' She indicated the bench on the far wall. 'How about lying down? A massage might help.'

After a moment, Cat acquiesced and lay face down with her head resting on her arms, adjusting her towel to maintain her modesty, such as it was.

Seconds later, she felt the woman's touch on her feet, using her thumbs and forefingers to work at her soles, her toes, before working her way along Cat's heels and ankles, demonstrating a strong, expert grip. And as she massaged, she spoke in steady, reassuring tones. 'Nothing will harm you here. As you relax, your breathing, your pulse will slow down.' Her fingers made crescent motions over the backs of Cat's legs, a repetitive pressure that provided the proper amount of force and seemed to sap the strength from her muscles. 'Your mind is beginning to rest now, to set aside the conscious and drift into higher areas.'

And, as if in physical illustration, Tara's hands moved up along Cat's thighs, to just below the level of her towel. An excitement shot through Cat, temporarily eclipsing her descent into relaxation, and she wished she could find the strength to raise a hand and loosen her towel.

Tara, however, still demonstrating her uncanny powers of perception, did it for her, just enough to expose Cat's back but not her buttocks, allowing her hands to work their magic on her shoulders and along either side of her spine. 'Visions, memories that are not your own, will be offered to you. Accept them, wear them and experience them. But you will be aware that you are in a vision. You will see something of yours that should not be there. This will be your reminder of who you are, a reminder that you can control what you are experiencing, and let it stop and continue as you please.'

Cat's eyelids felt heavy, and her perceptions did indeed drift, as she noted the beads of sweat running across her forehead, and the fullness of her breasts, how her nipples were hardening against the thick white cotton between her body and the bench. She felt wet – yes, inside as well as outside. More aware now, she could see her surroundings shift, expand, the walls of the sauna extending outwards to accommodate the crates against the walls and the large silver car on the platform in the centre of the boxcar, steam wisping around it like snakes . . .

* * *

...Suddenly, some of the water splashed onto Priscilla's skirt. She stepped back, glaring at the cause of the spill. 'Clumsy woman!'

Kerry stopped in place, the large yellow sponge in her hand dripping water and suds to the floor. 'Sorry, Miss O'Neill.'

Priscilla pouted, crossing her arms over her chest. 'Yes, you should be.' Not that she was as mad as she made out; it was just soapy water, and on what was hardly the most expensive outfit in Priscilla's considerable wardrobe. However, she had a persona to maintain.

'Yes, Miss O'Neill.' Kerry was medium tall, annoyingly skinny, with long blonde hair tied back and usually tucked under a grey chauffeur's cap, part of a man's outfit that Daddy preferred on her. Her jacket hung over a nearby crate with her tie, and she had the sleeves of her white dress shirt rolled up as she focused on her current task, cleaning her employer's latest toy: one of the new DeLoreans, a futuristic-looking silver sports car with a low body and gull-wing doors. Priscilla thought it gaudy in the extreme, but her father was a man with far more money than sense, and had to be one of the first in America to own one. Priscilla did not share her father's tastes.

At least, not in cars.

And he had insisted that his new 'chauffeur' (as if anyone believed that) Kerry collect it personally from the New York docks and accompany it across country to California, and clean it twice a day, whether it needed cleaning or not. It was Priscilla who had insisted on accompanying Kerry, an insistence that had made her father chuckle. He joked about apparent jealousy on Priscilla's part, jealousy regarding the attention he was giving Kerry.

Priscilla let him think whatever he wanted.

She stood in the cramped confines of the boxcar, watching

Daddy's other new toy give the DeLorean another good clean, the white silk of the woman's shirt picking up droplets of water, and offering more give than the grey trousers, which pulled tight over the woman's slim buttocks whenever she bent forwards.

Priscilla felt a familiar, welcome warmth growing, with sweat prickling the tops of her breasts and under her arms, a heat caused by more than the interior of the boxcar.

It was a heat she saw reflected in Kerry's eyes too, and in those full red lips, whenever the other woman looked over at Priscilla.

For a while, there was only the background clack-clack of the train wheels on the tracks as they raced through Illinois, the tinny sounds of Huey Lewis's latest on Kerry's portable radio and the slosh of soapy water in the bucket, some of it splashing onto Kerry's trouser legs now. She seemed to disregard it.

Priscilla wouldn't, however. 'Must you be so sloppy? You represent my father's organisation! How would it appear if someone saw his personal chauffer looking dishevelled?' Inwardly, Priscilla laughed at the absurdity of her question; Daddy published some of the filthiest men's magazines on the market.

'Sorry, Miss O'Neill.' Kerry continued working, still playing the demure type. 'But your father wanted his new car kept clean. I don't know what else I can do.'

'Well, I do. Take off your clothes.'

Kerry stopped and looked over at her, that affected look of innocence of hers making Priscilla's pussy twitch. 'T– Take off my clothes? In front of you? But I . . . I couldn't.'

'Why not? I know you do it for my father, your employer. And in his absence, *I'm* your employer. Isn't that right?'

Kerry swallowed, wide-eyed. 'I . . . I guess so.'

'Fine then: strip.'

Kerry stared at her a moment longer, then finally nodded in surrender. She unbuttoned her shirt to reveal a snow-white spaghetti-strap bikini top, straining to contain large, round, tanned breasts, above a flat stomach. She cast the shirt to join her other clothes, kicked off her shoes and socks, and then sent her trousers following. A tiny white bikini bottom cupped neat, taut buttocks and topped long, muscular legs.

Kerry stood there, coyly dropping her gaze. 'Will this be satisfactory, Miss O'Neill?'

Priscilla suppressed the expected pang of jealousy at the fitness of the other woman's body, preferring to relish the lust she'd felt for it since she'd first seen it, months ago. Outwardly, though, she nodded curtly and replied, 'Get back to work.'

'Yes, Miss O'Neill.'

Priscilla steadied herself, feeling the growing heat between her legs as she watched Kerry bend over for the bucket and sponge, the triangle of cotton of her bikini bottoms pulling taut across her tanned buttocks, and the swell of her breasts pressing into her top. She swung her hips as she walked about the car, now reaching for a bucket of clean water for rinsing, the metal clasps holding the bikini strips at her hips and breasts looking so flimsy. One quick snap . . .

It made Priscilla, clad in her charcoal power-dressing suit, feel overdressed, and so far removed from the flimsy cotton of her panties, now riding up into her aroused sex to embrace and tease it. 'You like working for my father, don't you?'

'He's very good to me, Miss O'Neill.'

A smile curled Priscilla's lips. 'I'm sure. He likes dirty sluts like you.'

Kerry stopped in her tracks, her demeanour changing from supplicant servant to something stronger, more defiant. She strode around the car towards Priscilla. 'Listen up, you: no one calls me that. Not your father. And certainly not his spoilt little bitch of a daughter.'

Priscilla swallowed, her breath coming short and her legs growing unsteady as Kerry stood tall before her, licking her lips, playing along with this familiar but still enticing game of theirs. Priscilla's voice broke. 'Y– You can't talk to me like that.'

'I can do anything I want.' She grabbed Priscilla by the lapels of her jacket. 'I can have anything I want. Or anyone.' She pulled her into a hot, hard kiss, their lips parting and their tongues thick and hot around each other, Kerry being as rough and as dominant as Priscilla craved.

Kerry leant against the side of the car, still dragging Priscilla along, pulling the young woman down to her breasts. 'Kiss them. Worship them.'

Priscilla obeyed, plunging into the swelling curves of the cleavage, tasting salty sweat as her hands moved up to unhook the top, freeing the breasts before clamping her mouth over one of Kerry's nipples. The flesh filled her mouth, and Priscilla licked and sucked greedily.

'Ooh,' Kerry cooed. 'It seems *you're* the dirty slut here, aren't you?'

Priscilla moaned into the flesh, her own nipples aching in her clothes and her pussy thickening and throbbing as Kerry pushed her to her knees. She reached up to undo the hip clasps on Kerry's bottoms, tugging them away to reveal the soft wet strip of hair on Kerry's pussy. Heartbeats later, her fingertips parted the woman's cleft, felt the heat and drank in her scent.

'Oh yeah!' the woman cried out in deep satisfaction, clutching Priscilla's head, riding against her mouth. 'That's it, you little bitch, do it like that! And don't stop!'

Priscilla heeded her paramour's demands. She worked up a

rhythm, her tongue darting inside, licking and lapping and drawing in her folds to suck on the flesh, until Kerry's whole body shook and heaved, breathless. 'Son of a . . .'

Priscilla's mouth felt damp with Kerry's juices. God, she was so horny for her! She gripped Kerry's hips and dived back into her sex, her only distraction the shiny gold badge at her knee.

Badge? She glanced at it, noted the shiny gold surface, stamped with the logo of the Internal Revenue Service. A special agent's badge . . .

'Ms Montoya?'

Cat blinked and looked up, finding herself pressing a nude Tara against the car, as if a layer of skin disguising the women had been stripped from them. Her face was still at Tara's sex, her tongue still pleasuring her, sensing how close the other woman was.

But still, Tara was reacting. 'You don't . . . Oh God, you don't have to –'

Cat shut her up with another stab of her tongue, relishing the sensual experience of it all, a part of her sensing the echoes of Priscilla and Kerry, decades before. She let her actions be guided by them, revelling in it almost as much as Tara was, feeling it build, build.

'Fuck!' Tara's sex spasmed, and she threw her head back as she came against Cat's lips. Or was it Kerry, on Priscilla's lips? Or did it matter at that moment?

The women clutched each other as Cat rose, aware of her own hungers but content for now to take in what was going on.

Tara, however, was not. She slowly turned Cat and herself around until Cat was up against the car now, and Tara slumped to her knees before her, reaching up and unzipping Cat's skirt at the side, lowering it and revealing black stockings and thin black panties.

Cat felt a twinge inside, and looked down at the woman. 'Tara, our bodies, in real life, are they ...?'

Tara nodded, as her cool hands pressed against the inside of Cat's thighs, gently but insistently urging them apart. 'We can stop at any time.' Then she buried her face against Cat's groin, breathing hotly onto her through the panties and making Cat quiver.

If Cat had any thoughts of stopping this, they had vanished.

She felt her skin flush as Tara's fingers teasingly pulled down the panties, helping one of Cat's legs out of them but leaving the underwear hanging around the other ankle.

Then she returned to Cat's pussy, her hot tongue trailing up and around the edge of her bush and over the slim curve of her belly. Cat let loose a growl as her sex throbbed impatiently, as her hands gripped the edge of the DeLorean.

Tara's tongue dipped, teasingly, playing with the roots of Cat's pubic hair, before grazing silkily along Cat's slit. Cat yelped with electric pleasure, her body writhing and her bare ass rubbing against the car, as Tara's tongue swirled around her cleft, the tip curling up to find and flick against her clit. Her back arched as tight as a piano wire. '*Madre de Dios.*'

Tara's tongue jabbed, delved and circled, and her moist hot breath caressed Cat's skin. Cat's hands became fists, which pounded against the stainless steel frame of the car. Tara grabbed her by the hips and jabbed deep into her, suckling on her clit, keeping a steady, tortuous pace, circling, sucking, circling and sucking repeatedly.

Cat came convulsively, her body shaking and slipping off its tenuous perch on the car, landing on her rear, her legs spread obscenely as she gripped Tara. Still riding high on her climax, she began laughing, hugging and kissing Tara, a part of her still able to see herself as Priscilla in 1981, fucking with Daddy's new toy . . .

. . . 'Cat?'
Cat looked up at Nathan.

12

Donnie lay on his berth bed, hands folded behind his head, a wide indulgent grin on his face as he looked up at the woman sitting at his side. 'Tonight, after the costume party, I'll be inviting Jack along to the Playroom. He likes to tie me up in there, and it's lockable and soundproofed. But tonight, he'll be the one in the chains. Then I'll let you in, and we can begin persuading him to sign the papers.' Her voice was as sweet as honey, catching his full attention.

The hand she had wrapped around his erection, languidly drawing his foreskin up and down, didn't hurt either. 'Papers, yeah.'

'Yes, the papers. I've had transfer of ownership papers printed out, and I know the right lawyers in New Orleans to make it legal. But we have to get him to sign over first.'

'Yeah.' His eyes were beginning to droop, even as his excitement was mounting. Since late last night, they must have fucked, sucked and licked a half-dozen times, each time Faye reinforcing her arguments and refining her – their – plans. It was as if she was conditioning him, eliminating any lingering doubts.

As it happened, she had him at the first orgasm.

'He's tough, but not that tough,' she continued, her thumb swivelling up to stroke his cockhead, smearing pre-come over the silky surface. She'd suggested just masturbating him rather than have a full fuck, citing her tired muscles, and Donnie couldn't help but agree to it, feeling too lazy for anything more strenuous. Besides, wasn't he gonna be doing the lion's share of the work tonight, putting the muscle on Wheeler?

'Do you have a gun?' she asked him, slowing down her stroking motions. 'Well?'

'Mmm? No, darling, never needed one.' Which was good, given that Uncle Leo repeatedly refused to let him have one. At first, Donnie thought he was being punished for that time he'd accidentally left the keys in one of Leo's delivery trucks, letting it be stolen. However, Leo had forgiven him for that – after all, it wasn't as if Donnie was just some nameless goon in his mob.

Leo and Donnie's father had been the prime movers in setting up their organisation in Tampa and, though his mother tried to shield him from the realities, the young Donnie had quickly learnt, and quickly warmed to the lifestyle. Especially to Leo, with his cheetah smile and dynamic confidence, and it shamed him those times when he felt even closer to Uncle Leo than his own father. And when Donnie was fourteen, and his dad had been killed in a police raid following a botched bank heist, it was Leo who had taken Donnie and his mother under his wing.

It was a sweet climb. But not without cost. April, for instance. She'd been generous, funny, beautiful.

And unfaithful. Leo, ever careful, had run some background checks, and provided harsh photographic proof of her infidelity. 'It's a stark lesson,' Leo had told him, with much sympathy, 'but loyalty is as necessary to us as breathing.'

Donnie couldn't face her; Leo had thoughtfully sent him on an errand, while he sent some of his boys to help April pack up and find someone else. But Leo had been right, such treachery could not be forgiven, and so he had stood his ground and cut her out of his life. She had been good to him, but not as good as Leo had.

And with this woman, this train, he'd get more from his uncle.

Memories of April – and that weird black chick name-dropping her last night – threatened to dampen his mood. Better to push the unfaithful bitch aside. She was history.

Suddenly Faye stopped masturbating him, rising. 'Hey.'

A look of regret crossed her face. 'Sorry, stud, but I'm late for a train activity, and I don't want Jack to get suspicious. You don't mind finishing yourself off, do you?'

'What? You gotta be kidding me, woman.'

She smiled. 'It's gonna be a hell of a turn-on for me, thinking of you in here, pleasuring yourself. And tonight, once this train is mine, we'll celebrate like we never have before.' She nodded to his waiting cock. 'Well? Go on.'

He grunted, smiled and reached for his own shaft. He enjoyed her watching him before she departed, determined to come and get some sleep before tonight. And as his pumping increased, he considered how much his fortunes had changed in the last few days: he had a hot woman hungry for him, a chance to take some frustration out on that dickhead Wheeler for looking down on him and the opportunity to make an indelible mark in Uncle Leo's eyes.

Who said crime didn't pay?

Nathan stood at the door to the sauna, the cool air he let in banishing away the images of the boxcar. 'What the hell is going on?'

Cat froze, as if by the cold air, and she realised she was on the floor of the sauna, naked and sweat-covered with Tara and her wrapped up in each other's limbs, as Tara pulled down their towels from the bench.

Nathan stepped inside, his posture tense as he approached Cat. 'Are you OK?'

With a sudden rush of acute embarrassment, Cat rose and wrapped the towel around her waist. '*Si*, I'm fine. Stop looking at me.'

'Oh, sorry. Didn't mean to disturb you in the privacy of this public place. Come back to the berth, we need to talk.'

'This is such a flashback to the high school prom.' Tara wrapped her own towel around her, raising a hand in his direction. 'Mr Ames, perhaps I can explain –'

'Perhaps not.' He never took his eyes off Cat. 'Mind your own business. All of you.'

Behind him, the Olivers, looking ready to intervene, stayed silent instead.

Nathan's unprecedented rudeness shook Cat from her lingering waves of euphoria and confusion. 'Hound, maybe you should calm down and listen –'

'This *is* me, calm, Agent Montoya.'

It was his deliberate use of Cat's proper title in front of Tara that convinced her to take this elsewhere. She turned to the woman. 'Sorry about this. I'll try to explain it to him.'

However, Tara appeared unoffended by Nathan's discourtesy, leaning in to whisper, 'Don't tell, show. And use your anger when it's needed. It's one of your greatest strengths.' Then she drew back and kissed Cat on the lips, a gesture of affection, a reminder of the remarkable sensual experience they had just shared.

There was another caress of cold air as Nathan opened the sauna door again, wiping sweat from his brow. 'Now.'

In the corridor, she turned to him. 'My clothes, in that box.'

He glanced down, picked up the box in question and held it, not offering to let her get dressed now. And such was her shock at his responses, that she didn't argue, preferring to make her way as swiftly as possible back to their berth, ignoring the curious looks from the few passengers they passed, as the storm outside lashed against the train windows. But as she walked back with Nathan directly behind her, her anger overcame her need to stay calm and rational. How dare he talk to her like that, and in front of the others! No matter the provocation, it was uncalled for.

She felt her fury boil within her, and she let it grow, until they were back in the berth, and she spun to face him. '*Idiota*! What the fuck was that about? Revealing who I was in front of civilians.'

For his part, Nathan's face seemed to mirror her own ire. 'Why not? You seemed to be revealing everything else to them in there, and to anyone else who might have come in.'

Embarrassment shot through her, but she took that and converted it to additional fuel for her anger. 'What's wrong, sorry you weren't invited to watch sooner? I'm not your wife, I'm not your child and I'm not your subordinate. I'm your partner, *comprende*?'

Nathan's scowl never wavered. 'I know that. And I was proud that you'd be my partner. I'm the one who defended your professionalism to all those dicks back in Miami.'

Cat tightened the towel around her. 'Give me my clothes.'

He dropped the box at her feet.

'Now turn around.'

He grunted, but relented. 'A little late to be showing modesty, don't you think?'

She dropped her towel, reaching for. '*Besame el culo*! What was I to wear in a sauna?'

'Was it hot too when you were fucking Wheeler?'

Cat paused, and then resumed drawing her panties up her thighs. 'That's not the issue.' She ignored her bra and slacks and slipped into her blouse.

'Then why keep it hidden from me? Everything hidden?'

His tone suggested knowledge to back this up, and she realised that he had learnt something. However, she remained defensive. 'Oh? And what the hell else do you think I've been hiding?'

'A request to Gordy about voodoo spirits, about a fifty-year-old Mob mystery, one that Wheeler is involved in, in some way? Trying to help a known criminal, one you're investigating? Someone who's been secretly monitoring us from the moment we boarded?'

'*What?*'

He'd walked over to the couch and picked up the disconnected camera and microphone, showing it to her.

Cat suddenly felt exposed, recalling the times Nathan and she had talked in here, when they'd made love, when she'd masturbated. She mouthed, 'Is it clear?' When he nodded, she asked, '*Dios*, how did you find this?'

'Faye mentioned it. Don't worry, she said they couldn't hear us. That's how Wheeler knew about the phone, but didn't know what was said.'

Relief sapped Cat's anger, a welcome substitute for the earlier mortification that their mission may have been compromised from the start, not to mention their integrity. But she couldn't shake off the acknowledgement that Nathan was right to be angry with her, that she had concealed things from him. She had her reasons, and she still stuck by them, but it didn't detract from the wrongness of it all.

Now, however, she felt more confident in her situation and her knowledge of it. Besides, if she kept silent any longer about what was going on, she would explode, or Nathan would come up with something far worse.

They had to trust each other again.

'Hound,' she finally breathed out, feeling her anger and anxiety subside, not leaving entirely but falling into a manageable state, 'if I tell you what's going on, will you promise to believe me?' It was a stupid question and she knew it. How can anyone promise something like that? Especially what she had to say to him.

Yet, Nathan nodded and replied immediately, 'Of course.'

It bolstered her confidence, a little. She breathed out again, and chose her words as carefully as possible. 'Nathan, I know this is going to sound like something out of *The X Files*, but ... this train has a spirit of its own. It carries the memories of people who have ridden in it, like echoes. What's more, people today can experience those memories, in the form of dreams or visions. I've been experiencing the memories of a woman from fifty years ago, named Valentina. She was married against her will to a mobster named Mickey, but her secret lover Enrique travelled with her. At first, I put these down to dreams, and then hypnosis or hallucinogens Wheeler might have slipped me. However, I was wrong. They're real. And I think I'm seeing them in order to solve the mystery of what happened to Val.'

She ran out of breath, and felt herself much better for finally getting it off her chest.

That feeling lasted all of three seconds, before Nathan spoke. 'Cat ... this is your first assignment. You've been under a lot of pressure –'

'*Dios*!' she snapped. 'I knew it. I knew you'd say that.'

'Of course. What did you expect? That I'd swallow some story of spirits and visions? Wheeler clearly has you brainwashed.'

'But I've talked with other people, and they've experienced the same things. The Olivers, Tara –'

'Oh, your fuck partners, well, that convinces me now.' Nathan paced around in disbelief. 'You ask me to believe what you say, and then shovel me something so patently unbelievable?'

'Yes. That's when I need you the most.' Frustration welled up within her, and she paced in the opposite direction, then stopped and stared out the window at the rain-lashed country-side speeding by. Damn it, she knew it would be difficult to tell him . . .

Don't tell, show . . .

She looked him over, an idea sparked inside her, one that was still blossoming as she sniffed the air around him. 'Pretty Persuasion. Cheap perfume on you, a scent Faye wears. And there are smudges on your trousers.' She was lying, of course, but it didn't matter. Her face went dark with a sudden fury. 'So, nothing happened between you and her, huh?'

Nathan frowned. 'What? I never said –'

'How dare you lecture me when you've been off fucking that tramp?'

Nathan's face was a picture of disbelief at the tangent their talk had taken. 'This isn't about me.'

But Cat was in the throes of a genuine tantrum, a Latin storm to match the one outside – and only partly affected for the benefit of her plan. 'Was she good, *pendejo*? Nice juicy ass on her? Did you get off?'

'I'm not gonna play this game.'

He started to turn away, but she reached out and pulled him back, desperate for him not to make the wrong move and leave. 'Don't even think of going to her, bastard!'

'I'm not interested in her.'

'Lying pig! Don't deny she's hot. Hell, *I'd* fuck her.' She grunted. 'Bet you'd get off watching that, wouldn't you, like you did watching me with Tara?'

His patience snapped at that. 'You little hypocrite! You have some nerve, after all you've got up to. You've been a bit of a *puta* yourself, haven't you?'

Cat snarled, pulled her hand back, ready to land a blow, knowing he would see it and stop her before she inflicted any real damage.

She was right. Nathan blocked her swing, and then another, pushed her up against the nearest wall and pinned her arms behind her as she tried in vain to pull free. Well, she tried a little, mostly struggling vocally with him, cursing and snapping. A few manoeuvres, and she could put up a better fight. And both of them knew it. But it wasn't about having a serious scrap with him.

She craved feeling him close against her, smelling him, feeling his erection pressed against her. Her breath was hissing hard and fast, and she gasped as he leant in and growled, 'I never wanted her. I never wanted anyone as much as I want you, you stupid little bitch.'

'Prove it, *pajiero*.'

Anger – and passion – blazed as he dipped his head and kissed her, hard and rough, pushing his tongue into her mouth. Cat kissed him back, matching his fury, arching her body against his as she still tried to pull her hands free from his grip.

Suddenly she bit his lip until he yelped and pulled back from her mouth, and she panted, 'Is that . . . Is that the best you can do, *pajiero*?'

'I haven't even started yet.' Nathan's free hand moved to the front of her blouse, yanking until fabric tore, and he dipped his head and captured one of Cat's now bared breasts between his lips.

She cursed as she felt his teeth clamp down, and a sharp burst of pain-pleasure shot through her. Fucking hell, this was delicious! It was reawakening her hungers, as her body responded to the feeling of his hard cock pressed against her hip.

Then Nathan withdrew, releasing her hands but holding her by the hips, watching her intently, ready for the next move she might make. 'Cat, what the fuck is really going on?'

'Shut up!' she snapped and, not trusting him to do that, pulled him back into another frantic kiss, tearing at his own shirt until she felt buttons fly like candy from a broken piñata. Then she was at his chest, biting hard on his flesh until he grunted and did something about it.

He pushed her back against the bed, Cat yelping as she landed on the mattress, smiling up at him, her breasts heaving inside her torn blouse, her panties pulled tight against her puffy sex. '*Vete a cingar.*'

'I'd rather fuck you instead.' He was upon her, tugging roughly on her panties. Cat struggled with him again, as if to escape, in reality to help him get them off her, and she was half onto her stomach when he'd succeeded. Nathan practically pinned her to the bed as he removed the remains of his shirt and kicked off his shoes. 'So, is your precious Wheeler this rough with you?'

She looked up at him from under tousled hair, feeling feral, feeling desired, her own desire overpowering, a driving force as unstoppable as the pistons driving the train or the forces sculpting the storm outside. 'You call this rough, dickhead? You're a *choca.*' She laughed, not with derision but with delight, until Nathan reached down between her cheeks and stroked the strip of fur between her inner thighs, grunting at finding hot wet flesh. Then his thumb found and teased her clit.

Cat ground her teeth and tried to move against his hand, but he remained enticingly relentless, rough without abuse, an unspoken agreement on the rules of the game woven between them. Little bursts of climaxes shot through her and she caught them all, enjoyed them all. She relished this. It was as if Nathan was fuelling her with each kiss, each nip, each time his fingers delved deeper into her. And he kept watching her, as if he would never be able to touch her again after this day, and wanted to remember the way she was, using all his senses. Maybe he genuinely thought that way. Maybe he thought that things would change irrevocably after this mission.

He might be right.

Now, though, Cat bit her lip with another mini-climax, and then looked up, panting. 'You said ... You said you'd rather fuck ... fuck me ... so where ... where is it?'

'Here,' he growled, easing off her a little as he withdrew his hand. He unzipped his trousers and moved faster as she helped him. The anticipation and excitement swelling within her seemed to fill her chest, making it harder to breathe. He kicked off his trousers and briefs, and his cock, now freed to extend to its full hard length, bobbed from side to side as he raised himself up to position Cat on the mattress beneath him. She opened her thighs and lifted her hips so that her pelvis was touching his, and the wiry hairs on his legs brushed against her own delicate skin.

She looked up into his eyes, seeing hunger and horniness as strong as her own, and at that moment didn't care if her ulterior motives for this act bore fruit. 'Fuck!' Nathan's first eager thrust made Cat suck in her breath sharply, and she tightened her thighs against his body and wrapped her arms around him until he was fully upon her, unable and unwilling to stop the thrusts he now made into her with his hips alone. She saw his eyes shut, his thoughts set aside to sate his passions, as he pushed himself into her, repeatedly.

She let her mind drift, their bodies knowing what to do, taking their cues from the actions of another couple from the past, in this very berth. She thought of them, thought of what they'd felt and what they'd did, half a century ago. She couldn't take any more ...

... Val couldn't take any more. She lay there, blindfolded, her hands bound above her – the only way Mickey would fuck her since he'd learnt of her mother – and kept as still as she could, unwilling to react to the hands running over her body.

Both pairs of hands. Mickey's, and those belonging to his new mistress, Yvonne. 'I don't think she likes this, Mickey.'

Beside her, Mickey grunted. 'She's not gonna complain.' The hand he had at Val's hip now slapped her there. 'Isn't that right? You like this, don't you?'

'Yes, Mickey.' Amazing how hard it was to push two little words from her mouth. And it was amazing how quickly their relationship had degenerated. The sex had grown rougher, but at least it was less frequent. In addition, her suspicions that he would be just like the other wise guys and get himself a mistress were soon confirmed. This, though – bringing the woman into the bed, a bold display of his contempt for her – was new.

She listened to them kiss above her, while she fought the urge to lash out, verbally or with her legs, no matter the provocation.

It was almost a relief to hear Yvonne suggest, 'Let's go back to my room, Mickey.'

'Mmph.' Val heard him pull back, could almost feel his eyes burn into her. 'What do you think, Valentina?' She started as his hand moved between her thighs, suddenly pinching her sharply when she didn't part her thighs for him. His fingers stroked the outline of her sex. 'Do you mind waiting here while Yvonne and I go away for a while?'

Val's whole body grew as taut as a piano wire. 'No, Mickey. I don't mind.'

'Good.' She felt him and Yvonne rise, gather their coats, and leave the berth.

Val lay there, wishing that if they were going to leave her tied up again, they could have covered her. Oh God, how long was this going to go on?

The door opened again, and she tensed once more, losing control only as she heard a far more welcome voice. 'Val?'

Oh God. 'Enrique.' It was as if his presence allowed her to be more honest with her feeling. 'Help me.'

She felt him rush to her, remove her blindfold. She gasped as she looked up into his face, saw his concern, his anger. He untied her hands and pulled the abandoned bedsheet up to cover her.

Val sat up and fell into his arms, clutching him almost manic-ally, wanting his arms to stay around her, forever, shielding her. Her limbs shook and her breath seemed to rush from her twice as fast as she could take it in, her relief palpable.

Then she heard Enrique mutter, 'I'm gonna kill him. I swear to God, I'm gonna kill him now.'

'No!' She pulled back, reached up and held his broad face in her hands. 'You're not going anywhere. You're not doing anything but being with me now.' She kissed him. 'Erasing the touch they left on me.'

Enrique tried to protest, but his will weakened with each subsequent kiss, with her hands unbuttoning his shirt.

The clothes lay in a tangled heap on the floor, as the couple kissed and embraced and fucked, Val feeling her spirits rise once more, feeling better than she had in a long time. She knew that they couldn't be long, and that Enrique would eventually have to leave her tied up like before. That was later. She clasped Enrique's buttocks, clenching her fingers into his firm flesh, and making him respond with a deeper thrust, a longer moan.

And a question. 'What the hell is this?'

Val had been staring up at the ceiling fan, twirling away like a hypnotist's wheel from some cheap horror movie. Now she glanced to her side, as Enrique pulled something from under one of the pillows. 'Tooth fairy visit?'

She glanced at the large silver coin. 'That's Mickey's hundred-dollar piece. Throw it onto the table.'

'Hundred dollar piece? There's no such thing.'

'He says it's rare. Took it from the Lebowskis last week.' She glared as he examined it further. 'Drop that right now and get back to work, you hear me?'

Enrique laughed and flung the coin away, driving back into her, lifting his belly up to let her hand return between them, find and please her clit.

'Slower for a moment.'

He nodded and followed suit, still watching her, enjoying the reactions on her face.

She looked up at him and announced, 'I'm leaving him.'

He nodded, obviously feeling his own need for climax, and fighting it. 'I know, *ma chère*, I know. Someday.'

'No. Not someday. Next week.'

Enrique slowed down even more, his eyes wide. 'What? You mean it?'

'Sure.'

'B– But why next week? Why not now?'

'We need time to prepare. Next week, Mickey's planning a big money delivery, over two hundred grand. We can take it and run.'

'But what about your father?'

'He'll come with us, of course. Let Mickey keep the club.'

'And where are we going?'

She smiled. 'Atlanta, first. I have relatives there, my mother's sister. Shall we stop fucking while I go get an atlas and plan further?'

'N– No.' The disbelief in Enrique's eyes quickly blossomed into an excited, infectious joy, one she shared, and he quickened his drive into her. It was as if her declaration alone had been enough to lift so much of the weight off both of them. They weren't out of the woods yet – there was so much to plan, and so much risk – but it was a tremendous start.

Val turned her head to one side . . .

. . . and saw the gold special agent badge sitting on the adjacent pillow like a hotel mint. Cat nodded at it, looking up again into Enrique's face, holding it again, relishing the sensual fullness of the man's cock in her. But it wasn't really him there. 'Nathan . . . Hound . . . you're in there. Come on, talk to me, Agent Ames.'

Enrique frowned in confusion. 'Cat, what are you . . .'

Then it was Nathan above her, stopping his thrusts to glance around at the berth as it was fifty years before. 'Cat, what are you . . .'

'Don't stop, *idiota*!' Snarling, she rolled him to one side, taking advantage of his confusion to get him on his back, so that she was on top, looking down. She smiled with satisfaction that they were on the same level now.

'It's . . . real,' he murmured, stunned. 'You were right.'

Cat smiled. 'And now I claim my prize.'

And she rode him faster, ignoring his pleas for her to slow down before he came. She wanted him to surrender here too, surrender to the acknowledgement of this phenomenon.

Nathan's hips were beginning to buck upwards, and he pushed up with his cock, his moans reaching a familiar tone that told her his climax was imminent. Cat threw her head back and looked up triumphantly at the ceiling fan, as Nathan's come coated her insides and seeped from her with her own spasming walls.

She fell forwards on top of him, shuddering and laughing with weak delight.

13

'Do you know why you're here, Miss Wright?' Leo Kolchak said.

'Uh, yes, Mr Kolchak.' April stood there, dressed in her finest clothes, as bowled over by the older man's charm, his charisma, as by the fact that her introduction to him was while he sat there, receiving a blow job from a scantily-clad woman.

She supposed it helped that around the rest of the room onboard the train, other minimally dressed women milled about, attending the rest of Leo's guests for this private party. April wore a small, revealing, navy-blue party dress, but still felt overdressed in comparison. And definitely on the spot.

'Are you certain you wouldn't care for some champagne, my dear?' he asked her in that thick Baltic accent. He was a large man in a black turtleneck and trousers, whose girth and trimmed silver hair and beard suggested Santa Claus by way of a Russian submarine commander. On her knees before him, a slim, shapely woman with a mass of red hair bobbed her head slowly up and down at his groin, while he held her by her hair with one of his huge hands, guiding her pace. Leo could have been asking the woman attending him so intimately the question, except that he barely acknowledged her.

Instead, he was staring at April. 'Then I'll come to the point. My idiot nephew lost one of my delivery trucks. He cost me thirty thousand dollars.'

April swallowed. 'Mr Kolchak, Donnie wants to move up in

the organisation, do more than just courier work and odd jobs.'

'That's understandable. Suck, Miss Halliday, suck,' he added, glancing down at the woman before him. 'But he still lost my truck.'

'Yes, sir.' Her heart pounded, suspecting what would be asked of her. 'Mr Kolchak, we'll pay you back. Donnie always talks about you in the highest regard. He's –'

'An idiot. My nephew's a fucking idiot.' Now Leo glanced down again at the woman with his dick in her mouth, as if to make April look down as well. 'Like his father. Clumsy, loud-mouthed, boorish idiots, the pair of them. Neither of them deserved Laura, as either wife or mother.'

April felt hot, as stunned by the man's assessment of Donnie as by his insouciance as the redhead continued to service him. 'Mr Kolchak, Donnie loves you.'

'So does my dog. But if my dog cost me thirty grand, I'd shoot him. I demand compensation. Are *you* willing to do that and save him? Starting now?'

And here it was, her last chance to back out. April thought she'd prepared herself for this, too. She may have been a small-town girl, but she wasn't a child. Still, she trembled.

She reminded herself that she was doing this for him, not for herself. 'I ... anything, Mr Kolchak. So long as Donnie doesn't find out.'

The man responded with a smile that never reached his eyes. 'How romantic. Miss Halliday, off.'

The woman rose back onto unsteady feet, not looking at anyone as she moved quickly and silently to the bar at the far end of the carriage. April's attention moved to Leo's dick, a thick, glistening column of flesh sticking up from between the folds of his trousers, pointing in her direction. A chuckle from Leo made her look back at his face, his smile, as he silently indicated the place where the other woman had just been.

April's heart raced and her mouth filled with cotton. Her legs shook as she approached, and then knelt before him. Oh God, she'd wanted to be so cool about this, but now she felt like that mousy little schoolgirl who'd run away when her first boyfriend had touched her breasts while they were kissing.

'Don't worry,' Leo reassured her, never touching his cock himself but making it flex teasingly before her, 'my idiot nephew need never know.'

April wanted to faint, or to let her body carry on while her mind went elsewhere. However, she remained terribly conscious as she breathed in the scent of his sex, his male musk. She tentatively clasped his cock at the base, before parting her lips and taking him inside. It seemed to swell and pulse further, growing hotter and thicker. She leant forwards experimentally, accepting more and more of him, and then her movements grew more confident, even as she reminded herself that, as he'd just come, she could be here for ages. Her eyes felt heavy and wet, as Leo took her by the hair now, guiding her motions.

But it was the man's words that made her heart race and made her realise that this would be the longest night of her life. 'No, my dear, my idiot nephew need never have to hear about your noble sacrifice. We can keep him in the dark about many things. About my contempt for him and his father. About the times I'd had his mother, my brother's wife.' His voice dropped an octave. 'I don't suppose we even need to mention who tipped off the police about his father's location, do we?'

A flash to her right made her look up, seeing someone with a camera. Panicking, she tried backing off Leo, but he forced her back down again. 'No, my dear. You're too good to waste on my idiot nephew. I have a place for you in one of my Tampa establishments. And if you don't want anything to happen to little Donnie or yourself, you'll agree.'

April struggled, her eyes thick with tears and more flashes . . .

. . . Donnie sat up to a flash of lightning outside, gasping, choked with shock and nearly falling off his bed. Oh my God . . . that *happened*. He was as certain of this as he was of anything in his life. It had happened. Here. He even knew when it had happened: the weekend April had said she was visiting relatives, the same weekend Uncle Leo had also left for one of his parties.

And the reasons he knew this, or how he had received this revelation, never entered his head, as if it had filled to capacity with thoughts of what Leo had done to April. And of the times Donnie had thanked Leo for exposing her.

He was certain he'd never felt so stupid, or so ashamed.

Tara knelt naked on the floor of her berth, the furniture pushed to the ends to make space for the vévé of talcum powder she'd made on the carpet, the vévé to summon Papa Legba, one of the older, more beneficent spirits, who guarded the crossroads between this world and the next. She was missing much – dancing, a sacrifice – but at least she had some sugar-coated beignets from the kitchens as an offering, and the train wheels gave her a suitable drumlike rhythm.

In the end, she knew that it was intent, and ability, which swayed the forces. Besides, she didn't want power, revenge or protection, merely knowledge. How dangerous could that be?

Very.

Tara gasped, her eyes still shut, her mouth still voicing

chants, but her mind sought out the voice that caressed her. Papa Legba?

The papa has kept me from the crossroads for a long time.
Belle?

No answer.

Tara persisted. Who are you? Why are you on this train? Why do you offer these memories of those who have come before us?

She shivered, as something moved across her breasts, and the voice touched her mind again. *I am passion, Great-great-granddaughter. I am power. I am fury and storm and night. And I am here to fulfil my obligations.*

The touch slipped down between Tara's legs, even as other forces held the rest of her in place. Her pussy cried out as tendrils stroked her, teasing, loving. But she barely noticed, her mind filling with overwhelming images: a storm ravaging the sky, a maelstrom of wind and rain bound together with thunder and lightning, which seemed to shake the earth to its core, and send all things away seeking shelter. All but the train, a single defiant force cutting through the night, her beam of light lancing the blackness ahead of her as she raced so fast and sure her wheels barely touched the rails.

And perched upon her prow rode a woman, a woman nude but for the eldritch fire dancing around her.

She drove the train.

She *was* the train.

And she drove onwards, to a destination of her own choice, and woe betide anyone foolish enough to stand in her way.

Cat jerked in place, blinking and gasping, immediately calming down as she felt Nathan's arms around. 'Did you ... Did you dream that?'

'Dream what?'

'A naked woman riding on the front of the train.'

'Naked? Tell me more.'

'Never mind.' The sky was dark outside with the continuing storm, and grew darker as Cat and Nathan lay wrapped around each other, sweat binding them together. Cat's head rose and fell as it lay on Nathan's chest, as she listened to his heartbeat. 'Hound – Nathan – when I was with Jack, I –'

'Cat,' he murmured, 'you don't have to explain yourself.'

'Can I do it anyway? What I'm trying to say was that when I needed to come, he just happened to be there, and it helped that he was so good at what he did. I mean, *Dios*, the way he could –'

'Is there a non-humiliating point to this?'

'Yes, dickhead.' She turned her head to face him. 'He's good. But you're better. Isn't that what you wanted to hear?'

'Nope. I wanted to hear that he was crap, and that you sent him home to play with his coins.'

Cat smiled, playing with his chest hairs. 'Men.' Her smile dropped. 'We should get up.'

'No, let's stay in a bit longer.'

'Why?' Then she nodded as if in understanding. 'Ahh right, you older guys need more rest.'

He twisted suddenly, half on top of her, invading her mouth with his tongue, wrapping one leg around hers, pressing his erection into her thigh. His hand moved up and caressed one of her breasts, enjoying the fullness of it, its heat and softness. Their tongues danced together, and Cat melted and squirmed under his attentions, wrapping her arms around him.

When their mouths parted, Cat gasped and asked, still teasingly, 'So, you remain in peak condition, Agent Ames?'

'Dunno.' Pressing his erection harder against her, Nathan shifted his hand down along her belly, dipping once into her navel before continuing its descent, cupped her mound, feeling the heat, the wetness of individual strands of her bush, and the puffy flesh against his palm. 'Let's find out.'

Cat's eyes widened in response, and her mouth gasped out as Nathan entered her with his middle finger, gently but insistently penetrating her to the hilt, the walls of her sex tightening ferociously around him. Nathan smiled and leant in close to whisper, 'Let me know if you find me flagging, right?'

Cat's eyes opened wide each time his finger went deep, and she bit her lip before replying breathlessly, 'Ah . . . ah fuck . . . bastard.'

He drew closer to her ear and licked it. Cat's body undulated like waves, her limbs spasming, and a reply she tried to make was lost somewhere. But he still spoke. 'If I want to stay in bed with you, sleep's usually the last thing on my mind.' As his finger continued to thrust into her, his thumb swivelled up to tease and rub against her clitoris. Cat closed her eyes and clenched her teeth in acute concentration. 'And I don't want anyone else touching you.'

'Ah . . . ah . . . you . . .' Words became yelps, yelps became cries, rising, galvanising like her body in the throes of climax, suffused with sensation for what seemed like hours.

Then she collapsed on the bed, her pussy having squeezed out Nathan's finger, her head spinning, but her hungers driving her to part her thighs and help Nathan as he rose above her, his cock brushing against her inner thigh, seeking the warmth of her damp, sensitised pussy, moaning as he drove into her. Fully onto her but keeping his weight off her, he pumped with a furious abandon, keeping her on the cusp of another climax. Cat's pussy squeezed around him, clutching him once more, their mouths grinding with an almost frightening intensity, his grunts as he fucked her a honey coating to her ears.

As Nathan began losing control, thrusting harder and faster into her, Cat urged him onwards, wanting his seed inside her again. He gave it, moaning and shooting into Cat and completing the circuit for another of her own orgasms, a sustained wave of bliss that sent her flying for the longest time...

Cat dropped back to earth when Nathan's cock wilted inside her, and she moved off him to clench her thighs and keep his seed inside her. They clung to each other, neither speaking, neither opening their eyes, but remaining close, their skin glistening with sweat. Cat absently reached down and stroked his flaccid shaft, moist and shining with their fluids. 'Bastard. Now I *do* have to rest.'

'Aww, poor baby, maybe –'

'Coins?'

'What?'

She rose a little, frowning. 'He collects coins?' It didn't seem to fit the man's personality. Perhaps he really had turned over a new leaf?

'Well, I didn't see any, but he's got books and notes on them.'

And with that, it all fell into place for Cat.

She cast off the bedsheets and padded naked over to where the phone sat, wincing with sweet discomfort at the after-effects of their sex, and aware of his come beginning to seep from her.

'What are you doing?' he asked.

'Calling Gordy. I have another request I hope he'll fulfil.'

Nathan smiled as he watched her. 'Just describe in detail what I'm seeing now and he'll move mountains. But are you going to let me in on it this time?'

She turned back to him and winked. 'Listen and learn.'

Nathan did both.

*　　*　　*

There weren't many in the reception carriage at that hour, with most passengers in the rear of the train, availing themselves of the wardrobes to select costumes for the party that evening. At the nearby tables, Richard Newholme sat alone as always, still wearing the suit he wore when he'd boarded yesterday, as if his costume of choice was commuting businessman; he nursed his brandy and otherwise kept to his own thoughts. Ben and Hannah were clad in a white tuxedo suit and red sequin dress, respectively, an echo of Bogart and Bergman.

Wheeler held out his arms to display the billowy black sleeves of his silk shirt, part of an ensemble of brocaded leather waistcoat, bandana, breeches and knee-high leather boots, threatening a potted plant with his rapier. 'Louisiana has traditionally been a haven for pirates and privateers, and extends to the moonshiners of Prohibition days. Belle herself has carried a number of modern scoundrels –'

Tara, dressed in a very attractive biker chick's outfit of tight leathers, ripped T-shirt and studded belts and collars, looked distracted and annoyed, and sounded it. 'You talk a lot about Belle, Jack. But you have no idea what's really behind her. If you did, you wouldn't be so flippant.'

Wheeler looked bemused at the interruption, glancing at the door. 'Is there a problem, Miss Gilbrand?'

'You're waiting for Cat and Nathan.'

'Uh, yes. I sent someone to their berth inviting them to join us here.'

'Don't worry; they're on their way now.'

'Excuse me?' He turned again; seconds later, Catalina and Nathan Ames entered, striding purposefully towards him. They were dressed in plain dark clothes, a black skirt suit on Catalina and a trouser suit on Mr Ames. Cat reached into her jacket and produced a gold badge and ID card. 'Jonathan Wheeler, I'm

Special Agent Catalina Montoya, and this is Special Agent Nathan Ames. We're with the Criminal Investigation Division of the IRS.'

Wheeler smiled and offered light applause. 'Well presented and very authentic sounding. But a little tip for you: FBI agents are sexy, tax agents aren't.'

'I've had both types,' Nathan informed him with a smile. 'And you are dead wrong.'

'And you're dead wrong about these being costumes.' Cat put away her badge. 'They're real. We're real. And you're under arrest, *pendejo*.'

Faye stormed into the dining carriage, pushing past the curious, seeking that son of a bitch. 'Donnie!'

The man sat alone near the dining-car bar, nursing a shot glass and acquired bottle, looking as if his world had collapsed upon him.

She drew closer. 'What the hell are you doing?'

He never looked up from the glass in his hand, his face flushed with previous shots and his voice was slurred. 'Getting drunk. Can't you tell?'

Faye tried to control her temper, turning on the sweetness as she sat beside him, lowering her voice. 'Stud, if you get drunk, you won't be able to help me.'

He nodded. 'That's true.' He downed his shot in one.

She leant in closer, anger and panic vying for dominance, and set down the folded documents she was carrying. 'Donnie, I've got the transfer of ownership papers ready. But if I don't take over, you won't have anything to tell your Uncle Leo.'

Mention of the man's name finally brought out a response from him – a face of tight contempt. 'I've got enough to tell him. I'll tell him to go to hell, for starters. And I'll follow.'

Faye looked around, in case anyone was close enough to

hear, before whispering, 'Donnie, if it's a case of nerves, you're not going to get courage from a couple of shots of JD.'

'It's not about fear.' He swallowed. 'It's about shame. Leave me alone, will you?'

'Donnie,' she started, reaching under the table to touch him.

Now he looked up. 'Leave me alone, or I'll tell Wheeler about your plans.'

Faye saw the harsh look of truth in his eyes. She departed quickly and found a vacant lavatory to enter and vent out her frustrations, smacking her fists against the walls. *Goddamn it!* What had happened to him in just a few short hours?

Then she calmed down, checked out her appearance in the mirror and nodded with satisfaction. This was just a temporary setback. She'd find some other loser. Maybe Ames? Then this shitty train would belong to her. She promised herself that.

Calmer now, she moved to leave.

But the door wouldn't unlock.

She tried it repeatedly, cursed, pounded her fists against the door, called out for help until her voice went hoarse, even tried the emergency button.

Nothing.

Twisting with rage, she lashed out, kicking the toilet bowl and bruising her toes through her best shoes.

And that was when the toilet erupted its contents like a geyser.

'Arrested?' Wheeler smiled, looking to the few other passengers in the carriage, most pretending not to be interested. 'On what charges?'

'Conspiracy to steal government property.'

'Ooh, sounds impressive, but of course I have no idea what you mean.'

'Of course you do, honey.' Cat walked about, deliberately taking in the other passengers. 'Let's talk about the Silver Bell.'

'My ownership of this train is clearly and legally established.'

'I don't mean Belle with an "e" at the end, but then you know that anyway. In 1875, the US Treasury was looking to produce a commemorative coin of legal tender, to honour the upcoming American Centennial. One prototype – a silver coin worth one hundred dollars – went as far as having a proof run of sixty-four made, but the government rejected the idea due to silver devaluation. The Treasury ordered all but one melted down, sending the last for display in the Smithsonian in D.C. However, it went missing while in transit from the Mint in New Orleans. I'll let my assistant Agent Ames continue.'

Nathan shot her a good-natured glare, before proceeding. 'Over the following decades, various secret service agents had tried tracking it down, with no success. And its reputation among collectors has grown.' He produced a page, detailing the obverse and reverse sides of a silver coin. 'From one of your own notebooks. Because of the picture of the Liberty Bell on one side, the coin has earned the nickname of . . . the Silver Bell. And, with the 1933 Gold Double Eagle and the 1781 Ortega Dubloon, it's considered one of the most valuable coins in the world, with an estimated value among collectors exceeding eight million dollars.'

'Unscrupulous collectors, that is,' Cat amended. 'Since the coin is considered stolen Treasury property.'

'Is this charming narrative going anywhere?' Wheeler asked, his face now taut.

'*Si*, Jack. The coin was last rumoured to be in the possession of a Chicago mobster named Ira Lebowsky – the same mobster robbed by one Mickey Uscione in 1958. You know all about Mickey, of course, your office is full of notes on him, and his wife, and her lover. You've been using the echoes of these three people, not to help them find some peace, but to find the coin. There are no ghosts.'

'What?'

All eyes turned to Newholme, who'd risen from his chair and approached the group warily, his face an expression of confusion and pain. He fixed a stare at Wheeler. 'A fraud? This is all a fraud?'

Wheeler swallowed, looking embarrassed. 'Mr Newholme, I never intimated that your wife's spirit was onboard.'

'Bastard. You bastard.' The old man stormed out of the carriage.

Wheeler turned back to Cat. 'Very fanciful story, Catalina, but you have no proof, no witnesses.' He raised the rapier.

Nathan immediately stepped in front of Cat, his posture defensive, his face hard. 'Drop that, bud. *Now!*'

Wheeler smiled and released it, letting it hit the carpet with a clang. 'How gallant, but I think the lady can defend herself. She's fit, and I know from personal experience, quite limber.'

'Save it, Jack,' Cat advised, stepping around Nathan and patting him on the arm. 'Down, boy. He won't try anything. He'll be too busy calling his driver to stop at the next station.'

Wheeler frowned at her, but to his credit nodded and walked to the internal phone by the front of the carriage, Nathan following.

Ben and Hannah Oliver drew up to Cat. 'Um, Agent Montoya, is it?'

'It's still Cat.'

OK. Are we in any trouble?'

She smiled. 'No. This is strictly a Federal matter. We'll arrange to have the passengers transported back to their points of origin on another train.'

Now Tara spoke up. 'But what about the mystery? Val and Enrique?'

'Sorry, but they'll have to wait with Mamselle Belagrís –'

Tara paled. '*Belagrís*? Belle is Belagrís?'

'I don't know,' Cat admitted. 'Val thought of that name often. My sources tell me she was some sort of spirit protector.'

'She is.' The younger woman's face took on a new look, not one of disappointment, but unease. 'This might not all be over, Catalina.'

Before Cat could ask what she meant, Nathan drew up. 'The driver's not answering. The phone seems to work, but . . .'

'Get to the locomotive. I'll try some of the utility phones in the neighbouring carriages.' To Wheeler, she added, 'You're coming with me. The rest of you, please stay here.'

Wheeler kept up his enigmatic expression as Cat escorted him to the next carriage in the train, finding no one and no working phone. 'You'd better get these things functioning, Jack.'

'Nothing to do with me, Special Agent.'

The second car, the kitchen/pantry/storage carriage, was also empty and without a working phone. 'Jack, you'll be charged with obstructing Federal agents in the course of an investigation.'

'I'm telling you, it's not me.'

When they reached the accessway to the next carriage, they found the safety door shut, refusing to open. Cat pinned Wheeler to the nearest wall. 'Enough of this, *pendejo*! I'm gonna put you away for so long.'

'*It's not me!*' he practically yelled. 'Belle does these things!'

Such was the sincerity he showed, the fear, that Cat released him. 'You're serious?'

Wheeler straightened up again. 'She can disrupt the cameras and microphones, lock doors, lose things on me! She's mercurial, obstreperous, stubborn – the quintessential female!'

From the far end of the carriage, Nathan appeared. 'Cat! You'd better come see this!'

She did, as did everybody else, it seemed. There was another secured door separating the locomotive from the rest of the train, but a small thick window allowed one to look in and see the intricate workings of the locomotive controls, and the driver himself.

Except that in this instance, there was no driver.

Cat was stunned, but turned to see an equally surprised Wheeler. 'Have you put this thing on some automatic pilot?'

'The old Imperial IIIs didn't have such features,' Ben Oliver noted, looking around him in awe, if not fear. 'They have dead man's switches, so if something happens to the driver, the train comes to a stop.'

'Last I saw them, the driver and his assistant were in one of the staff berths, from this morning,' Wheeler noted. 'Once everyone was back onboard in the afternoon, they start up with a signal from us. Maybe they're still back there, trapped?'

Like the rest of us, Cat told herself. She scowled at him. 'Why the hell are you smiling?'

Wheeler looked insufferably smug. 'Isn't it obvious? Belle's protecting me. She doesn't want me arrested.'

'She doesn't give a damn about you, Jack.'

All eyes turned to Tara, who continued, 'This is about fulfilling a generations-old pact. She wants the mystery solved. And she won't let go until it's done.'

In the main carriages of Belle, the collective passengers and staff, ignorant of the situation in the front of the train, enveloped by heat and red light and the throbbing waves of the guitarist at the peak of his energies, danced and bobbed and fucked in a collective mass, a bacchanal of energy that fed the force which drove the train into the night.

Unstoppable.

13

They'd returned to the reception carriage to plan their next move – all except for Wheeler, who sat alone in one corner, content to look more insufferable now than before.

'Our own phone can't seem to get a signal now, and we can't get to any of the phones in Wheeler's office,' Nathan was saying. 'Maybe we can break a window here, and I can climb outside to the rest of the train?'

'That would be too dangerous, Agent Ames,' Ben warned. 'We're going too fast, in the dark, in a storm.'

'*Si*, Hound. You're not Bruce Willis.'

'Bruce Willis climbed out of buildings, Cat, it was Steven Seagal who climbed outside of trains.'

'Steven Seagal *es un cabrón estúpido*.' Cat's eyes locked with Wheeler's. The man was definitely hiding more than he had told, although she was convinced that, as bizarre as it was, Belle had indeed taken control of itself – herself? – though her brain had started to turn to porridge when Tara had started flinging about technobabble such as 'psychokinetic manifestations' and 'poltergeist-level electromagnetic fields'.

'We might find something in the kitchens to get the safety doors open,' Nathan suggested.

'Like what, a can opener against the inch-thick steel?'

'Why not just wait it out?' Hannah asked, sounding a little fearful now. 'There's limited fuel, and the rail authorities can sideline us, once they fail to contact us. Belle won't ... crash us, will she?'

'If Belle is really Mamselle Belagrís, then she's one of the Guédé loa,' Tara warned, looking wary. 'They're spirits of the dead. They have nothing to fear.'

Memories of Val and her charm, and that vision of the spirit driving the train, returned to Cat. 'Tara, if this concerns magic – voodoo – I need to know more about it than what I've already picked up from the midnight movies.'

'Well then, throw away what you've already picked up, because it'll be false. We don't make zombies or voodoo dolls or curses. When we invoke the spirits, it's for harmony and peace, birth and rebirth, increased abundance of luck, material happiness, health, protection –'

'Tara,' Cat interjected, trying to be patient, 'I accept that the majority of believers are decent, intelligent people. But we need specific information.'

The girl nodded in concession. '*Voudon* is the oldest religion on Earth, one that travelled from Africa in the hearts and minds of those slaves transported to the New World. Here it blended with the shamanist beliefs of Native Americans, and added elements from Catholicism to appease the slave owners. It recognises one distant Creator, and a pantheon of angel-like spirits known as the loa, who act as intermediaries between the Creator and man, as they are ancestral and archetypal embodiments of the forces of nature and the human psyche. There are many families of loa, all with their own personalities and powers, rituals and symbols.'

'And Belagrís is a member of the Guédé loa?'

'Yes. The Guédé loa as a family are loud, rude, very sexual and, well, fun.'

'Fun!' Nathan exclaimed wryly.

'Yes. They like to party. No wonder she likes it here.'

'What do you know about Belagrís herself?'

'Not much, to be honest, apart from the fact that she's a

New World spirit, created by those born into slavery in America. You have to understand, there's hundreds of loa, sought for many purposes. Earthly families powerful in magic can "adopt" them as guardian spirits, and the service can last for generations.'

'A family,' Cat echoed. 'Like Val's.'

'But Belagrís has been all but forgotten. I've never even seen her vévé.'

'Her what?' Nathan asked.

'Her symbol, like an astral formula. Every loa has his or her own individual vévé. Reproduction of the astral forces represented by the vévés obliges the loa to descend to Earth.'

'You've already seen it,' Cat assured her, indicating the cross-like figures on the walls, the Southern Spirits logo. 'My sources confirmed it.'

Everyone looked around, as if seeing them for the first time. Cat looked over at Wheeler. 'The name, the Southern Spirits logo, all connected to Belagrís. You used these deliberately, to accentuate her power. *Idiota.*' She turned back to Tara. 'Is there a spell you can work, a prayer, to appease her somehow?'

The girl shook her head. 'I've tried. She's not listening.'

Cat was afraid of that. She looked to the men. 'Perhaps we can disable the electricals somewhere?'

Nathan looked to Ben, considering. Cat left them to it, not expecting any success – stopping this force was going to take more than just unplugging a few wires. She approached Wheeler, sitting close beside him to speak quietly. 'Belle wants the mystery solved. To do that, we need access to the right hotspots, though she's blocked us from most of the rest of the train. That suggests there's a hotspot I haven't experienced, where the answer lies. You know this train better than anyone else. Where is it, Jack?'

He regarded her. 'And I'm going to assist you, and expedite my arrest? Thanks, my Latin beauty, but no thanks.'

Cat eyed him, understanding where this was going. 'What do you want?'

Wheeler glanced past her to the others, then leant in closer, his voice a murmur. 'You and I go to the secret hotspot, the place where Val and Enrique were killed. We experience what they did, discover what happened, Belle's satisfied, she stops – and you drop the charges about the coin against me.'

Cat smirked. 'You've had access to that area all this time, and you haven't solved it yourself, or brought someone else along to help you?'

'I've tried, darling. I've not found anyone as adept at experiencing the visions as you, anyone Belle has liked as much as you.'

'And then you expect me to just lie there and let you fuck me and get away with your crimes?'

'It seems fair. You'll not let me get away with the coin, will you?'

'And you definitely know where this hotspot is?'

'Cat,' Nathan approached. 'What's going on?'

She stayed focused on Wheeler, who took on a serious, no-nonsense aspect as he responded, 'It's pretty strong, since it's where the couple died. The few times I brought a perceptive female there, they tended to, ah, react badly to what they felt, and became unresponsive.' He looked her over. 'You, however, should be strong enough not to give in to your, shall we say, feminine weaknesses?'

She pictured how he'd look with a broken nose, before turning back to a still-watching, still-concerned Nathan. 'I'm taking Wheeler elsewhere. He has information he'll give to me alone.' Before he could reply, she pressed her forefinger softly against his lips. 'I can handle him, and by myself, this time. Trust me.'

It took some visible effort on his part, but Nathan only replied, 'Be careful, Catalina.'

'Keep everyone here.' Her fingers lingered, and she smiled, proud that he didn't seem to notice what she'd taken from his jacket pocket.

Cat followed Wheeler into the latter half of the kitchens carriage, to one of the pantries and, as soon as he had escorted her inside its cramped confines, she spotted the incongruity. 'Too small in here. It should be bigger.'

'Give the lady a cigar. No one else has ever noticed.' He reached behind one of the shelves, unlatched something, and the entire wall swivelled on a hidden axis in the middle, like some passageway entrance in a mystery-novel mansion. The space beyond appeared much like any of the other berths on the train: narrow bed, old-fashioned furniture, a ceiling fan and small pictures on the walls. Cat recognised the decor from the period of Val and Enrique. Wheeler stepped inside. 'It was better to keep this section hidden, in case anyone accidentally discovered the hotspot and was troubled by it.'

'And in case they also learnt where the coin was, right, Jack?'

'Don't get all high and mighty with me, sweetie. I'm losing out on an eight-million dollar deal, and my chance to get away from this ... thing.'

'What a way to refer to Belle,' Cat mocked. 'After your spirited defence of her during this trip.'

'Like flesh and blood women, after a while she becomes smothering, overpowering. Take off your jacket.'

After a moment, she did so, setting it on an adjacent chair. 'I hope you were going to spend some of that money on therapy to deal with your issues regarding women.'

He was removing his waistcoat, and his boots. 'I have no

issues, Agent Montoya. I know what to do to please women, and to get them to please me. And I know what to do to keep them from getting too clingy, possessive. As they inevitably do.'

She grunted. 'So much for your graveside confession about envying Enrique's passion, his love. What now?'

He reached into a cabinet and withdrew a pair of silver handcuffs. 'Put your hands behind your back.'

'*Besame el culo.*'

He held up the cuffs like a necklace. 'We have to recreate the conditions as they were fifty years ago. Come on, we both know you're no stranger to bondage.'

Reluctantly, she walked towards him, her hands clenched into fists as they moved behind her back. She felt him draw up, felt the cool metal clamp around her wrists with a treble click. Her arms gave a reflexive tug to test the amount of give.

It wasn't much. 'This doesn't mean I trust you, Jack –'

Before she could finish, Jack caught her by the arm, twisted her around to face him, and kissed her full on the mouth, his other hand clasping the back of her head. He pressed his lips down on hers and plunged his tongue into the warm wetness between them. Cat was taken by surprise, but recovered quickly, sucking on his tongue as she felt the same electric sensations she had experienced in the sling room, the heat of passion quickly drowning out her other feelings.

'F– Fuck,' she muttered, her lips moving against his, the words almost impaled on his tongue. 'I'm –'

'You're going nowhere,' he informed her as he pulled back, moving his lips down to her neck. 'Except where I want. Doing what I want.'

The feeling of his lips and hot tongue made her throw her head back, tightening the sinews in her throat. That made it easier for Wheeler to fasten his mouth on them, sucking the skin in as the hand at the back of her head grabbed her by the hair.

He took his hand away from her arm and fumbled with the front of her blouse, trying to unbutton it before losing what little patience he had and tearing at it. Her breasts heaved from the frilled tops of her white lace bra, and he was reaching around and unclasping her bra, before returning and freeing her breasts entirely from the cups. He dropped his mouth to each one, taking them in turn, sucking at her flesh, concentrating on the nipple, rubbing it against the edges of his teeth.

Cat's arousal grew, her whole body quivering, and though his actions were expected, the intensity was pushing her closer to the edge, making her crave this ravishment. As his teeth created a delicious torture on her nipples, twin flames of pain and pleasure combining, indistinguishable, her sex seemed to catch fire as well.

Wheeler drew back and dropped to his knees, looking up at her as he reached up under her skirt and over the tops of her stockings to find the sides of her panties. With a wanton grunt, he yanked them down, dragging them to her ankles, only letting her step out of one leg band.

He smiled up at her as his hand returned to her sex, the smile broadening further as his finger stroked her bush, his other hand steadying her at the small of her back. His fingers dipped along her slit and sunk shallowly into her folds.

Cat gasped and swayed, as his forefinger moved to the crest of her sex, finding her hard, swollen clit. Cat felt it throb and pulse like a signal, seeking attention. It made her moan as he nudged against it. Behind her, her hands struggled between each other.

Wheeler sensed her apparent fighting. 'Save your energy. You're mine. And you're not getting away – *owww*!'

Before he knew it, he was pinned face down on the bed, one arm twisted behind him, as Cat straddled him, freeing her remaining wrist with the universal key she'd taken from Nathan's jacket. 'Come on, Jack, you think I'm stupid? That I wouldn't be ready for something like this?' When he struggled some more, Cat put a little more pressure on his arm. 'Calm down, *nino*. You're going nowhere, except where I want. Doing what I want.'

Wheeler turned his head and looked up at her, panting. 'Lemme . . . go . . . I don't . . . play this.'

'No?' Cat had both his wrists cuffed together now, and turned him onto his back, then straddled his groin by rucking her skirt up until it was around her waist. She took her time slipping her breasts back into her bra and refastening it, and then inspecting the rips on her blouse. 'You're paying for this one, Jack. Anyway, where was I? Oh yes.' She ground slowly onto his groin, genuinely enjoying the pressure against her bare clit, sometimes leaning forwards as if to kiss him, her voice a sultry murmur almost lost to the sounds of the train wheels. 'I bet your body can play just fine like this.'

Wheeler, darkening with this blow to his masculine pride, began struggling again, until she bent forwards, gripped him by the chin, and warned, 'You keep fighting me, and I'll keep you on edge for hours, with no relief. You know I can do it. Is that what you want?'

The man looked petulant enough to remain defiant. Fortunately for him – for them both – he finally replied, 'N– No.'

'*Bueno.*' Cat sat up straight again, reaching down to her sex as she continued to grind against an ever-growing erection she could feel through his clothes. 'But I'm still not going to fuck you. Not until you ask. I might even make you beg.'

'Fuck you!' His face was a picture of the fight between his ego and his libido.

And Cat enjoyed that, almost as much as she enjoyed touching her clit lightly, tracing a tight circle around it as her stockinged thighs clenched around his captive legs, making his cock betray its master and throb for attention. Cat grew bolder, delving further down to part her folds and dip into her wetness, gathering it as her pussy reacted to this provocation with a necklace of tiny contractions.

When she withdrew her glistening fingers, she leant forwards once more, offering them to Wheeler's nose, his lips. 'Remember this? My scent? You'll want a taste as well.'

Amusingly, he tried to remain rebellious and keep his mouth shut, despite his obvious reaction to her musk.

'It wasn't a request, by the way, *pendejo*,' she informed him sweetly. 'Now open up and suck, like a good little *puta*.' She ground harder against his groin, imagining the friction and pressure would soon grow more painful than pleasurable for the stubborn *cabrón*.

She was right; Wheeler parted his mouth and Cat decided to move to the next step, feeling herself suitably aroused. She lifted herself up and eased back until she just kept his knees trapped. She unhooked her skirt and threw it aside, finding it a nuisance now. Then she reached for the belt and zipper on his trousers, noting the intense bulge and the tiny damp patch that she'd left on him.

Demonstrating the same roughness he'd shown to her blouse, Cat undid and pulled down his trousers and briefs to his thighs, letting his cock spring free into the air, proud and thick and erect, some pre-come seeping down the underside of the shaft, not being absorbed by his cotton briefs.

'Oh my,' she teased, 'looks like somebody *does* like playing the submissive one for a change.' She licked the tip of her middle finger and gently moistened his cockhead, making the shaft twitch and try to flee her. 'Well? Do you want to be fucked?'

He didn't answer. She leant back and dipped forwards, until her mouth was enticingly, maddeningly close to his member, and it was as if she was speaking directly to it, repeating, 'Do you want to be fucked? To feel the hot embrace of my pussy around you, squeezing, releasing, milking you of every drop you're carrying?' Her hand reached out now and brushed through his clump of pubic hair to grasp him at the base of his cock, stroking slowly upwards. 'Well, *puta*?' She applied some more pressure, watching him closely, careful not to let him go too far before she was ready. '*Well?*'

'Y– Yes,' came a whisper.

Her tongue darted out, the tip running along the rim of his cockhead, collecting his pre-come. 'Yes, what? What do your want? Spell it out for me. I'm just a stupid little woman.' She blew gently on him, feeling his whole body quiver.

He snarled at her through gritted teeth. 'Fuck me! *Fuck me!*'

'Well, since you're begging now.' Cat rose up, her own eagerness barely hidden, as she positioned herself over his staff, feeling the heat radiating from her parted sex like air escaping from a balloon. She dealt with this by slowly sinking down onto him, letting her mind open ...

... It was so hot ... so hot, even in just her pink teddy, but Val didn't care. She was happy, more happy than she had been in a long, long time.

'I have something for you,' Enrique announced, close to her.

'What, besides your love, and our freedom – and some stolen money?' She was undoing his tie, and unbuttoning his shirt, and something behind it caught her eye, her eyes widening. 'Sweet God, you found it!'

Behind his shirt sat her charm, the one Mickey had torn off

her a month ago and threw away. It was hanging around his neck as if it had been there all along. 'Where'd you get it?'

Enrique grinned with delight at her response. 'One of the porters found it in the garbage, and actually tried to sell it to me. I was going to surprise you.' He cast off his shirt. 'After this.' He reached into his trouser pocket and produced a small box, dropping to one knee before her.

Val's heart raced. 'Enrique.'

He opened the box. It was a ring, a simple wedding band. His voice near cracked. 'I...I know you're technically still married...'

'Only in the eyes of one faith.' She reached for the more expensive ring from Mickey, cursing for not removing it sooner as she flung it across the room, with the same contempt Mickey had shown her charm. She accepted Enrique's ring, the love she had for him so overpowering it threatened to make her cry. 'As far as anyone else is concerned, we've been married for years.'

He smiled, reaching behind his head for the chain holding the charm. 'I'd better give this to you as well.'

'Later.' She pulled him back up and continued kissing and undressing him, their bodies receiving the attention they demanded.

To the hard pounding rhythm of the train that carried them, the lovers moved their bodies together like pistons: Enrique driving deep into her, again and again, Val clutching and squeezing him as another climax rushed through her.

The heat in the berth was stifling, unrelieved by the ceiling fan directly above them, and sweat matted the tips of her russet hair to her neck, before rolling down beneath the salmon-pink silk of her teddy. She wanted to take it off and be as naked as her lover, but he wouldn't unwrap his huge arms from around her, wouldn't stop using those full, strong lips and tongue.

She didn't have any problem with that.

They were free. Well, nearly. They had left Mickey back in Chicago, taking with them two hundred thousand dollars of Mob money, destined for the Cuban casinos. But it would never reach them. Her father was prepared, and would meet them when they arrived tomorrow morning in New Orleans. From there, they would take the train to Miami and, from there, a boat to Europe, under assumed names and fake passports. The Mob could keep the club.

And Mickey? Mickey could kiss the imprint of her ass that she left in their marital bed back in Chicago.

She sat in Enrique's lap, her thighs straddling his hips as he pushed up into her, repeatedly, the tip of his shaft stroking the walls of her sex in all the right places. She felt like such a small thing in his embrace, something that could easily be crushed without due care. But she knew him better. He would never hurt her. One of his hands had descended along her spine to cup her cheeks, squeezing hungrily and sending tiny jolts through her like sparks on the rails.

But her teddy had become distracting enough for her to pull back and motion silently until her lover got the idea and relaxed his hold on her. When she cast it aside, however, he bent her backwards until she thought she'd fall from him, then he bent forward and engulfed one of her nipples in his mouth, sucking sharply and making her yelp. Her hands gripped his arms for support, and she stared upwards, the whirling wooden blades seeming to mesmerise her.

And still Enrique drove into Val, even as she drove back, meeting him thrust for thrust, while his free hand manoeuvred between their bodies, touching her bush, then her clit, his thumb providing a gentle but insistent teasing that made her weak with the sensations running though her.

'Oh sweet God!' Riding the crest of it, she leant forwards

once more, wanting to kiss him again, to push him harder, faster. She wanted him to lose control, wanted him to surrender to her for once, and fill her with his seed. She knew it would all be over, before either of them knew it.

Neither of them heard the berth door open, and then close.

However, they did hear the voice. 'Adulteress.'

Val and Enrique froze in mid-coitus at the sight of Mickey at the doorway, automatic pistol in hand, eyes cold, dark and disbelieving of what was before him. Val's heart skipped a beat as her husband's murderous glare flicked between the two lovers, as if unsure which one to focus his fury upon first. 'Mickey –'

'Get off him.'

Val felt Enrique's wilting cock withdraw from her, as she slowly untangled her limbs and rose onto shaking legs. Enrique moved to stand in front of her protectively.

'Back away,' Mickey ordered, chilling Val with the sheer deadness of the tone. She'd heard it before, more than once, and always before he was to go out and commit some terrible action.

'Mickey,' Enrique started, holding up his hands, 'it's not her fault. I forced myself on her. I threatened her.'

Mickey gestured with his gun to make him shift further to one side of the berth. '*Silencio.*' Then he looked back at Val, who was reaching for a shirt to cover herself. 'No. Whores should be used to nakedness. Well? Is it true? Did he force himself on you?'

An escape, at least for her. A last chance at staying alive, though Enrique was doomed.

She wasn't surprised, really, at her response. 'No, Mickey. He didn't. I love him.' She had her hands covering her breasts and bush; now she dropped them to her sides. Modesty before her husband and lover seemed pointless now – especially if she was about to die. 'I always have.'

'I know. I had my suspicions for a while, and eventually learnt about an Enrique Cazenove.' He raised his pistol, and his voice, at her. 'How could you betray me?'

Disbelief crept through her, threatening to paralyse her, but she couldn't let herself slip into shock now, and let her anger at his attitude galvanise her. 'How could you think I wouldn't? You took me. *Took me!* Threatened my father's life if I didn't marry you. You made me think you'd treat me different from the other Mob wives, but you went and got yourself a mistress.' She swallowed, calmer now, knowing her next words could be her last. 'This was never about betraying you. This was about getting back what you took from me. You'll never own me again.' She said the last without spite, without malice. After all that had happened between them – what could still happen – she didn't want to hurt him.

And she saw that he saw it, too, saw the truth unfold in Mickey's eyes. And the anger began to drain from him, eclipsed with a numbing grief. Mickey had done bad things, but he was no monster, mindless and unreasoning, and she hoped that when things calmed down, they could . . .

Movement to her right made her turn, as Enrique took the opportunity to charge at Mickey. Mickey turned too, raised his pistol at the other man and, for the rest of her life, Val would wonder what made her go after them both, reaching for the gun, when common sense dictated she dive out of the way. The men grappled . . .

And someone punched her in the chest, making her fall back and drop almost comically to her knees, her ears ringing as shots filled the berth. How did Mickey punch her? He still had the gun in his hand. Maybe it was Enrique. Accidentally, of course, but she'd still make him pay, in back rubs and chocolates.

She tried to catch her breath, but failed and fell to her side. The wind must really have been knocked out of her.

From behind her hair, she saw Mickey fall as well, onto his back, staring upwards, also gasping for breath like a fish out of water. And then Enrique was at her side, gently lifting her into his arms to cradle her, his face as white as a sheet and his body cold against hers. 'Val? Oh God, Val, I'm sorry, *ma chère* ... I'm so sorry.'

Confusion made her frown, and her chest tightened in pain. She couldn't bear to see the tears streaming down his face, but she couldn't look away either. Or speak, though her mouth did open. She saw the charm still hanging around his neck, and thought mildly that she should have taken it from him earlier, she would have saved herself a punch.

She wanted to tell him that everything would be all right, but he looked so upset. She prayed to Mamselle Belagrís to give him peace. Just give her a moment to rest, and then they'd be up and leave Mickey to sleep it all off ... just a moment ... she loved being in Enrique's arms ... there was nothing as sweet ... oh, there was the crossroads ahead ...

... Papa Legba taking Cat in hand ...

'Catalina!'

Cat opened her eyes again to look up at Nathan, the pain in her chest a white noise of sensation that nevertheless was drowned out by the sound of this strange man holding her, shaking her. 'Agent Catalina Montoya! Wake up, damn it! Don't stay locked in the vision. You could die with her.' He slapped her face. 'Damn it, talk to me!'

'H– Hit me again, *pajiero*, I'll have your *cojones* for breakfast.'

Nathan's face was a picture of intense relief as he hugged her, and she let him, still trying to collate the knowledge and feelings she'd experienced. There was a pain in her chest, perhaps some psychosomatic echo of the bullet that had torn into Val, but it was already ebbing as she regained control. 'I thought . . . I thought I said I could handle myself.'

'I knew you could. But you didn't have to.'

'You big *chocha*.' She pushed him away, aware that Wheeler was still lying on the bed, hands cuffed behind him and trousers around his thighs, his cock limp and nestled against his balls, and aware that she was bereft of skirt and panties. She tugged at her torn blouse as Wheeler stared blankly upwards, obviously having been caught up in the vision as well. 'Nothing. Nothing about the Silver Bell.'

Cat's sympathy for him was nonexistent, as she reached for her skirt and looked to Nathan. 'It was Mickey who died with Val, not Enrique. Enrique must have disposed of the bodies, took the Mob money and ran, afraid of retribution from Mickey's friends.'

Nathan nodded. 'Makes sense. I wonder what happened to him after that.'

'Ask him yourself. He's right behind you.'

Nathan twisted in place, following her eyes to see Richard Newholme standing, holding a revolver in an echo of events on this spot, years before. He glanced around uncomfortably, as if taking in how close the decor was to the original design, but kept the gun fixed on the two agents on the floor.

Wheeler looked up now, as best he could. '*You?*'

Cat never took his eyes off the newcomer, or his weapon. 'Cazenove. New House. Newholme, anglicised. It seems obvious now.'

He shrugged. 'You're the first person in fifty years to spot it, so something must have worked.'

'When we talked last night about the woman you loved, who died in a "train accident", you called her "my Cher", which

I'd assumed was her name, but you meant it as the Creole term of affection: "my dear". And you may have lost a lot of body mass, but I can still see the exact same expression now that Val did, all those years ago.'

The old man's voice was like dried leaves, crackling underneath footsteps. 'I bribed the night staff to arrange for the train to stop along a deserted route, and buried Valentina and Mickey in the woods. And I ran, ran north, changed my name, and even went to college. But I never forgot.'

'Of course you couldn't.' Cat leant on Nathan and slowly helped herself to her feet, trying to present as non-threatening an image as she could to the man. 'You went into the antiques and memorabilia business. Wheeler contacted you about purchases for Southern Spirits, you visited one day, and experienced the echoes of Val and yourself.'

'Yes.' And Newholme's eyes lit up, his free hand loosening his tie and unbuttoning his shirt, enough to reveal a familiar brass charm, one he tugged free from around his neck to hold out. 'She should have worn this. It would have protected her. Belagrís swore to protect and serve all the Sauveterre family. But being here, feeling those memories again... it was like... like I had a second chance. A second chance to...'

'Forget the mistake you made. I know. So why the gun?'

Enrique indicated Wheeler. 'You arrest him, you confiscate the train. I'll lose her. Again.'

'Um,' Wheeler interrupted. 'Not that I'm ungrateful, but can you get one of them to at least pull my pants up?'

The others ignored him. Cat continued, 'It's over, Enrique. The running, the hiding.'

'No!' Desperation made him look as if he'd been struck. 'The train wants me here!'

'Yes, Enrique. But not to keep reliving old memories. It kept you coming back until we arrived, so that we could learn the truth. So I could then tell you what I learnt, what I saw and felt, from Valentina herself. And I can tell you this: there was no pain. No fear. No thoughts of betrayal or disappointment in her heart. All she felt, until the end, was the love she had for you. How much she loved being held by you, how you kept her close and safe.'

Cat approached, and kept speaking. She wasn't very conscious of her words, but it seemed to be having the desired effect. The restraint of a half-century's guilt seeped from him along with his strength. And by the time she'd gently taken the gun from him and tossed it to Nathan, the tears running down Enrique's face turned into sobs, and he almost fell into Cat's supportive arms.

15

Jack Wheeler had gone for a shower and change of clothes, while the people who had upturned his work and ruined two years' planning carried out their boring legal proceedings. Not long after Catalina had disarmed Richard Newholme – or Enrique Cazenove – Belle allowed access to the rest of the train, not that anyone had even noticed. The train driver and his assistant, trapped for many hours in their berth, accepted the story that some drunken passengers had taken over the loco-motive. It was a serious incident, but they accepted a small monetary gift to help them forget it.

They had arrived in New Orleans Sunday morning, on schedule, an amazing feat considering the circumstances. The Federal agents had contacted the local police to be at the station, ready to take Newholme into custody, where he would eventually lead them to the location of the bodies of Valentina and Mickey. Wheeler wondered if the coin would still be with Mickey's remains, or if it was lost along the way. Damn, eight million dollars . . .

He shook his head as he combed his hair. No, there was no point in crying over spilt milk. At least he still had Belle, a sweet little moneymaker. Now that the coin was out of his reach, perhaps he could use the cameras and microphones for a little judicious blackmail of the right influential people?

He left his quarters and proceeded to his office, wondering where Faye had gone. Most likely she was still in someone's berth, sleeping off a night of drink and sex. He wasn't in too great a hurry to find her. Cat, however, was another matter, even if she was a Fed.

He entered his office to find the current woman of his thoughts waiting there, sitting at his desk, staring at a spread of Tarot cards. Wheeler strode over to her, studied her activity. 'That's usually Faye's domain.'

'She's busy at the moment. Tara dealt this spread out, gave me an interpretation.'

He leant in closer. 'Seeking your future?'

'Yours, actually.' She indicated each card. 'The Tower: sudden, unexpected change. The Lovers, Reversed: betrayal. The Fool: new beginnings. The Two of Swords, Reversed: caution when dealing with others. And the Six of Swords: an imminent journey.' She picked up the Fool card, looked at it, and then him. 'I can see the resemblance.'

'Amusing. But I'm not going anywhere.'

'No?' She leant back and looked up at him. 'Sorry you never got your hands on the Silver Bell?'

He grunted. 'It's probably sitting in some mud patch in the middle of nowhere.'

'Actually, it's closer than you think.' She reached into her pocket and produced a small shiny coin, moved it in her fingers.

Wheeler's jaw dropped, and he drew closer. 'That's ... That's it?' He stared, as if hypnotised. It was ... well, not beautiful. It was just a coin. What it was worth, however, was another matter.

'*Si*. Eight million dollars of coin. And you had it all along.'

'*What?* Where?'

'In that voodoo display case in the reception carriage, in the gris-gris bag. You see, when Enrique, as Newholme, was equipping your train with memorabilia, and you wanted some authentic materials, he put together a bag based on his own knowledge of the faith. I'm told they're meant to protect the wearer from harm or bring good luck, and should contain oils, stones, bones, hair and offerings like silver to appease the spirits. Newholme put an old silver dollar in the bag, one he'd had for decades.'

Wheeler stared at the coin again, laughing softly and shaking his head at the irony. It was almost too much to accept. 'I've had it ... had it all along?'

'Tara speculates that Mamselle Belagrís took its value and uniqueness as one hell of an offering to her, and that this boosted her powers and influence as much as the sexual energy generated onboard since Southern Spirits started.'

'And now it's going to gather dust in a museum.' Wheeler's heart ached.

'I'll honour my agreement, and pretend this was a lucky find.' Cat slipped the coin back into her pocket. 'Oh, and you should know that Donnie and Faye are being taken into custody.'

Wheeler paled. 'Faye? What for?'

'Attempted extortion. It seems that Donnie had some sort of epiphany last night, and when he learnt our true occupations, he came confessing his sins – including how Faye had planned to use him to force you into signing over Belle and ownership of the Southern Spirits company to her. By force, if necessary.'

The news made Wheeler's blood run cold. *Faye?* Faye of all people? Yes, she had a temper, but had never shown any overweening greed or ambition. 'Are you sure?'

She nodded. 'We found her with some legal papers ready for your signature. She'd been trapped in one of the public toilets for most of the night – and at one stage, the toilet had erupted its contents.' She smirked. 'Her fragrance matched her mood.'

Wheeler grunted. He still didn't know whether to be appalled or impressed with the woman's audacity. 'Well, nice to know the law was onboard to protect me.' He smiled, drawing closer until he was almost brushing against her. 'So, my delightful one, why are you here? If it's to continue what we started last night –'

Cat smiled up at him. 'I'm here to help you.'

That put him on an unexpected edge. But he remained cool. 'That's most beneficent of you, but I don't see how.'

'Donnie's prepared to testify against his uncle, Leo Kolchak. In particular about the money laundering.' She leant back in the chair until it creaked. 'Once you're named, I intend to have you indicted for your part in the operation.'

'That'll be his word against mine.'

'No, that'll be his word, plus the files we downloaded from your PC, against your word.'

A chill ran down his spine. 'What? You had no right!'

'Sure we did. It came with the warrant.'

He swallowed. 'But what about our deal? You'd drop the charges –'

'That concerned the conspiracy to steal the Silver Bell coin and smuggle it out of the country. I honoured that agreement. The laundering charges remain. However, if you are no longer the owner of this train and company, then there will be little point in pursuing an indictment against you.' She folded her arms across her chest. 'You sell Belle, and you'll stay free.'

Wheeler's head ached from the offer. Sell everything he had here, start over? It was one thing to be able to do that when he had millions from the coin sale at his fingertips, but . . . 'Please, enlighten me as to the part where you "help" me.'

'Why, by finding you a willing buyer already: Tara Gilbrand. I've spoken with her about this, and she's prepared to take Belle off your hands, and employ the Olivers to help her. There's no reason Southern Spirits shouldn't keep running – albeit without those illegal cameras and microphones you installed. Naughty, naughty, Jack.'

Wheeler studied her, even as his heart sank. It was so abrupt. But, knowing Tara's wealthy family connections, at least he'd get a decent price. 'That seems ... acceptable. But I won't settle for anything less than –'

'Three hundred dollars.'

He blinked. 'Excuse me?'

'You'll settle for three hundred dollars, the same amount you said you had when you first found Belle. Nothing more, not even that money you have in the safe. And you'll be off the train and away from it within the hour, or the deal's off.'

Disbelief at the woman's casual words boiled into indignation, and then anger. 'Are you *serious*? After all I've gone through?' He shook with rage. 'You think you can get away with this? *Do you?*'

Cat, however, remained perfectly composed. 'I think I see you standing there with a fist, Jack. I suggest you use it, lose it or I'll break it off at the wrist, *puta*.' Before she gave him a chance to respond in any way, she swiftly rose to her feet, facing him. 'And don't blame me, blame Belle. She played you like a fool from the start.'

'What?'

'*Si*. She tempted you, encouraged you with tantalising visions of the coin, persuaded you to refurbish her and bring others onboard, until the right combination of passengers were there. Passengers who could reveal what happened to Val. Passengers who could convince Enrique, the man Val loved so much, to finally give himself up and live his final years with a clearer conscience. And ultimately, for you to find Val's descendant.'

'Descendant? What are you talking about?'

'Belagrís is a protectorate spirit, bound to the Sauveterre

family. Val's closest blood relative on her mother's side was an aunt who'd moved to Atlanta and later married; Tara's one of their grandchildren. Now Belle can continue to fulfil her obligations to the family. The circle is complete. Oh, and you still have that fist, Jack. And I have nine ways to put you on the floor, none of which you'll enjoy.'

He grunted, thoughts of walking away from this sweet business still stinging him like a bastard. Was she right? Had Belle played him for a patsy all along?

If so, then, given his own successes in deception, he had no right to feel resentful when someone better could do it to him.

He released his fist, offered it as a handshake. 'Looks like we have another deal, Agent Montoya.'

After a moment, Cat accepted it. He leaned in, smelling her hair, and his voice dropped to a whisper, though they were alone in the office. 'And how about we seal the deal with a little breakfast in my room? To help ease the pain I'm feeling over the enormous losses I'm taking?' He reached out, fingertips tracing the outline of her hips as he drew even nearer. 'You can't deny how much you enjoyed yourself with me, can you?'

Cat smiled again, wetting her lips and fixing him with a hungry expression that made his cock stir in his slacks. Until she spoke. 'No, I can't. But I've literally had better – and with someone I can trust afterwards. Oh, and Jack? You try getting any closer to that coin, and you'll lose something far more precious to you than Belle.'

She stood perched against the taxi, hers and Nathan's bags packed and in the trunk, and the coin signed over to the local authorities. There was a break in the rain, though the air remained thick and humid. But she ignored it as she stared at the locomotive that had carried her further than just a few hundred miles. After a moment, she walked over to it, staring at the single round light at the prow as if it was an eye. Cat felt the need to say something to her, some admission of how her perceptions had expanded, how her beliefs were questioned, about the world, about Nathan, about herself. She hated it. She relished it.

In the end, she settled for: 'Nice trip.'

Belle said nothing, of course.

'Agent Montoya!'

She turned as Tara, the Olivers and Nathan approached, Tara beaming with barely-contained excitement. 'Well, the papers are signed, and Belle's ours!'

'Or we're hers,' Ben joked. 'And yes, we'll get the cameras and microphones removed immediately.'

'And then everything will be as it should be.'

'You really believe that, Tara?' Cat asked.

'How can you not, after all you've seen? Most practitioners of magic believe that there are no accidents. They believe that everything is intertwined with and interdependent on everything else. We're often just characters in someone else's story, we just don't usually see it.'

Cat shrugged. 'Guess I just need a little bit more convincing.'

Tara laughed. 'I've already thanked Mr Ames, but I wanted to thank you as well.' She leant in, kissed and embraced her. 'And to offer you both lifetime memberships.'

'Sounds good, huh, Wildcat?' Nathan winked.

Cat pulled back. '*Gracias*, Tara, but as Federal agents we couldn't accept gratuities from businesses that have been the subject of an investigation.' Then she waited a beat before adding, 'I'll pay for my own.'

'Agent Montoya!' All eyes turned to Wheeler, dressed for the road and carrying a shoulder bag, as he stopped at the entrance into the station and waved to her, smiling. 'I hope you don't think you've seen the last of me?'

She smirked. 'I can still hope.'

Nathan drew up beside her, as if Wheeler would somehow reach out across the distance to them and grab at her. 'The local police have left with the perps. We've got to get over to the airport.'

She sighed. They were set to fly back to Miami that evening, and be ready for work Monday morning, though they had a few more days to finish their reports. '*Si.*'

They said their goodbyes hurriedly. Cat glanced over to the empty spot where she'd seen Wheeler only seconds before. *Adios*, Jack. Try to learn something from all this.

Like Miami, New Orleans seemed built in and around water, whether it was the winding Mississippi feeding its way to the Gulf of Mexico, or the many large lakes surrounding. In the taxi ride from the station to the International Airport, Cat found it a sprawling city with architecture reflecting its centuries of French, Spanish and American influences, and with none of its beauty diminished by recent disasters or by a sky blanketed in billowy clouds of grey and black which occasionally fought with bellows of thunder and odd bursts of rain. It made Cat want to find some excuse to go exploring for a day or two.

Beside her, Nathan leant closer. 'Penny for your thoughts.'

'Oh, I'm just dreaming.'

'Thought you'd have had enough of that this weekend.'

She looked to him, smiling, and then dropped her smile. 'Nathan, I'm sorry I didn't let you in on what was going on sooner.'

'Forget it.'

'No more secrets, then?'

He paused, looked ready to say something serious, before settling for: 'Agreed.'

Cat knew something was amiss when they entered the airport and found masses of people staring up at the electronic boards, many of which displayed the same two words: DELAYED or CANCELLED.

Nathan confirmed the worst with the check-in desk. 'The storms surrounding the city are lingering. All flights east have been cancelled until at least tomorrow.'

He couldn't keep the grin off his face.

A grin she quickly matched. 'We'd better beat the crowds and find a room in town.'

It proved a more difficult task than anticipated, with many having a head start, but Cat left Nathan to carry on with the quest, while she sat near the check-in section minding the luggage and calling the Miami office to inform them of the news. Visions of a night and morning in this city with Nathan danced in her head and made her pussy twitch, as she sat checking her phone's power, memory ... Strange. There were several large audio files stored in her phone's temporary folder. She chose one and heard Nathan's voice. She smiled.

The smile evaporated as she listened to what he said: 'Interim report on Agent Montoya, continuance: during the course of the investigation, she has made an informal acquaintance of the subject, engaging him in friendly dialogue while also utilising her natural charm and physical features. Her manner, while requiring polish that only experience can provide, proved efficacious in establishing a rapport with the subject.'

She felt a chill run through her as she stopped the recording, and checked another. It was another account from Nathan. About her.

Reports. He was secretly reporting on her. She checked the history folder, and found he had uploaded copies of the files to a number that looked like a secured voicemail box, like the one available to directors like . . . Hausmann.

Son of a bitch. Hausmann obviously didn't trust her to manage this operation, so he had Nathan secretly keep tabs on her. After all his condemnation of her this weekend for keeping secrets from him, he'd been doing this all along.

She thought she'd be screaming at this point. Instead, she felt a sadly familiar sense of betrayal.

And already her mind was working on her next course of action.

Nathan returned. 'Found a room, down near the French Quarter. Don't know what it's like, but any port in a storm, right?'

'Right.' She made a move for her bags, remaining silent and emotionally distant as they hailed and obtained a taxi, which under Nathan's guidance took them in a different direction than they had taken before.

'Hope it's not on a steamboat or something,' Nathan joked. 'I get seasick.'

'Yes.'

'You OK, Cat? Tired?'

'Tired, yes.' It was true enough; they had been awake for nearly twenty hours and fatigue was gnawing at her. She stared out the window as the glass began steaming up, watching the sudden bursts of rain, the heavens finally opening up in full symphony, matching her mood.

The taxi took them into an older part of the city, one with narrower streets and buildings that were more regal: townhouses, French and Spanish colonial designs, and hybrids of two or more styles. She watched pedestrians dash here and there, their umbrellas and newspapers scant protection from the rain. The heat was growing stifling in the taxi, but she dared not roll down the window and risk being drenched.

After an eternity, they appeared to arrive at their destination, a run-down looking three-storey red-white brick establishment, with decorative wrought-iron rail balconies on the second floor, hanging tropical plants swaying in the wind and a crowning tower resting on the angled slate-swathed roof. Absently she looked for the name of the establishment, but its sign was dark and kept rocking, and she wasn't ready to speak to Nathan unless necessary.

It was a quick dash from the taxi to reception, and the interior confirmed her fears that the run-down nature of the place wasn't just confined to the exterior: it was all hardwood floors or threadbare carpets, with dozens of pictures on the walls leading to a dark bar where patrons huddled in from the rain and blues played on a jukebox.

She carried her own bags up to the room on the second floor, a stark enclosure dominated by a large bed sitting high on a brass frame, with an old-fashioned chest of drawers and cheval mirror, a table with some fresh peaches, and glass balcony doors draped in gauzelike curtains. And, of course, more pictures. She had to admit the place had a sense of history. She just wished she were in a better mood to appreciate it.

Nathan closed the hotel-room door. 'You go ahead and unpack first.'

'No. Leave them.' She took off her jacket, calmer now that she'd made her decision, and not wanting to waste time packing up again later. 'Get your clothes off.'

'Excuse me?'

She'd stopped at the balcony doors, as if ready to step out of them, but instead began unbuttoning her blouse and slipping out of her pumps. 'Take off your clothes. I want to fuck.' She looked back at him. 'Is there a problem with that?'

'Are you sure you don't want to eat first, or shower up –'

'No.'

He stared in bemusement for a moment, and then smiled and began unknotting his tie. 'OK.'

For a moment, there was only the patter of rain on the balcony and music seeping in through the floorboards, and the rustle of their clothes. Cat turned away as she continued undressing, steeling herself. Doing this was turning out to be more difficult than expected, so she forced herself to approach him when she was down to her bra and panties, and Nathan to his briefs. 'Get on the bed.'

'Cat.'

She turned to face him. 'I want to fuck, Nathan. I want to fuck, and then –'

'And then what?'

She looked down, saw his cock tenting his briefs, and reached out for it. 'Nothing. Just do as you're told, and –'

He reached out, removing her hand. 'No. I want to know what's going on. Why are you acting like this?'

Cat's face tightened, angry that he was going to deny her even this. 'I know about your reports.'

He froze. 'You do?'

'Yes. You were sloppy, failing to check if the phone left copies in temporary folders of whatever you send. Maybe I should write up my own performance reports on you for Hausmann?'

'Hausmann? What's he got to do with this?'

'Stop playing the innocent!' Her blood boiled, and the feelings she'd contained since the airport now burst forth, not helped by her exhaustion. She took a swing at him, connecting with his jaw.

Nathan, however, rolled with the punch a little, saving his face and her fist too much pain, and was ready for her when she tried again, turning and slipping a restraining arm around her, even as she struggled in his grip. 'Fucking *puta*! *Cabrón*!'

'Cat, will you cut it out? Jesus! I wasn't reporting to Hausmann.'

'Oh? Who was it, then? Internal Affairs? CIA?'

'Alan Mortimer.'

Cat froze at the unexpected name. 'Mortimer? The regional commissioner of the FBI?'

'Ex-commissioner, or soon to be.'

'What the fuck is this about?'

'If I let you go, will you promise not to hit me again?'

'No!'

The answer made him chuckle for a few seconds, and he released her, stepping back as she turned to face him, his hands raised towards her in a conciliatory gesture. 'Mortimer's going to head Miami's new top secret Financial Intelligence Taskforce. He's recruiting the best from all the agencies – FBI, Homeland Security, the IRS, of course – for both office and field work. I was recruited six months back and, in that time, they asked if there was any suitable additional personnel in my department. You were among the top of my recommendations list.'

Cat's mind reeled at the revelations. She'd heard rumours about the taskforce, had even considered applying for it, but such was the secrecy and protracted news about it, that she assumed it had become another government project mired in focus group limbo. She still stood there, hands balled into fists, her knuckles aching. 'Just "among the top"?'

'Yeah, well, there was some question regarding your lack of field experience, which is why you were given a chance with the Wheeler assignment, and I was given a chance to provide covert reports on your performance. There was also some issue about your temper.' He touched his jaw. 'Not that I've seen any instances of it.'

The news defused much of her anger, leaving only some mortification on her part. 'So why the fuck didn't you tell me about what you were doing sooner?'

Now Nathan's voice and anger rose. 'Because there's a reason they call them "covert reports". Damn it, Cat, I wasn't delighted to do it, but it had to be done, and it was hardly the worst act I could commit. And if you can't accept that, then you can *besame el culo* for a change!'

'OK, OK, down, boy.' Feeling embarrassed by her outburst, she offered him a conciliatory smile. 'No need to lose your temper like that.'

'Lose *my* temper?' Nathan snorted, though he was obviously not as outraged as he sounded. Then his brow creased with thought. 'If you suspected something like that, why were we about to ... Jesus, you were gonna pull a Cliff on me, weren't you? You were gonna fuck me and dump me like you did your boyfriend, right?'

'Hound.'

'Son of a bitch.' He turned and reached for his clothes.

And it was that image, of Nathan leaving, of leaving her, all because of a stupid misunderstanding, which filled her with an unprecedented dread, a fear that drove her back to him. 'Nathan, wait, please. I'm sorry – really.' Her body shook as if from the cold, and she clung to him as if he were a lifeline. She held her breath, her whole being, until he responded, wrapping his arms around her and holding her tightly. And her tension bled from her, leaving an intense relief, relief that the faith she had developed for him had not been misplaced, relief that he had been able to put aside his own anger.

After a while of just standing there in each other's arms, Cat murmured, 'Do you think your report will be enough to sway Mortimer?'

He chuckled. 'He's already swayed, the report was just a

formality. He should make the offer in a few weeks. You could be at the seminars with Gordy and me in a month.'

'Gordy? *He's* been accepted? *Dios*.' She rolled her eyes. Of course, she didn't have to accept. She supposed she could stay where she was, working with Hausmann and Leewood and Chaney, maybe taking secondments, working her way up to assistant chief in ten years' time, assuming others with more seniority weren't ahead of her, while Nathan went off some-where . . .

To hell with that.

She breathed in his scent, and began kissing his chest and shoulder, feeling his cock begin to stir again in his briefs as her fingertips moved up over his shoulder blades. She felt him reach up and draw her hair away from her neck, before planting his lips there, his strong hands moving down to stroke and cup her cheeks. Cat's nipples and sex were burning, and the entire surface of her skin had become unbearably sensitive. Slowly, deliberately, she turned around in his embrace, his hands still gripping her, his hips and cock now jutted against the smooth swell of her ass. His embrace tightened, and his lips returned to her neck, and then her ears.

She studied the patterns on the wood panelling behind him. 'It's been a strange weekend.'

'No kidding.' A glint of cocky humour showed in his voice.

'We'll have to seriously edit our reports.'

'Oh, I agree – hey!'

Cat had pulled out of his embrace, as if she was off to start writing. Instead, she glided over to the balcony doors, unlatched and opened them.

'Cat, you're not on the train now, you can't just go out like that!'

'No? Better come out and get me then.' She took a step out, then looked back at him and smiled mischievously. 'It's bucketing out here. No one's looking up. Besides, we're in New Orleans. Take it easy.'

The balcony itself was small, with just enough room for two chairs, and was surrounded by black wrought-iron railings in elaborate designs and potted foliage that Cat felt offered sufficient cover – unless and until someone looked at them from a window across the street. It was scarcely cooler out here than inside, despite the rain and the mild breeze.

Cat rested her forearms on the balcony rail and looked down, seeing an old man sitting on a box under a balcony across the street. He was playing a guitar, with an upturned hat at his feet. She leant in, trying in vain to hear his music over the sound of the rain pounding into the street and on the surrounding roofs. Despite her own assurances, it was scary – and thrilling.

She braced her feet in her heels, slightly apart, hearing Nathan draw behind her. 'We should leave out any reference to Belle, the hotspots –'

'That's a given, if we want to keep our new appointments.' Nathan's hands gripped her as if she'd fall off the balcony, his hips and bulge pressed against the smooth swell of her buttocks. 'And what about the sex?'

Heat and sweat rolled from her shoulders, down her breasts and over her belly. She pushed back against him. '*Dios*, yes, or we'll give those *pajieros* back in Miami endless inspiration.'

Nathan's erection rubbed at the cleft between her buttocks, as his mouth moved back to her ear. 'Like that business in the Dungeon, when I was forced to tie you up, spank you, and then –'

'I know the rest. "Forced", huh?' As she leant further on the railing, her breasts threatening to spill out of her bra and over her arms, she smiled, as she seemed to catch the attention of the old man. 'I'd better also leave out the incident in the sauna as well, where Tara and I were naked and fucking on the floor.'

'Actually,' he was murmuring, 'I was hoping you could write that up and let me have a copy.'

'Why am I not surprised? Men.' She felt Nathan kneel down out of sight behind her, kiss the backs of her legs, his fingers trailing ahead of him to her rear. She grinned to the street below as he drew down her panties to her knees, the tip of his tongue dancing along the strip of skin between her cheeks, playing with the entrance to her rear. She thrust back against his face. 'Get off that. You've had too much of my ass this weekend.'

'I can never have enough,' he declared, rising back to his feet.

'Oh yeah? I'll buy a strap-on and let you find out for yourself – *fuck!*' Cat felt herself pressed hard up against the rail, its cold, wet metal struts pressing against the front of her thighs, as Nathan's hand reached around to her bush, her puffy sex, and he growled in her ear. Standing this close, she could smell him again, tangy and musky and rough.

She parted her thighs further as his hand slipped between them, one long, short-nailed finger probing up into her hot wetness. She adjusted her position slightly, giving him better access, the lips of her pussy throbbing hotly. His hard, curved finger slid in and out of her slowly, teasingly, as his other hand rested on the back of her neck, keeping her in place. She gripped the balcony rail, leaning further forwards until the rain just about caught the top of her head, steadily soaking her hair as Nathan fingered her on the balcony of a New Orleans hotel. Her pussy was deliciously hot and hungry for satisfaction, enjoying his finger but aching for the irreplaceable fullness that only his erect cock could bring.

'Fuck!' she called out again, straightening up and pulling up her panties, not caring who saw her breasts. 'Let's get to bed!'

She spared a final glance at the man across the street, who had evidently heard her, to judge from his laughter. Then she disappeared back into the room with Nathan, leaving the balcony doors open. She unclipped her bra and slipped out of her panties, as Nathan removed his own briefs. The mattress springs creaked as she lay back, and her eyes rolled at the noise.

'I hope that doesn't put you off,' he said with a smile as he looked down at her.

'Me? No. I'm just feeling sorry for our neighbours. They won't get any sleep tonight.'

'You're such a saint.' He brought the hand that had been at her sex to his mouth, taking in her scent, tasting her juices on his finger. He smacked his lips, increasing Cat's own hunger as she cupped her breasts, her thumbs touching the crests of her nipples, circling, pinching and rolling them, adding to that desperate need pounding through her body.

He bent down at the bedside to engulf one of her nipples in his mouth, sucking hard and making her cry out. She swept upwards, her cry becoming a moan as she was tossed into an intense whirlpool of sensation, parting her thighs further as he climbed up onto the bed, his hand returning to her sex. His mouth was hot, and his tongue licked her breasts like a flame, the lightest touch a shock. He swept it around each nipple, as his fingers brushed between her folds in long wide upward strokes. Cat found herself so sensitive that she was gasping as she felt him move downwards. He parted her thighs as his mouth replaced his fingers, licking her, piercing her, before moving up to her clitoris, pressing it back just as his fingers had done moments before. But his tongue was a hot and sticky thing, feeling more organic, more alive, than his finger had, and it was as if the tempo of its pulse transferred itself to her, increasing the pressure, the pleasure.

An orgasm broke free from Cat. She cursed, her head pressing back against the goose-down pillow, her hands reaching out to grip his hair, as his tongue and lips conspired to keep her on that pinnacle for as long as she could stand it.

It seemed ages before she started drifting down again. But she became aware of Nathan rising above her, up on his knees, licking his lips and watching her with undisguised lust.

Cat looked up at him from under her dishevelled hair, focusing on his cock, glad that it hadn't lost its firmness while he was orally pleasuring her. She licked her lips. 'Agent Ames, that piece looks dangerous, you'd better holster it. Think you can find a place for it?'

'I've got one just in mind.' With a wicked laugh, he was upon her, lifting her legs up and guiding his cock towards her.

Cat wriggled on the mattress, providing as much ease as she could for him penetrating her – only to find it wasn't needed, as she felt so wet, the walls of her sex gripping him and maximising sweet resistance. 'Come on, just let go. We're gonna be stuck here for a while.'

He began pumping in and out of her, Cat gripping him, overwhelmed by the ferocity of his pistoning. Her mind seemed to envelop him as well as her sex and limbs, and her senses focused towards their joined sexes, like light through a lens. She stared upwards at the ceiling fan, one like on the train, in the visions of Belle in her younger days. A part of her wondered if Nathan and she had added any hotspots of their own during their time on Belle. Maybe, if Belle's still running fifty years from now, someone could experience what they had and thought and felt this weekend.

It was strange, but even as her body was riding with Nathan's, relishing the sex, the closeness and security, her mind was active, wondering how much of what had happened onboard Belle really happened. She could imagine her mind already coming up with rational and faux-rational explanations for it all, anything that was better than the idea of spirits guiding hers and Nathan's and everyone else's actions. And, being away from the influence of the train, it became easier. There were remarkable coincidences, yes, but only so many –

Suddenly, thunder made one of the framed photos overhead drop to the bed, nearly hitting her. '*Cabrón!*'

Nathan stopped pumping. 'You OK, Cat?'

She followed. 'Yes. Fucking thing.' She lifted it up, set it standing on the adjacent side table, and looked up at him as he chuckled at her. 'Have you stopped for the night then, *pajiero?*'

Nathan's lips curled into a smile, and he flexed his cock inside her, making her curse again as he began thrusting back into her, his lips at her neck, his arms wrapped around her, trapping her and keeping her as if by some slim chance she might have wanted to go elsewhere.

Cat let her body return to that sweet rhythm she shared with her lover, even as her eyes drew back to the picture, an old black and white photo featuring what Cat clearly recognised as the front of their hotel.

There was a young couple, the young man's arms wrapped around the woman's.

Val and Enrique.

This hotel was Val's father's club, or used to be.

There were coincidences in life, but ... getting a room here? Had Belagrís arranged the storm, arranged the reservation here, of all places in the city? Just to remind Cat of the power of the Southern Spirits around her?

Dios, wait until she told Nathan!

Later.

Cat ground her pelvis against Nathan's, exerting as much pressure on her clitoris as she could in this position. Her body had carried on while her mind had been distracted and now it was beginning to lose control. The moment had taken over, and Cat's whole being was trying to pull him closer, closer, further into her body, until the spasms that she could not and would not hold back any longer swept over her, and her head jerked backwards into the pillow, cursing with each bullet he spurted into her.

In the distance, a train sounded its departure.

Visit the Black Lace website at
www.black-lace-books.com

FIND OUT THE LATEST INFORMATION AND TAKE ADVANTAGE OF OUR FANTASTIC FREE BOOK OFFER! ALSO VISIT THE SITE FOR . . .

- All Black Lace titles currently available and how to order online
- Great new offers
- Writers' guidelines
- Author interviews
- An erotica newsletter
- Features
- Cool links

BLACK LACE – THE LEADING IMPRINT OF WOMEN'S SEXY FICTION

TAKING YOUR EROTIC READING PLEASURE TO NEW HORIZONS

LOOK OUT FOR THE ALL-NEW BLACK LACE BOOKS – AVAILABLE NOW!

FORBIDDEN FRUIT
Susie Raymond
ISBN 978 0 352 34189 17

The last thing sexy thirty-something Beth expected was to get involved with a much younger man. But when she finds him spying on her in the dressing room at work she embarks on an erotic journey with the straining youth, teaching him and teasing him as she leads him through myriad sensuous exercises at her stylish modern home. As their lascivious games become more and more intense, Beth soon begins to realise that she is the one being awakened to a new world of desire – and that hers is the mind quickly becoming consumed with lust.

To be published in July 2008

JULIET RISING
Cleo Cordell
ISBN 978 0 352 34192 1

Nothing is more important to Reynard than winning the favours of the bright and wilful Juliet, a pupil at Madame Nicol's exclusive but strict 18th century ladies' academy. Her captivating beauty tinged with a hint of cruelty soon has Reynard willing to do anything to win her approval. But Juliet's methods have little effect on Andreas, the real object of her lustful obsessions. Unable to bend him to her will, she is forced to watch him lavish his manly talents on her fellow pupils. That is, until she agrees to change her stuck-up, stubborn ways and become an eager erotic participant.

AMANDA'S YOUNG MEN
Madeline Moore
ISBN 978 0 352 34191 4

When her husband dies under mysterious circumstances in a by-the-hour motel, Amanda inherits a chain of shoe shops that bleeds money. But luckily for Amanda, the staff are bright and beautiful young people, ambitious to succeed and eager to give her total satisfaction. As she sets out to save the chain, and track down the woman involved in her husband's death, Amanda also finds time to amuse herself with lovers – young ones, and lots of them. Heels, hose, and haute couture have always been parts of Amanda's life, but now she's up to her dimples in duplicity, desire and decadence.

To be published in August 2008

WILDWOOD
Janine Ashbless
ISBN 978 0 352 34194 5

Avril Shearing is a landscape gardener brought in to reclaim an overgrown woodland for the handsome and manipulative Michael Deverick. But among the trees lurks a tribe of environmental activists determined to stop anyone getting in, led by the enigmatic Ash who reagrds Michael as his mortal enemy. Avril soon discovers that on the Kester Estate nothing is as it seems. Creatures that belong in dreams or in nightmares emerge after dark to prowl the grounds, and hidden in the heart of the wood is something so important that people will kill, or die for it. Ash and Michael become locked in a deadly battle for the Wildwood – and for Avril herself.

ODALISQUE
Fleur Reynolds
ISBN 978 0 352 34193 8

Set against a backdrop of sophisticated elegance, a tale of family intrigue, forbidden passions and depraved secrets unfolds. Beautiful but scheming, successful designer Auralie plots to bring about the downfall of her virtuous cousin, Jeanine. Recently widowed, but still young and glamorous, Jeanine finds her passions being rekindled by Auralie's husband. But she is playing into Auralie's hands – vindictive hands that drag Jeanine into a world of erotic depravity. Why are the cousins locked into this sexual feud? And what is the purpose of Jeanine's mysterious Confessor, and his sordid underground sect?

ENCHANTED
Janine Ashbless, Olivia Knight, Leonie Martell

ISBN 978 0 352 34195 2

Bear Skin

Hazel is whisked away from her tedious job and humdrum life by the mysterious Arailt, to be his lover. The only problem is there is more to Arailt than meets the eye – much more.

The Three Riddles

The elves, they say, know the secrets of events – but the queen has no time for superstitions. As her kingdom crumbles, she longs for her lost love, but can she risk her country on a whim?

The People in the Garden

Strange things are happening in the grounds of Count and Countess Malinovsky's Gothic manor house. Local people tell of fairies, goblins and unnameable creatures, and there are stories about a ghostly girl with an uncanny resemblance to the decadent couple's beautiful servant, Katia.

Black Lace Booklist

Information is correct at time of printing. To avoid disappointment, check availability before ordering. Go to www.black-lace-books.com.
All books are priced £7.99 unless another price is given.

BLACK LACE BOOKS WITH A CONTEMPORARY SETTING

☐ THE ANGELS' SHARE Maya Hess	ISBN 978 0 352 34043 6	
☐ ASKING FOR TROUBLE Kristina Lloyd	ISBN 978 0 352 33362 9	
☐ BLACK LIPSTICK KISSES Monica Belle	ISBN 978 0 352 33885 3	£6.99
☐ THE BLUE GUIDE Carrie Williams	ISBN 978 0 352 34132 7	
☐ THE BOSS Monica Belle	ISBN 978 0 352 34088 7	
☐ BOUND IN BLUE Monica Belle	ISBN 978 0 352 34012 2	
☐ CAMPAIGN HEAT Gabrielle Marcola	ISBN 978 0 352 33941 6	
☐ CAT SCRATCH FEVER Sophie Mouette	ISBN 978 0 352 34021 4	
☐ CIRCUS EXCITE Nikki Magennis	ISBN 978 0 352 34033 7	
☐ CLUB CRÈME Primula Bond	ISBN 978 0 352 33907 2	£6.99
☐ CONFESSIONAL Judith Roycroft	ISBN 978 0 352 33421 3	
☐ CONTINUUM Portia Da Costa	ISBN 978 0 352 33120 5	
☐ DANGEROUS CONSEQUENCES Pamela Rochford	ISBN 978 0 352 33185 4	
☐ DARK DESIGNS Madelynne Ellis	ISBN 978 0 352 34075 7	
☐ THE DEVIL INSIDE Portia Da Costa	ISBN 978 0 352 32993 6	
☐ EQUAL OPPORTUNITIES Mathilde Madden	ISBN 978 0 352 34070 2	
☐ FIRE AND ICE Laura Hamilton	ISBN 978 0 352 33486 2	
☐ GONE WILD Maria Eppie	ISBN 978 0 352 33670 5	
☐ HOTBED Portia Da Costa	ISBN 978 0 352 33614 9	
☐ IN PURSUIT OF ANNA Natasha Rostova	ISBN 978 0 352 34060 3	
☐ IN THE FLESH Emma Holly	ISBN 978 0 352 34117 4	
☐ LEARNING TO LOVE IT Alison Tyler	ISBN 978 0 352 33535 7	
☐ MAD ABOUT THE BOY Mathilde Madden	ISBN 978 0 352 34001 6	
☐ MAKE YOU A MAN Anna Clare	ISBN 978 0 352 34006 1	
☐ MAN HUNT Cathleen Ross	ISBN 978 0 352 33583 8	
☐ THE MASTER OF SHILDEN Lucinda Carrington	ISBN 978 0 352 33140 3	
☐ MIXED DOUBLES Zoe le Verdier	ISBN 978 0 352 33312 4	£6.99
☐ MIXED SIGNALS Anna Clare	ISBN 978 0 352 33889 1	£6.99

- ❑ MS BEHAVIOUR Mini Lee ISBN 978 0 352 33962 1
- ❑ PACKING HEAT Karina Moore ISBN 978 0 352 33356 8 £6.99
- ❑ PAGAN HEAT Monica Belle ISBN 978 0 352 33974 4
- ❑ PEEP SHOW Mathilde Madden ISBN 978 0 352 33924 9
- ❑ THE POWER GAME Carrera Devonshire ISBN 978 0 352 33990 4
- ❑ THE PRIVATE UNDOING OF A PUBLIC SERVANT ISBN 978 0 352 34066 5
     Leonie Martel
- ❑ RUDE AWAKENING Pamela Kyle ISBN 978 0 352 33036 9
- ❑ SAUCE FOR THE GOOSE Mary Rose Maxwell ISBN 978 0 352 33492 3
- ❑ SPLIT Kristina Lloyd ISBN 978 0 352 34154 9
- ❑ STELLA DOES HOLLYWOOD Stella Black ISBN 978 0 352 33588 3
- ❑ THE STRANGER Portia Da Costa ISBN 978 0 352 33211 0
- ❑ SUITE SEVENTEEN Portia Da Costa ISBN 978 0 352 34109 9
- ❑ TONGUE IN CHEEK Tabitha Flyte ISBN 978 0 352 33484 8
- ❑ THE TOP OF HER GAME Emma Holly ISBN 978 0 352 34116 7
- ❑ UNNATURAL SELECTION Alaine Hood ISBN 978 0 352 33963 8
- ❑ VELVET GLOVE Emma Holly ISBN 978 0 352 34115 0
- ❑ VILLAGE OF SECRETS Mercedes Kelly ISBN 978 0 352 33344 5
- ❑ WILD BY NATURE Monica Belle ISBN 978 0 352 33915 7 £6.99
- ❑ WILD CARD Madeline Moore ISBN 978 0 352 34038 2
- ❑ WING OF MADNESS Mae Nixon ISBN 978 0 352 34099 3

BLACK LACE BOOKS WITH AN HISTORICAL SETTING

- ❑ THE BARBARIAN GEISHA Charlotte Royal ISBN 978 0 352 33267 7
- ❑ BARBARIAN PRIZE Deanna Ashford ISBN 978 0 352 34017 7
- ❑ THE CAPTIVATION Natasha Rostova ISBN 978 0 352 33234 9
- ❑ DARKER THAN LOVE Kristina Lloyd ISBN 978 0 352 33279 0
- ❑ WILD KINGDOM Deanna Ashford ISBN 978 0 352 33549 4
- ❑ DIVINE TORMENT Janine Ashbless ISBN 978 0 352 33719 1
- ❑ FRENCH MANNERS Olivia Christie ISBN 978 0 352 33214 1
- ❑ LORD WRAXALL'S FANCY Anna Lieff Saxby ISBN 978 0 352 33080 2
- ❑ NICOLE'S REVENGE Lisette Allen ISBN 978 0 352 32984 4
- ❑ THE SENSES BEJEWELLED Cleo Cordell ISBN 978 0 352 32904 2 £6.99
- ❑ THE SOCIETY OF SIN Sian Lacey Taylder ISBN 978 0 352 34080 1
- ❑ TEMPLAR PRIZE Deanna Ashford ISBN 978 0 352 34137 2
- ❑ UNDRESSING THE DEVIL Angel Strand ISBN 978 0 352 33938 6

BLACK LACE BOOKS WITH A PARANORMAL THEME

☐ BRIGHT FIRE Maya Hess   ISBN 978 0 352 34104 4
☐ BURNING BRIGHT Janine Ashbless   ISBN 978 0 352 34085 6
☐ CRUEL ENCHANTMENT Janine Ashbless   ISBN 978 0 352 33483 1
☐ FLOOD Anna Clare   ISBN 978 0 352 34094 8
☐ GOTHIC BLUE Portia Da Costa   ISBN 978 0 352 33075 8
☐ THE PRIDE Edie Bingham   ISBN 978 0 352 33997 3
☐ THE SILVER COLLAR Mathilde Madden   ISBN 978 0 352 34141 9
☐ THE TEN VISIONS Olivia Knight   ISBN 978 0 352 34119 8

BLACK LACE ANTHOLOGIES

☐ BLACK LACE QUICKIES 1 Various   ISBN 978 0 352 34126 6   £2.99
☐ BLACK LACE QUICKIES 2 Various   ISBN 978 0 352 34127 3   £2.99
☐ BLACK LACE QUICKIES 3 Various   ISBN 978 0 352 34128 0   £2.99
☐ BLACK LACE QUICKIES 4 Various   ISBN 978 0 352 34129 7   £2.99
☐ BLACK LACE QUICKIES 5 Various   ISBN 978 0 352 34130 3   £2.99
☐ BLACK LACE QUICKIES 6 Various   ISBN 978 0 352 34133 4   £2.99
☐ BLACK LACE QUICKIES 7 Various   ISBN 978 0 352 34146 4   £2.99
☐ BLACK LACE QUICKIES 8 Various   ISBN 978 0 352 34147 1   £2.99
☐ BLACK LACE QUICKIES 9 Various   ISBN 978 0 352 34155 6   £2.99
☐ MORE WICKED WORDS Various   ISBN 978 0 352 33487 9   £6.99
☐ WICKED WORDS 3 Various   ISBN 978 0 352 33522 7   £6.99
☐ WICKED WORDS 4 Various   ISBN 978 0 352 33603 3   £6.99
☐ WICKED WORDS 5 Various   ISBN 978 0 352 33642 2   £6.99
☐ WICKED WORDS 6 Various   ISBN 978 0 352 33690 3   £6.99
☐ WICKED WORDS 7 Various   ISBN 978 0 352 33743 6   £6.99
☐ WICKED WORDS 8 Various   ISBN 978 0 352 33787 0   £6.99
☐ WICKED WORDS 9 Various   ISBN 978 0 352 33860 0
☐ WICKED WORDS 10 Various   ISBN 978 0 352 33893 8
☐ THE BEST OF BLACK LACE 2 Various   ISBN 978 0 352 33718 4
☐ WICKED WORDS: SEX IN THE OFFICE Various   ISBN 978 0 352 33944 7
☐ WICKED WORDS: SEX AT THE SPORTS CLUB Various   ISBN 978 0 352 33991 1
☐ WICKED WORDS: SEX ON HOLIDAY Various   ISBN 978 0 352 33961 4
☐ WICKED WORDS: SEX IN UNIFORM Various   ISBN 978 0 352 34002 3
☐ WICKED WORDS: SEX IN THE KITCHEN Various   ISBN 978 0 352 34018 4
☐ WICKED WORDS: SEX ON THE MOVE Various   ISBN 978 0 352 34034 4
☐ WICKED WORDS: SEX AND MUSIC Various   ISBN 978 0 352 34061 0

To find out the latest information about Black Lace titles, check out the website: www.black-lace-books.com or send for a booklist with complete synopses by writing to:

Black Lace Booklist, Virgin Books Ltd
Thames Wharf Studios
Rainville Road
London W6 9HA

Please include an SAE of decent size. Please note only British stamps are valid.

Our privacy policy
We will not disclose information you supply us to any other parties. We will not disclose any information which identifies you personally to any person without your express consent.

From time to time we may send out information about Black Lace books and special offers. Please tick here if you do not wish to receive Black Lace information. ❑

Please send me the books I have ticked above.

Name ....

Address ....

....

....

....

Post Code ....

Send to: Virgin Books Cash Sales, Thames Wharf Studios, Rainville Road, London W6 9HA.

US customers: for prices and details of how to order books for delivery by mail, call 888-330-8477.

Please enclose a cheque or postal order, made payable to Virgin Books Ltd, to the value of the books you have ordered plus postage and packing costs as follows:

UK and BFPO – £1.00 for the first book, 50p for each subsequent book.

Overseas (including Republic of Ireland) – £2.00 for the first book, £1.00 for each subsequent book.

If you would prefer to pay by VISA, ACCESS/MASTERCARD, DINERS CLUB, AMEX or SWITCH, please write your card number and expiry date here:

M ....

Signature ....

Please allow up to 28 days for delivery.